MW01173004

A BOOK LADY MYSTERY BY JOSEPH D'AGNESE

She sells books, eats well, and has a very large brain. Criminals fear her.

Meet Beatrice Valentine, a larger-than-life bookshop owner with a penchant for three things in abundance—delicious Italian food, *vino*, and murder.

For decades she has sold used and rare books from her stylish-but-cluttered domain on New York City's legendary Book Row.

But when the eccentric antiques-and-books dealer next door is found dead, it's time to put down the cannoli and get to work. Aided by her long-suffering private eye nephew, corpulent Aunt Bea launches an investigation using her irrepressible talents for snooping, meddling, and outthinking the police. Pitted against Aunt Bea's brilliant deductions, murderers don't stand a chance.

Murder on Book Row is the first in a delightful series of light-hearted whodunnits set in a world of rare books and abundant snacks. Written by a winner of the Derringer Award for Short Mystery Fiction. If you like charming puzzle mysteries, witty banter, and fiendishly clever solutions, you'll love getting to know the Book Lady.

Get *Murder on Book Row* today and sink your teeth into a delicious case that's one for the books!

JOIN THE VIP CLUB

Members of The Daggyland VIP Club get a free Starter Library of Joe's books, not to mention advance news on upcoming books and specials. See the back of the book for details on how to sign up.

MURDER ON BOOK ROW

A Book Lady Mystery

JOSEPH D'AGNESE

For Denise

BATTER UP

On the fifth day of the New Year, my Aunt Beatrice adhered strictly to her usual morning schedule. She rose at five, read a book till six, was showered and dressed by six thirty. By seven she headed north on her morning constitutional toward the colorful streets of Greenwich Village.

Aunt Bea is fond of saying that she walks briskly every morning to keep in shape. But I can't say this approach has yielded sterling results. Her shape and carriage hasn't changed one bit in thirty years.

The weather had been miserable these last few weeks, with rain, sleet, or snow in irritating abundance. It was officially The Winter Everyone Hated. After only minutes of traipsing through the slush, Bea sought the comforts of the warm, butter-scented interior of Anzotti's Bakery on Thompson Street. She barreled up to the display case and began surveying the morning pastries. Behind the glass counter she saw everything from coffee cakes and English muffins to turnovers and sixteen types of doughnuts, cream and jelly-filled. They even had an international delights counter, complete with little paper flags of the world's pastry-loving nations. My aunt's eye beheld Irish soda bread, Mexican flan, Viennese strudel, not to mention Italian grostoli, cannoli, strufoli, sfogliatelle, biscotti, farfallette dolci, amaretti, panettone, and pasticcini.

Aunt Bea inspected all these things and said, "I'll take three prune Danish."

In other words, her usual order.

She got one for herself, the others for her two longtime business associates, Amos Horne and Milo Barski.

"That one looks a little flat," she said, rapping the counter with her knuckles.

"This one?" said the salesgirl, peering over the top. She knew my aunt by sight. Bea was the tall woman of a certain age, with a single stripe of white running through her thick, jet-black hair. She wore a wide-brimmed wool hat, a green puffy down jacket, a thick orange cardigan, and a flowery garment that some would charitably call a caftan and others would call a sheet.

You might say that my aunt is legendary in this neighborhood. A legendary pain in the butt.

"You talking about this one?" the salesgirl said, waiting.

My aunt smiled. The sales clerk was a sleepy little thing, flour-faced and pimply, but Bea had no patience for her chicanery. "No," she said, rapping again. "The one you slipped in the bag when you thought I was looking at the Bundt cakes."

"You want another one?" the girl said.

"If you're asking if I'd like the offending Danish replaced with a plumper one, then yes, I would."

The girl rolled her eyes and made the switch. My aunt said later that she was glad she'd spoken up. She knew Milo and Amos would kick up a fuss if their pastries were second rate. Had she known what was in store for her, she would have skipped the munchies altogether.

She left the bakery, unfolded her gigantic umbrella—the one with the pink-and-yellow duck print—and walked a few blocks in the freezing rain to Broadway and Eighth Street, where she waited at the top of the subway steps. She glanced at her watch. It was 8:04 a.m. Amos was late. Figures. It was six minutes later, 8:10 a.m. precisely, when she spotted her arthritic friend slowly climbing the steps to the sidewalk.

He was a small, neat, elderly man with a bristly gray moustache, wearing a tan overcoat and thick red scarf looped around his neck. On his head was a jaunty blue beret, dripping rain from its little tail. He looked ready to burst into "La Marseillaise." He said, "You been waiting long?"

Bea said no, of course not. She'd just gotten there. She used one of her oversized pink handkerchiefs to wipe droplets of rain from her face, and they were off. They walked four blocks up and two over to Fourth Avenue. My aunt unlocked the door of Book Lady & Friends Bookshop, and stepped into a cavernous space filled with used and rare books that stretched from floor to ceiling. It's the sort of place that makes you feel as though you've fallen into a well whose walls are lined with paper and ink.

Scented geraniums grow in the front windows in such profusion that they have pressed their thick leaves across the glass and climbed ever upward, blocking the view of all but the tallest of passersby. The ceiling is the original tin, painted bright screaming yellow. There's a front checkout area with a cash register, a table to wrap purchases and sort new acquisitions, and a little conversation area in the back left corner, presided over by a giant spinning globe and a surly bronze bust of Giuseppe Verdi.

Theoretically the bookstore carries a volume on every subject under the sun, but you don't have to look far to glean my aunt's true area of expertise—and her passion. The most striking thing about the Book Lady bookshop is the fully stocked demo kitchen situated at the back half of the store. There, cast-iron skillets and copper pots dangle overhead and threaten to brain anyone who wanders too close.

My aunt installed the kitchen decades ago, at a time when many of her culinary heroes still lived and thought nothing of stopping by the shop to sign old copies of their backlist cook-books and whip up a soufflé while they were at it. I remember one time walking in to find my aunt in deep conversation with Julia Child and Craig Claiborne. Each of them was wearing a pair of white gloves and taking turns carefully paging through some old book on culinary herbs that Aunt Bea had scored on a buying trip to London. The book later sold to a collector in Chappaqua for an undisclosed sum, but not before Child, Claiborne, and Aunt Bea made a careful transcription of the "receipts" preserved in those fragile brown pages.

Fourth Avenue's Book Row was like that once, a mile-long string of bookshops that was a tourist destination unto itself, drawing bibliophiles from all over the world. It was said that it could take you an entire Saturday to work your way down one end of the avenue to the other and back up again, browsing through store after store with all their little specialties. Once, there had been stores that sold nothing but travel books and maps, stores that specialized in biographies, ones that carried the poshest art and coffee table books you've ever seen, and ones that cared for nothing but poetry, the stranger the better.

Years ago, the city had strangely decreed that the booksellers could no longer sell from carts on the sidewalk. They were a public menace! They blocked the flow of pedestrians! Anyone found in violation of that ordinance would be fined. Most book-sellers complied, but after those long New York winters, who could blame them if they rolled out a cart or two on the first warm days of spring? In seconds, thanks to a couple of stir-crazy bookmen and ladies, that little stretch of New York City looked like Paris. I gather it must have been a pretty sweet thing to shop for books while the sun warmed your back and the planetrees on the sidewalk unfurled their crimson bulbous flowers.

But that magical world had largely faded into the past. One by one, many stores closed due to rising rents and unsympathetic landlords, until there were just a few left. Hangers-on like my aunt and a few others.

She stood in the kitchen now—that crazy wide hat still on her head—firing up the temperamental espresso machine and setting out the store-bought pastries on mismatched plates of bone china. As she started the first of her morning cappuccinos, she peered over the kitchen counter toward the front of the store.

Amos Horne stood in the doorway with a frown on his face. "You know," he said, "that's peculiar."

"What is?"

"You know how he's always in before us? Well, he's not."

"Nonsense. He's always in."

Amos threw up his hands. "What can I tell you?"

Aunt Bea glanced at her watch: 8:19 a.m. She switched off the espresso machine and stepped out of her shop with Amos to the storefront next door. She stopped when she saw that the ribbed metal security door in front of *M. BARSKI ANTIQUES* was down.

"How strange!" she said. "The door's down but the padlocks are missing."

"Maybe he forgot something at home," Amos said.

My aunt waved that remark away as if it weren't worth her time. She slid up the metal like a garage door, revealing the darkened windows of Barski's shop. In the window she saw the usual: odd pieces of furniture and ceramics doing their darndest to look desirable. My aunt peered once through the window and said, "Oh dear."

"What?" Amos said. "What's oh dear, dear?"

Aunt Bea tried the door. It was locked. But the light on the little box attached to the door was dimmed, indicating that the security alarm was off. She excused herself momentarily and returned to her shop. She emerged seconds later, swinging wood.

"What's that?"

"This, Amos, is what is known as a Louisville Slugger. Kindly get out of my way, please."

"What are you gonna do with that?"

"Well," my aunt said, "seeing as the Mets haven't exactly picked up my contract this year, I guess I'm going to have to take my game elsewhere. Are you moving?"

Amos scurried to the street, fiddling with his scarf.

"Thank you."

Beatrice took a few preparatory swings, stepped up to the imaginary plate, and proceeded to smack a line drive through the glass window of Barski's shop door. The time was 8:22 a.m.

"Goodness, you're nuts!" Amos yelped. He watched Aunt Bea wrap her hand in her damp handkerchief, reach in and unlock the door. Then she stepped into the shop.

"Milo ...?" she called.

She took two steps before clapping the handkerchief to her mouth. Amos was right behind her. They entered the cluttered kingdom of one Milo Barski, miser, Jack of all trades, grouch. Amid pricy relics of the past, they found a Milo sprawled out on his back under a stack of books. He looked as if someone had taken a Louisville Slugger to the side of his head. There was a good deal of blood.

Amos gulped twice, his moustache twitching. "Oh sweet mother of God. Is he ...?"

My aunt bent once to touch Milo. The temperature of the poor fellow's cheek told her everything she needed to know. She straightened up and nodded. "Don't touch a thing. Come with me! We can call the police from my place. Heavens, what terrible timing! Who's going to eat that extra Danish?"

That's how I got invited to breakfast.

❧ 2 ❧

SNOOPS AMONG THE DEAD

W hen I was a kid, Milo Barski used to sell these exquisite little train sets imported from Germany that he'd set up in the windows of his shop, along with Japanese pasteboard houses and Neapolitan nativity sets and vintage nutcrackers. Everything sort of mismatched, but still enticing to a kid's eye. If we were lucky, he'd get busy with a host of other projects and forget to take down the holiday village until spring.

Even though our mother had admonished us repeatedly to view those cunning creations from the street, my sisters and I could not resist slipping inside to take a closer peek. He kept a watchful eye on us and tolerated our visits, so long as they were brief, probably because he wanted to stay on good terms with Bea and other proprietors on that wondrous stretch of Fourth Avenue.

Even now I can still see Barski—pot-bellied and tweedy, gray-haired and ponytailed—scuttling up and down the aisles of his shop, picking his way through the junk. I see him griping at customers who were foolish enough to bring their kids along. "Don't touch! Let me help you with that. It's *very* delicate. *Very* rare." Throughout the shop, he leaned hand-lettered signs written on pieces of dry-cleaner's cardboard, which warned customers in stern red Magic Marker, *You break it, you bought it!*

He had always been serious. So serious that we kids took turns doing impressions of him when the grown-ups weren't around. "How much?" a customer might ask, and out came his bifocals, which were repaired with first aid bandage tape. The whole while he was inspecting a price tag, one of his eyes would rove the shop on the prowl for shoplifters.

On occasion he'd chase my sisters and me back to my aunt's shop. I'd run and hide in European history because there was a big brown armchair there that hid my height perfectly. My sisters would climb into the ground-level kitchen cabinets and huddle amid the pie plates and mixing bowls. I was closer to the sitting area, and thus prime witness to the gentle way my aunt calmed Barski down, offering him an anisette cookie from her stash, or pouring him a little nip from whatever bottle was hidden in the make-believe books on the shelves near her desk.

Barski would nip and nibble, then wander back to his place a much more subdued man. When I was close to becoming a teenager, my Aunt Bea threw her arm around me after one of these incidents and said, perfectly innocently, "I know it's great fun to torment him, but haven't you outgrown him? There's a whole *world* of people waiting to be tormented by the likes of *you*, Dante. Do yourself a favor. Leave poor Milo alone and go find *them*. No doubt they will be infinitely more interesting."

I didn't realize until I was much older that that conversation marked one of the last times I ever stepped into Barski's shop, until I was much older and was occasionally looking to impress a girl by sprucing up my apartment with some kind of knickknack.

It was a little after nine when I reached Fourth Avenue. The cops had put up their bright yellow party streamers, and a few patrolmen were keeping the onlookers back. Through the windows of the shop I could see my aunt and Amos, looking like a pair of gawkers on their way to cash their Social Security checks.

Barski's was the corner shop with two windows in an otherwise dingy tenement. The Book Row I'd grown up hearing about has been largely rent-hiked out of existence. Most of the bookstores have been replaced with overpriced boutiques selling leather, pottery, wall hangings, or bizarre contraptions of twisted metal you stick in the corner of your loft.

The patrolmen outside didn't give me much of a hassle. Took a peek at my license and let me slip under the tape. When I got inside and smelled the place, I wanted out. The air was hot and stifling, smelling of mothballs and death. In the vicinity of Barski's checkout area footprints were clearly visible in the dried blood, running almost to the front door. They were small prints, size six or seven, and judging from the way the forensics photographer was snapping away, they were marked for the highest scrutiny.

Amos looked wet and shocked and scared. My aunt looked indignant. She's a large woman who often has trouble deciding what to do with her hands. Digging them into her hips is her usual solution, though it makes her look like the peeved headmistress of some snooty private school. I'm told that in youth she was regarded as a beauty, though people nowadays more often describe her as handsome. I don't know if that's a compliment, but I do know that she doesn't often care what people think. To me her best features are her piercing dark eyes and that sharp nose of hers, the kind a Roman statue would envy. That morning, she looked like a very angry statue indeed, leaning on my old baseball bat.

"You guys okay?" I said, dripping rain onto the cheap industrial carpet.

She drew her lips up into a fleeting impression of a duck. "Are we *okay*? Do you hear him, Amos? Do you know the state has seen fit to license this man?"

JOSEPH D'AGNESE

"Have the police told you what happened yet?"

"I don't need the police to tell me *that*, dear boy. Isn't it obvious? Someone brained him and locked up after themselves. They flipped the bolt on the door so it would lock on their way out, or they scampered out the back exit. There are no wet footprints besides our own, which suggests no one entered the shop this morning. The police, I am told, agree with my assessment."

"Well, either they do, or they're afraid to disagree with you, Aunt Bea."

"It's an outrage, if you ask me." Amos said. "What have I been saying for years? The neighborhood's going downhill. This is proof of it!" The little birdlike man's eyes were moist, and he kept tugging at his face. I've often theorized that if indeed the meek will inherit the earth, then Amos may someday make a killing in real estate.

A big plainclothes cop with dark hair and eyes came over. "You gentlemen and lady want to step this way? I got some more questions."

We followed him a few steps into the store, losing sight of the body. The Crime Scene Unit prowled the shop, dusting for prints, measuring, collecting, fiddling with something hidden behind Barski's sales counter.

Memories flooded me. Barski with his stooped shoulders, doing his crab-walk through the artifacts at the end of another day. Cleaning up, dusting, straightening picture frames and chairs. Pouncing on paper clips and hoarding them in the pockets of his ratty Harris tweed, the one with the leather patches.

Though the sign out front proclaimed that you were entering an emporium devoted to books and antiques, I always regarded it as a high-end junk shop. It's just that the little white tags fluttering from every object never reflected the going price of junk.

Overhead a few chandeliers and a pair of large fluorescent lamps dangled from the ceiling. The chandeliers, strung up on J-hooks, seemed capable of braining us at a sneeze. The floor was a maze of early American furniture. An oaken dining room set. A grandfather clock. Secretary tables, settees, a collection of brass headboards, and more lamps. Most of the tables held little breakable knickknacks and wind-up clocks, tea sets, nautical trinkets, jewelry boxes, porcelain and brass animals, china sets and spice jars all as perfectly cluttered as a doting grandmother's living room. The walls, wherever they were free of bric-a-brac shelves, were covered with water-stained prints and framed photos. It was unsettling to find that we had an audience of sorts. Behind their glass, dour-faced, sepia-toned people stared down upon us.

Only two images had captivated me since childhood, and they were never for sale. They were two massive black-and-white photographs in black frames that hung in recesses along the north wall, illuminated by overhead lights. One showed Grace Kelly in a little black dress, her head thrown back in laughter, while a gaggle of nameless men ogled her. They appeared to be at a cocktail party in some California modern house. Everyone in the photo clutched a drink except Grace herself.

The second photo might have been taken at the very same party. It showed a door in the act of being closed on the photographer. Most of the image was in shadow, except for the part the door hasn't closed on yet. In that bright chunk of space you could see a man glaring at the person taking the picture. Without a doubt the man behind the door was a young, petulant Marlon Brando. Over his shoulder you could just make out the image of a young beautiful woman checking herself in a compact mirror. (No, it's not Grace.) All my life I've always wondered what went on behind that closed door.

The cop tapped two fingers on my trench coat. "Who's this?" he asked, almost as if he were inquiring about the price of one of the items. He was built like an athlete, maybe forty. Under his overcoat he wore a tan woolen blazer and a reddish tie crawling with stylish paramecia. These days cops dress well for murders; hourly guys like me are the slobs.

Bea navigated around a red velvet ottoman and did the honors. She didn't have to. When the cop flashed his shield and ID, I learned that I had just had the pleasure of meeting Detective Luis Munoz. He looked at me and skipped the handshake. "Sleet," he said, repeating my name. "Do I know that name?"

"You do now."

His mouth was a broken line. "Hah. You a book dealer, too, Mr. Sleet?"

"No, I'm not."

"You sell antiques?"

"Nope."

"You knew the guy?"

"Back in the day, sure."

"Did you see him last week, before or after his little accident?"

"No."

"You didn't see him fall?"

"No."

"Did you see him yesterday?"

"No."

"Have you seen him anytime in the last seventy-two hours?"

"I haven't seen him in years."

Munoz grimaced. "Pardon my French, Mr. Sleet, but why the heck are you here?"

"I'm providing moral support for my aunt. Also, I heard there'd be snacks."

Behind me I heard my dear Aunt Beatrice inhale sixty-three percent of the oxygen in the room. Munoz's eyes clenched. He towered over me, and that's no easy feat. He gave me his back and glared at Bea. "I thought you said he knew something."

"I said he *might*. He's grown into a very astute young man."

Munoz patted down his hair and took us a few more tentative steps forward, stopping at the end of the checkout area. Barski had constructed his command station out of three different pieces of furniture. There was a desk, which held a blotter and cash register. This was flanked on the left by a cheap folding table stacked with bubble wrap, sheets of newspaper, and brown wrapping paper. Behind the desk, against the wall, was a tall breakfront cabinet with glass windows.

Together, these three pieces of furniture formed the U-shaped station from which Barski lorded over the shop. From here he could ring up someone's payment, wrap the object if it was small enough, and tuck it into a plastic or paper bag for the journey home. But making that U all the more snug was the fact that Barski had placed another piece of furniture—a drop-leaf table— to the right of his desk. It was marked with a yellow tag that read SOLD.

The top of the drop leaf table held a silver-plated Sheffield water pitcher and what looked like a hand-painted chamber pot done up in red flowers. From the blood streaks on the carpet, it looked as if one end of the drop-leaf table had been temporarily placed right against the breakfront cabinet. So close that Milo would have been obliged to slide the drop-leaf table out of the way to open the breakfront.

Barski had an obsession with locks and chains and childish systems of security. The links of a long chain ran through the pulls of the breakfront, and were locked in front with a hefty padlock. We used to think it funny, watching him lock up, snapping the padlock shut, letting it rest left of the center doors, as it was now. And he had no qualms about sliding other pieces in front of it. The drop-leaf table was there now, but back in the day it was stuff like lamps, statuary, picture frames—stuff he was planning to wrap for a customer, refinish, or repair. He had so much stuff in his work zone that the only space he had left to position his chair was the size of a twenty-five-cent stamp.

But whoever had been here last hadn't bothered with the locks and chains. They'd simply conked Milo on the head, slid the drop leaf table away, and smashed the glass. Two of the peacock feathers that Milo had so carefully preserved inside that breakfront were scattered underfoot. Feather No. 3 had floated down into the chamber pot.

Munoz stood at the far end of the desk. The tan cash register and credit card machine sat on a wide piece of faded red felt near a phone and desk blotter. Papers littered the desk. Munoz studied a group of objects spread out on a white handkerchief. A wallet, some coins, a batch of keys, a shiny black comb. He frowned, then looked at Aunt Bea. "Miss Valentine, do you mind stepping over here, please?"

"*Ms.* Valentine."

"Fine, have it your way. Easy now, *Ms.* Valentine, careful of the books."

Bea stepped forward slowly. From that end of the desk, she could see Milo's feet under the chair and pile of books. She didn't cringe or flinch. Munoz asked if that's how she found him. My aunt said yes—feet towards the back of the store, head and arms splayed out toward the front.

"How long was he wearing that bandage?"

Bea's face was stone, her cheekbones damp with sweat. "As I've already indicated, he fell last Thursday, New Year's Day, and broke his nose. Or so he said."

I leaned over the desk, craning to get a peek. Barski wore a jacket and tie, coal pants, and a stiff bandage on his nose. The nose didn't look too bad, but someone had given him a new wound to worry about on the left side of his head. His glasses had flown off.

Munoz gestured at the drop-leaf table. Next to the Sheffield pitcher and chamber pot was a bloodied brass statue of a pudgy peacock. The bird's feathers jutted out at odd angles from a squat body as big as a bocce ball. It weighed six or seven pounds and sat on a short pair of scrawny brass legs.

"That bird," Munoz said. "Was that his?"

"Of course," she said. "It's been a fixture here for years."

I recognized it instantly, though it had been years since I'd seen it last. Barski had kept the peacock right on the corner of his desk. It was never for sale. Now his prize was spattered with blood. Streaks in the blood showed how the killer had dragged the drop leaf table away, closer to Barski's head.

"I gather he came in on the holiday to clean up the shop," my aunt said without being asked. "He said he was hanging one of these lamps and fell off the ladder. He told us about it when we saw him Friday, adorned with that sad splint."

My eyes rolled up to the chandeliers. In the glare of the fluorescent lights, their crystal teardrops seemed coated with peach fuzz. Just think—one low price bought you the chandelier and thirty years of dust.

Birk waved his chin at the breakfront. "What kind of books did he keep up there? Anything valuable?"

"That's the thing," Amos said, "I never got the impression that he *loved* books or did much trade in that area. My God, just look at the place!"

Munoz didn't. He looked at Amos instead, peering at him as if for the first time. His eyes went from Amos's beret to his shoes, and lingered there a moment. Then Munoz looked at the other plainclothesman, a wide, puffy-faced cop with a slick head of coppery hair. Sweat coursed down his face. "He's been rolled," this detective told Munoz. "No cash in the wallet, nothing in the cash register. There's a safe out back, but it's locked. Whoever killed him did it for the cash on hand."

Munoz scowled at his partner. "Of course there's nothing in the register. Look at the sign out front. He didn't open on Sundays. Probably just stopped by yesterday for some reason, and they hit him then."

"ME hasn't looked at him yet," his partner reminded him. "Dead guy could have come in early this morning."

Munoz shook his head. "Birk, you think I need a doctor to tell me how long he's been dead? Rigor's starting to pass, blood's all down ... what else you need? It happened sometime yesterday and he's been stewing in this heat all night. He's lucky the place wasn't looted."

"Some luck," Amos snapped.

Munoz waved a hand at his partner. "Go find the thermostat or call the landlord. I'm dying over here."

Birk pushed past a technician and clunked off. Munoz used a handkerchief to lift Barski's keys. He came around the desk and skipped daintily over Barski's outstretched arm and the puddle of blood to try the keys in the padlock on the breakfront. Nothing doing. The CSU guy watched him. We were silent. He finally gave up and barked, "How you making out, Birk?"

Birk poked his head out of a back room and announced, "Hey, we got a darkroom back here, Luis."

A damn fine deduction, I thought. Two points for the detective. Munoz looked at us. "Man took pictures?"

"Yes," my aunt said impatiently. "In another life he was a photojournalist with a newspaper out west, and a stringer for one of the European agencies." She pointed at Grace Kelly and Brando on the wall across from us. "Those were his. All this ..." she said, waving at the shop, "came later."

Munoz studied Grace and Brando almost as closely as he'd studied Amos Horne's shoes. "Hmmph," he said. "Those aren't bad. You would have thought he'd open a photo gallery, not an antique place." He turned his attention back to the breakfront and the padlock. He worked his way through all of Milo's keys, and when he came empty, he shot a look at one of the forensics guys. "You find any other keys on this guy?"

"No, sir."

"Detective," my aunt said. "You'll find the keys to the padlock in the right top drawer of his desk. One of those keys in your hand unlocks the drawer. I can show you if you'd like—"

He waved her off curtly. "I don't need your help, lady. I got it."

My aunt took no offense at his brusque manner. She tilted her head wistfully at the ceiling. "You're quite correct about him, by the way. You'd think a man would adhere strictly to his area of expertise, but that isn't Milo. He prefers to dabble."

"You're getting your tenses confused, Ms. Valentine," Munoz said snarkily. "That *wasn't* Milo. He *preferred*. Past tense."

Following her instructions, he unlocked the drawer. He took out scratch pads, pieces of Barski's blue-edged writing paper, a wicked-looking letter opener, lots of blank price tags, a Rolodex. But no key.

"They took his watch!" Amos said, glancing over the items spread out on the handkerchief. "Do you see it, Bea? He *loved* that pocket watch. Crooks took it too!"

All along, I'd thought Munoz had done a great job shrugging off my aunt and Amos's comments. But now, for some reason, he snapped. "Okay, Boy Scouts, that's enough!" he said, shooing us out of the dead zone with his notebook. "Single file, up front. Everybody out!"

❧ 3 ❧
ENTER THE YUP

The doc arrived with an assistant DA who looked like a high schooler who'd gotten lost on his way to the Debate Team meeting. I guess it was a dull Monday downtown. I watched them work, felt my bad leg start to stiffen up on me, and looked out the front door. People shouting. A guy my age was picking a fight with a cop at the door. It took me a while to make him.

Kenning.

He'd changed. Looked neater, more presentable. No beard and moth-eaten sweaters. New glasses, too; round, wire-rimmed ones that made him look like he wasn't actually an art geek. He wore a beige overcoat and gray fedora and struggled as the cops tried to keep him out.

"Bea!" he yelled. "Would you tell 'em to lay off?"

Munoz wiped his forehead. "Who are you?"

"Kenning. Walter Kenning," he was saying, shaking them off to fix his tie. He had a tie bar under the knot, very crisp and snappy. "You people make it a point to rag on everyone? Hey, Dante, Bea. Amos, how's it going?"

Munoz whirled to face Bea. "Another one of your friends, Ms.

Valentine? Why don't you send out some invitations while you're at it, have a tea party?"

"Tea," she scoffed. "It's not yet time for tea, young man. I have excellent coffee waiting for me next door. But you'd be remiss to discount our visitor. This young man worked for Milo for some time."

"Partner?"

"Intern, assistant, whatever," Kenning corrected him.

"Fine," Munoz said. "Fine, pal, you come walking in here, you wait for someone to let you in. This is crazy, all these people in here. You," he said, looking at Walt. "You know anything about a darkroom?"

"He sent out a little catalog every quarter to a small mailing list. He'd photograph some of the pieces he was most proud of," Kenning said. He turned to my aunt. "What are they looking for? Don't they know who did it?"

"No," my aunt said, surveying Barski's desk. "And at the rate they're going, they probably won't."

"I heard that, lady," Munoz snapped.

"Gosh, look at the place!" Kenning said. "Cops trash it?" Kenning hadn't lost his Midwestern accent; his voice rose and dipped like hilly farmland.

"Whoever killed Milo did this," I told him. I was getting self-conscious in his presence. I reached up and straightened my tie. In general I would describe my sartorial style as *unformed*. A few years back, Kenning and I had looked unformed together. Back then, we had plenty of things to talk about, plans for the future. I used to worry he'd grow up and become Barski No. 2. Judging from appearances I needn't have worried. I wondered if he still painted.

Munoz finished bagging the contents of the dead man's pockets and came over to break up our chatting. "Again, mister, from the top?"

"Well, like I was saying, he had that little catalog," Kenning said, "and sometimes, if he got in good with certain customers, he'd photograph and appraise their pieces for insurance purposes. Insurance riders can get pricey, but almost anyone who collects seriously adds them to their homeowner's policy. They just need to have proof of the object's value. That's where Milo came in."

"There's a safe back here. You know the combination?"

"No. Milo kept that to himself."

"Any of you know the combo?"

Blank faces.

Kenning extracted a light blue handkerchief from his fancy gray suit and dabbed at his eyes. He was a little shorter than I was, maybe six feet, with the dashing good looks of a Sharper Image model. Hand the man an exploding briefcase and he was ready for a photo shoot. The glasses, though, made him look nebbishy.

Munoz opened his notebook. "You worked here how long?"

"Three years? I was going to school. NYU."

"Uh-huh. And you last saw him when? Heya, you got a problem, Ms. Valentine?"

Bea had been staring at Barski's desk blotter. Under a blotter flap were sheets of fine white tissue paper for wrapping delicate pieces.

"Look," she said.

Munoz swiveled his head, unreasonably flustered. "At what?"

"The top sheet is ripped," my aunt said. "Milo often used them for scratch paper when he was on the phone. One might theorize that if he had a sensitive note there in plain sight, the killer—"

Munoz exploded. "Get them out of here! All of them!"

As we filed past him on the way out the door, he stuffed his hand in his coat and came up with a plastic bag. "See, *Ms.* Sherlock?" he said, shoving it in Bea's face. "We got it, okay? How about letting us do our jobs? Birk, get them next door and take their statements."

Out on the sidewalk, Walt said out of the side of his mouth, "People are soooo sensitive."

Through the broken glass of the door, we heard Munoz chucking a fit. "Hey! We got a couple of junior G-men here! You believe this? Lock that door!"

"The glass is broken, sir."

"Lock it anyway!"

I could breathe much easier in the cold air of the sidewalk. The rain had let up, the sky a shifting mass of gray clouds. We moved past the patrolmen and headed to the Book Lady bookshop. Amos and Walter Kenning went in, but Bea stopped out front. She produced a tiny spiral notebook from the pockets of her down jacket and wrote in it with a tiny silver pen.

"Are you free to run an errand of the utmost urgency?" she said.

"Why?"

"*Why*, he says. I love when you say *Why*. Why can you never do what I ask without giving me an argument?"

"Why do you insist on making an ass of yourself? What was that cute stunt you pulled in there just now?"

She chewed the tip of her tongue as she wrote. "Shall we try again? We shall have need of a cab."

It was a rainy day in Manhattan, and the likelihood of hailing a cab was as good as becoming drinking buddies with your proctologist. "I can try," I said, adding, just for the heck of it, "Why?"

When she didn't answer, I looked at her notebook. In that bizarre penmanship she learned from a deranged teacher decades ago, she had written:

FRI. Haverstrom Grouser Club 3p

"What is that?"

"Milo's note. I memorized it when that ignoramus showed it

to me. Now, would you kindly summon a vehicle while I fetch my umbrella and feed a little white lie to Amos and Walter?"

❦ 4 ❦

THE MYSTERIES OF BROOKLYN

It had taken me years to learn what my parents had always known; my aunt had a notion that she was a genius, a notion that unfortunately prompted her to stick her pointy nose into everyone's business. I couldn't argue with her intelligence. I just wished she'd keep it to herself. So far the morning had been one piece of theater after another, and I knew she was only getting started.

After some legerdemain I managed to land a cab, and we headed south in silence, me sulking, her scribbling. After a while she put down the notebook, dried her hair and face with a fresh handkerchief from her massive purse, and offered me a pastry from a small white bag. When I declined, she persisted, using a word that was always tossed around in our family.

"*Mangia*," she said.

"I don't want to *mangia*," I said. "You *mangia*."

She shrugged as if *I* were the sensitive one, and bit into Barski's turnover. I hoped she'd choke. "At least drink the cappuccino," she coaxed, offering me a small paper cup with a plastic lid.

I sipped as the cab joined the stream of cars heading down the

West Side Highway. Was it my imagination or did the city look dirtier after a rain?

"Why can't we stay out of it this time?"

"Because something's wrong about the whole thing. You saw the chandeliers. Their significance failed to impress the detective," she said.

"Yeah. The chandeliers were dusty and the rest of the place looked like a mother-in-law just gave it the white glove treatment."

"Precisely. If Milo had fiddled with those chandeliers last Thursday as he claimed, it would have been to clean them. They were in the shop for months. So he *didn't* clean them. He lied. Now I ask you," she said, wagging a finger at me. "Why would he lie?"

"You think someone popped him in the face."

"Yes, *pop*."

"And they came back and did it for good?"

She shrugged and stared out the window. I let her stare. Traffic was bad, and I kind of wished I had something to occupy my thoughts. My mind kept unspooling the scene in the shop. When we reached the entrance to the Brooklyn-Battery Tunnel, she said, "Our poor fool is dead."

"I know. And we always made fun of him. He was one big joke to us."

"Children are that way," she said, deflecting.

"You did, too!"

Her cheeks turned scarlet. "You needn't remind me. What can I say? He is—er, he *was* an odd bird, *wasn't* he? A bizarre, unusual man. The quirks of his character are what we'll always remember about him. To be honest, I thought him a poser, but I am bound by our friendship, such as it was, to look into the matter. By now, that should be simple."

Sure it would—for her. Last summer she'd stuck her nose into the strange kidnapping of the daughter of one of my employer's clients, and ended up sending the cops on the right path. Before that, it was the mysterious case of an investment banker who had stepped into an empty conference room on the thirty-eighth floor of a Financial District skyscraper and disappeared. Before that, it was a diamond dealer and his missing bucket of ice (not what you think). Two Christmases ago, it had been the bit with the drunken Santa and the arsonist from Corona, Queens. No matter how you looked at it, Aunt Bea was becoming an excellent meddler.

"But if you never liked him much, why bother?"

She looked stunned. Crossing her arms, she said absently, "Like it or not, we were in the same line of work. He was vain, cheap, a bit of a charmer. I considered him a phony, but I suppose he had to be in order to wheedle his way into his clients' homes and take pictures of their precious objets d'art. But he *was* a bookseller in part, and that association must be honored in some way. It is—how shall we say?—a necessary obligation."

"Amos liked him, played chess with him," I said dreamily. "Walt won't admit it, but I think he was locked in kind of father-figure-slash-mentor scenario with Barski. But you? You hated the guy."

"Untrue! That's a hurtful thing to say. He just rubbed me the wrong way. Did you ever hear him talk? *I* was a bookseller, but he sold *antiquarian* volumes. He knew furniture, I give him that. His family was in the trade for years. But only a man like him would have the effrontery to think that he could easily add books to his repertoire. He knew only what Amos and I taught him."

Several minutes later, while I was digging in my wallet, she peered through raindrops at a simple two-family house, redone in awful white siding and white brickface. Barski's Brooklyn chateau.

"Do you have a key to his place?"

"What key?"

She paused at the front steps and ran her fingers along a

spiked fence around a square of yellow grass the size of a burial plot. In the street in front of the house, she studied the windshield of a red Ford Escort; it had two parking tickets. Behind it, a green Dodge Aspen blocked a fire hydrant and sported one ticket on the windshield. The Ford was Barski's car, hit with two counts of illegal parking, two days in a row. I didn't recognize the Dodge. But Bea plucked the ticket from its wiper. Her eyes glanced up at the windows of the house, still lined with colored lights and a gold banner proclaiming, FELIZ NAVIDAD!

Bea's eyes brightened. She winked at me. "Mrs. Gutierrez … lovely lady, but a poor driver. Shall we?"

I followed her up, watching her fuss with her hair, practice her smile, hand gestures, and mode of attack. All the while she studied the house like a chef sizing up cuts of beef. I loved this woman. She was a bit of a phony, true, but a *charming* phony. I suppose you had to be in order to wheedle yourself into people's homes.

The door was opened by a tiny dark-haired woman in a blue skirt and lavender blouse. She was in her mid-forties, but her hair color had graced a store shelf earlier that week.

"How are you, Mrs. Gutierrez?" Bea said.

"Señora! So nice to see you. We never thanked you for the wine. You been okay?"

My aunt brushed the air as if she gave bottles of wine to strangers every day, never expecting a word of thanks.

"I'm not very well today. You heard the bad news?"

Mrs. Gutierrez hadn't. She screamed when Bea told her. Her tenant was dead. Gone. Hasta la vista. Bea slipped effortlessly into Spanish, explaining the morning's gruesome discovery, then launched into the equally distressing news about Mrs. G's parking ticket.

The little woman stepped back so quickly you'd think Aunt Bea had presented her with a dead skunk. "What idiots!" she said in English.

Two minutes later I ascended the stairs behind Aunt Bea's bobbing rump. I heard her panting, and I braced myself at each step in case she made an involuntary backflip. At the top of the stairs I realized that Mrs. Gutierrez was crying. She turned to us and said, "Who did this thing to him?"

Bea said she didn't know, but no one who could perpetrate such a heinous act could escape justice for long. "Now, Señora," Bea said, "the police will come soon, wanting to look at his apartment. It would be best not to mention that we came looking for my nephew's scarf."

"Nothing!" the woman said in English. "They get nothing from me!"

She inserted a key into a little box at the side of the door. The red light went out. An alarm system here too. What a strange little man. In my experience, New Yorkers tended to protect their homes with objects that required brute strength to hack—high-security locks, bars on windows and doors—not alarm systems.

The landlady opened the door. We entered a small kitchen and flicked on the lights. I smelled bacon fat. Sunday morning's garbage hadn't been tossed out. To our right was a refrigerator, a sink, and a gas stove. Mrs. Gutierrez plopped herself down on a kitchen chair to collect her thoughts.

Huffing and puffing from the long climb, Bea nevertheless lost no time searching. For what, I couldn't say. She ventured down a small hall that led to a bedroom and living room. She paused before a hall closet and pulled it open. She found two tripods, a set of portable spotlamps, a camera case that held three cameras, a batch of colored filters, lenses, and plenty of 35mm film.

Aside from a few summer jackets wrapped in dry cleaners' plastic, the only other items in the closet were a trio of banker boxes on the floor. They were filled with old fashion and home decorating magazines. The magazines dated from the late 1940s. I flipped through the titles. *West Coast Living. California Style. Antiques Owner.*

Bea pulled one out and leafed through it. Fancy homes, funny-looking people in outdated clothing. Women showing off pricy gewgaws. A woman in flouncy pink stood beside a huge mantle-piece stocked with porcelain figurines and antique clocks. A man with a pipe and ascot lounged against a shelf of books and bottled ships. Their faces twisted into a silly grin. See how rich I am?

I found a leather portfolio and unzipped it. Newspaper clippings from something called the *Los Angeles Sun-Chronicle*. The earliest images in the portfolio were feature pics. Teens necking in movie theaters. Or else hanging out at night in the parking lot of drive-in hamburger joints. Movie premieres. Gradually, the images progressed to the gossip and society columns. Debutante balls. Charity functions. The latest, from the sixties, showed dolled-up models on the fashion pages of the women's section. In every case the credit line read: M. BARSKI.

"Didn't know he had it in him," I said.

"People never fail to surprise," Bea said.

The last newspaper was dated 1962. The magazines stretched to 1964, but there were fewer photos credited to Barski. At the back of the box we found a large color photo mounted on cardboard, with a plastic overlay and the words *Spitting Image*. It showed a bare-chested guy in jeans standing before a set of triple mirrors, like the ones you see in department store fitting rooms. A red flag with the anarchy sign fluttered in his back pocket. A pretty, dark-haired girl peeked around the edge of the mirrors, showing a bit of her face and even more of her thigh.

"What is it?" Bea asked. "An ad?"

"Could be. Subliminal. You're supposed to feel sexy and buy the jeans."

My aunt held up the photo at arm's length. "I do not feel sexy. I rarely feel sexy. I feel like sticking him back in the box."

And so she did.

❧ 5 ❧

MISS PEACOCK

The living room was furnished cheaply with a single armchair and sofa covered in green corduroy. An end table near the couch was laden with tiny figures of brass animals, smaller than the brass peacock that had ended Barski's life. A large folding table stood nearby. An old manual typewriter sat on it, next to a stack of Barski's blue-edged fine stationery, spiral notebooks, an empty fruit bowl, and more tagged objects, probably destined for the shop. Facing us was a tall, five-shelf bookshelf loaded with books. A massive Magnavox TV loomed in the corner across from the armchair. The place was immaculate, well lit, and lonely. A copy of *TV Guide* rested on an ottoman, neatly folded to Sunday night's schedule.

"Oh boy," I said. "Big night ahead."

My aunt waved her hand. "Please. Don't joke." Her voice was serious, almost offended.

I left the examination of the books to the expert and went to the bedroom, where I found a double bed squished between a worn bureau and a low dresser. A suitcase lay on a luggage stand under the only window. I took the bureau first. The top drawer held some bank books, envelopes, and some papers on a field of green felt. The bank books told me that Barski had closed his Manhattan savings account on Friday, withdrawing $4,553.39. On the same day he'd withdrawn $9,000 from his Brooklyn savings account. He'd returned Saturday to close the Brooklyn account, in the amount of $6,000 and change. But he left untouched his Brooklyn *checking* account, which still held $3,453.56.

I glanced at the top of the bureau and locked eyes with a porcelain piggy bank hiding behind a mother-of-pearl jewelry box. Both were empty. Two books sat beside the pig. The pig didn't blink as I moved on to the next set of drawers.

In his shirt drawer I hit gold: a folded sheaf of paper that read, LAST WILL & TESTAMENT. Signed, sealed, and witnessed last July 15. I read it fast. When the estate cleared probate, an entity called the Eunice K. Mauro Trust Fund in Allentown, Pennsylvania, would be one ecstatic fund. Amos and Walter would feel touched. Bea would be one unhappy camper. I went back to the checkbook, which proved to be dull reading. I found something much more interesting in a thick envelope: receipts for postal money orders. Dozens, maybe hundreds of them. For two hundred, two hundred fifty, never more than five hundred dollars each. Judging by the dates, they came out to be one money order a month for ... geez, *plenty* of months.

Now, I have always been impressed by the ineffable beauty of money orders. Cash for cash, no names, no numbers. Untraceable. But Barski had played it straight. He'd filled in the blanks and kept the receipts. PAY TO: E.K. Mauro Trust Fund, c/o Millicent M. Eversman. First National Savings, Allentown, PA.

I dropped it all back in the drawer and slid it shut. I hopped over the bed and picked through the stuff on top of the dresser. Combs and a brush, hair oil, the usual. And a ceramic picture frame edged in gold leaf. Pressed behind the glass was an old black-and-white photo of a young, bearded Beatnik-type dude standing near a crouching woman, both of them showing their teeth to the world and not caring how goofy they were dressed.

Milo Barski, circa 1960-something, judging from the car they were leaning on.

The woman was pretty. Light brown hair, round face, darkish brow and pleated slacks. Yeah, she would call them slacks. She was almost on her knees, looking up at the camera, her hands stretched out before her ... feeding some kind of animal. I couldn't tell what kind of beast it was because its body was obscured by a faded memento at the bottom of the frame, trapped between the glass and photo.

Was it a flower of some kind? No. It was the tip of a peacock's feather.

I rifled quickly through the half-empty dresser. Nothing, but a bulge in the suitcase attracted me. Bulges will do that. I unzipped the top of it and tossed back the top. Ties, shirts, pants, and underwear all hid the bulge. I peeled back the clothes and found a stack of books tied with red-and-white string. I undid the string and picked up the first book.

The Era of Good Feelings, by George Dangerfield.

I opened the cover. Smack dab in the middle of the pages Barski had cut a neat six-by-two-inch hole. It ran down to the back cover of the book. I was looking at a homemade book safe. I tried flipping through the pages, but they were glued shut. The same thing was going on with the next book on the stack—a thick edition of *Sotheby's World Guide to Antiques and Their Prices*.

On the other hand, Friedman's *Monetary History of the United States* gave me trouble; the *cover* was glued shut. But after I'd ripped it open and mangled half the pages, I knew why. In the center of one of those neat little holes lay the puckish face of Benjamin Franklin, pleading with me to free him and his greenish brethren from a rubber band.

There were still two more books in the suitcase. I looked back to the top of the bureau. I reached for the two books next to the piggy bank. Herman Wouk's *The Winds of War* and Margaret Mitchell's *Gone with the Wind*. These two had been cut and glued to create book safes, but both were empty. In fact, the cover of the Mitchell book had been practically torn off the spine.

"Oh, Aunt Bea?"

Her voice, when it came, sounded like a grunt. I took the books into the living room. She stood on a kitchen chair near the bookshelf, staring at an oil painting hanging on the wall. It showed boats at sea and fishermen hauling in their wooden-slatted lobster pots.

In her hands, of course, was a book. When I came in, she replaced the book on the shelves and gave me her attention.

"Find something?"

"We are in deep you-know-what."

Her eyebrows arched. "Proceed."

I shook the pile of books against my chest. "Two of these are full of cash and four are sitting around with their mouths open, waiting to be fed."

She can be athletic when she wants to be. She pursed her lips and slowly lowered her ponderous body to the floor. I heard the fruit bowl rattle. "People do occasionally hide money in books," she answered. "A few dollars here and there is no big deal."

"How about *thousands* of dollars?"

Her olive face went yellow. "What?" She snatched the book from my hands and studied the cash inside. She slapped the cover shut. "Did you open the others?"

"Only one other is glued shut. I didn't see the point."

"Yes, you are right."

She sat at the folding table and paged through one of those marble-covered notebooks. She looked at me. "Relax. Here. Glue that book shut." She slid a bottle of Elmer's at me. "Very little glue. It must be dry for the police."

In the notebook Barski had catalogued his current shop inventory. Judging from the first page, it was a list of books—their descriptions, condition, dates of acquisition, and sale. While Bea read down the list, I glanced at a tiny white price tag on the fruit bowl. One side read $250, the other was gibberish. I slipped it in my pocket.

"Does that thing list just books?" I said.

"Yes. There's a second volume for antiques and so forth. Hmm … See? At least he had the good sense to convert his worst books into those book safes of his. Look at the condition of *these* …"

"This is no time to appraise the darn things, Bea!"

"On the contrary. Their condition is important. Look. Four books: Friedman's *Monetary History of the United States*, Munn's *Encyclopedia of Banking and Finance*, *Gone with the Wind*, and *The Winds of War* are all crossed off in the ledger. No sale date. That means he was taking them off the market, so to speak. Were they all in the suitcase?"

"No. The two Wind titles were on top of the bureau. *Gone with the Wind* is in bad shape. The cover's mostly torn off."

"Intriguing. And the other titles in the suitcase?"

"*The Era of Good Feelings* and Sotheby's price guide."

She ticked them off. Both had been crossed off in the notebook. "And the third book?"

"There isn't a third. Only two."

She gazed at me narrowly. "Are you telling me there's not a first edition copy of *An American Tragedy* in the suitcase?"

"No."

She smiled, "Then we are making progress."

I closed the book on dabs of glue. It was still a botched job. Any idiot, including Munoz, would know someone had wrenched the book safe open. "I'm not really seeing the progress, Bea."

She headed for the bedroom and attacked the suitcase with far more gusto than I had. She gave a cry of joy and held up an envelope from a travel agency.

"See? Money, a packed suitcase, and the final prop—a bus ticket to Washington, DC."

I swiped the envelope from her hands and stuffed it back into the suitcase. I tied the books together with the string, and replaced them too. I zipped up the suitcase and managed to leave a smaller bulge than I'd found.

When I turned around, she had the picture frame in her hands. "Interesting," she murmured. "You saw the woman and the bird?"

"I saw the woman and a *feather*. What bird?"

She held up the picture frame. She'd slid the glass out and was pointing to the corner of the image. The woman was feeding a peacock.

"We should leave, Bea. This is making me nervous."

We started to go, but she had to go through the bureau. Just had to. Ran her hands along the drawer bottoms and came up empty. In the kitchen she went through the drawers swiftly but methodically while my stomach churned. *Come on!* The kitchen door was closed. Mrs. Gutierrez was gone. I took out a handkerchief and rubbed the table and the chair where our gullible benefactress had sat. Bea was inspecting the freezer when I looked up. Nothing inside but two TV dinners and a half gallon of Sealtest's Heavenly Hash ice cream.

Bea went for the fridge. Two bottles of white wine cooled their rims near a quart of milk. She even checked the meat and vegetable bins. Empty.

"Are you ready?" I asked impatiently.

She was. On the way down we heard a vacuum cleaner droning in the landlady's apartment. She went to tell Mrs. G. that we were leaving, and would she kindly reset the alarm?

On the stoop, I said, "She squeals, we're dead."

"She won't," she assured me. "She is the soul of discretion. Last Wednesday on New Year's Eve, Amos and I brought Milo home drunk as a fish. She helped us sober him up and put him to bed. I gave her a bottle of wine from his fridge."

"You mean it wasn't even yours to give?"

She chuckled over that, while I tried to picture a drunken fish.

"On top of that," she continued, "today the police are dead to her. Ah! I see she has moved her car!"

I looked. Mrs. G. parked it up the block, right up against the rear bumper of one of her neighbors' vehicles. As we walked to the big street in search of a cab, I mopped the sweat off my face.

"The bottles," she mused. "He's drunk three since New Year's. That's only five days ... three for him."

"Did he have a problem with alcohol?"

"Not that I saw. There are three types of drinkers. Ones who get jolly. Ones who get mean. And ones who get silent. Milo was one of those. I can't imagine the secrets he kept clammed up inside that hairy head of his. Tell me, you didn't find a lone key anywhere in there, did you?"

"Key? No. What key would that have been?"

"The one missing from the shop. On Saturday I went in to ask if he wished to order lunch with me and Amos. He said no, he was going out. And he was just locking the key ring away in his desk. Now it's missing. If it's not home or on his person, where is it?"

"You're hilarious!" I said. "Why does everything have to be mystery with you?"

"I'm not manufacturing a mystery, my dear boy. We are solidly in the midst of one."

"Who cares?" I said. "Whoever killed him didn't use the key. They *smashed* the glass. Let me tell you, I don't like it. The whole thing back there with the money in the books? It makes me nervous. We shouldn't have come."

"I don't see why you are so upset. I admit it looks troubling, but it's hardly a sweating matter."

"Bea, come on. Last Thursday someone pushed in your pal's face and it scared him enough that he packed up, got all his money and planned a nice one-way trip to Washington. What is that? Before he skips town, someone smashes his head in. On top of that, it really looks like he's been shelling out money to someone for years, maybe decades. Two hundred a month back in the day, as much as five hundred two days ago. Who's been getting that dough? Miss Peacock 1958?"

Her eyes narrowed. When she was thinking, she looked like a cat on a search-and-destroy mission, and just as dangerous. "Who *was* she? Clearly a lover, but why keep her image on the dresser all these years? Why the undying devotion? He never married, and in twenty years I've never heard him mention a woman by name who wasn't a client."

"I got a name. Millicent Eversman. Only I think she might be married now. If not, there may be a child in this. A girl or woman named Eunice."

"Did you read the will?"

"It was drafted by one of those cheap firms that advertises on the radio. For fifty bucks you get a will and a ham sandwich. Amos gets the jade chess set, if the cops ever finish with it. Walter gets some furniture for his apartment. Eunice's trust fund in Allentown gets the rest. Who knows who Eunice is? If it's a love child by the peacock lady, she's got to be twenty, at least. Should be a nice piece of change, all those hundreds, even after the IRS gets its share."

"Is that all?"

"No. Guess who gets to be the executor of the whole freaking mess?"

"Who?"

I flicked a finger at her beak as I opened the cab door.

She was aghast. "Me? Heavens, what a disaster." She leaned forward and spoke into the plexiglass divider. "Driver—for heaven's sake, take us to Manhattan!"

❧ 6 ❧

GROUSERS ALL

W e returned to the Book Lady bookshop shortly before noon, after a brief stop in Little Italy. Chaos reigned on Fourth Avenue. The cops hadn't left; they'd simply moved next door to Bea's shop.

Amos was having a shouting match with a snooty guy in a homburg who demanded to see Mr. Barski. He *had* to see Mr. Barski. He had an *appointment* to see him, that wasn't a lie, they could check it if they wanted, and he didn't see what all the commotion was about. Amos was saying Milo wouldn't be seeing anyone, anymore, ever again, hoping that the fellow would catch his drift, which he didn't.

Meanwhile, the back door of the Book Lady was open wide, offering a chilly view of the alley behind the building. A bunch of blues wandered around outside, including the CSU guys. Munoz was chewing out Birk, telling him just where his grandmother purchased her foot apparel.

Altogether, I thought I'd rather be in Hoboken.

Bea foolishly asked Amos what seemed to be the problem, and ended up sparking a lengthy rant from the little man about the insensitivity of cops. Here he was, trying to congenially answer their questions, when he happened to mention that he'd been stationed in Washington during the war, just like Milo. And that only triggered the cops, who proceeded to question him for an hour more on that subject and a litany of others, such as his shoe size, which was Men's 7. Now, all of a sudden, they were going about in high dudgeon about some book. No, Amos didn't know precisely what book. "Ask them!" he snorted at my aunt. "What am I, the information desk?"

Apparently, though, Munoz's team had found what they were looking for just now in the alley.

All the while, as Amos prattled on, the homburg-er was yanking the sleeves of Bea's voluminous garments, demanding to see someone in authority. He was here to begin an independent appraisal of Mr. Barski's premises, which would soon be offered for sale or liquidation on account of the gentleman's upcoming retirement. Homburger had made the appointment last Friday. Ask that Walter fellow, he said. *He* set up the whole thing.

Boy, I thought. This is crazy.

Slowly, without a care in the world, Aunt Bea shucked off her down jacket and hung it on the coatrack at the back of her shop. She slowly tied on an apron and plugged in her panini grill. I peeled myself away from the drama of the shop and found her with her nose in the pantry, flicking through a little brown box of tea packets. She already had her chipped purple enameled kettle on one of the burners.

"I think Amos is requiring some chamomile," she said, without looking up. "I suggest you go, Dante. Save yourself. You have your marching orders."

I walked the few blocks to Union Square and called the agency on a payphone. Melinda was eating lunch, but she patched me through to Rawlsy's extension. I gave him everything I had on Barski, including the newspapers, magazines, and the vaguest hint of the Allentown moochers. I gave him Amos's and Walter's names and told him to have a ball. The cops would be on that trail, too, but I knew Rawlsy would get it first if he had a head start. He had a law degree and a license, too, and someday when all the bars in town closed for good he'd get around to hanging a shingle.

I had him look up an address for me, then I hung up and grabbed the Lexington Avenue line to Fifty-First Street. I walked across town in search of the Grouser Club. I stalked numbers along Fifty-Second Street between Madison and Fifth until I came to a three-story building constructed of red stone, its facade held up by two tan columns and its windows dripping with stone drapery.

The place surprised me. You can forget your ideas of a swanky, posh restaurant catering to the beautiful people. The Grouser Club was just that—a club. And its diners were not so much beautiful as they were decrepit and jowly. It was lunchtime, but I didn't think I could afford even a breadstick there. I waved off the maître d' to get across the smoky room to the pinewood bar. Behind the bar I found a flight of stairs that were blocked by a maroon velvet rope.

Near the stairs was a small secretaire, crammed with papers and two telephones with light-up buttons. A wiry, strapping guy in a tux and cummerbund stood by the desk, shuffling through papers, ripping into someone on the line. He looked about six feet, two hundred pounds, and moved with the slow precision of a baseball player. Pulled at his collar, scratched his short black hair, rolled his eyes restlessly around his desk. "Uh—huh, uh—huh," he was saying, "can you hang on? Good," he said, hugging the phone to his chest, and looking at me. "What?"

"I want to see Mr. Haverstrom."

"You a king or prince or Pope or something?"

I shook my head. "But I do on occasion use the royal 'we.'"

"How's that?"

"It's joke," I said, "told better by Mark Twain."

He ignored me and went back to his phone, telling someone he didn't have their darn briarwood, they must have left it upstairs. I waved at him, and slipped under the velvet rope.

"Hey!" he said, suddenly interested. "I said beat it. Judge doesn't see anyone."

"I forgot," I said. "I'm an archduke on my mother's side. Name's Franz Ferdinand. See my medals?"

I held up a twenty, half-expecting him to recoil with disdain. But no. He snatched the cash, punched the HOLD button on his phone, and said, "I appreciate the effort, but you're wasting this. The guy sees no one."

From my wallet I took out one of *my* cards and one of Bea's. I borrowed his pen, and circled the address of the Book Lady & Friends Book Shop. "Try this," I said.

He looked like I'd handed him a buffalo chip. But he told me to stay put and galloped upstairs.

I leaned on the balustrade and watched the restaurant and breathed smoke. Hunting scenes and woodcuts on the walls, none of them very impressive, but they certainly looked expensive. They had a few hand-tinted framed prints of pheasants or quail that were brown from age. Busy place. Waiters sailed in and out with trays. I watched a frail elderly man with spectacles come in out of the cold, shaking rain off his thick gray overcoat. He eased onto a stool at the bar, and peeled off his galoshes. He didn't say boo to the barman, who nevertheless quickly slid a mug of Irish coffee in front of him. It was that kind of place.

But the whole time I was watching, something bugged me that I just couldn't put my finger on. But finally it popped into my head with utter clarity. There wasn't a single woman in the entire place. Just men of a certain age, as wrinkly as their out-of-fashion suits.

Time flew by. When the stair guard came back, he asked me to follow him up. "Well, that's a new one on me," he said, shaking his head in disbelief. "The Judge will see you in the Recreation Room."

I followed him up to a pair of heavy oaken doors. He opened the one on the left, and ushered me into a room full of round tables covered with white tablecloths. A swarm of busboys was setting a buffet table along some windows that looked out over Fifty-Second Street. More waiters buzzed around, fussing with knives and forks and soup bowls. He led me through the room to another set of tall double doors. He opened one, waved me in, and shut it after us. It shut snugly, like a stone over a tomb.

I didn't think places like this still existed, places where old gents sat around and stank up a room with their cigars. It might have been the ward of some geriatric hospital; its noises were the typical male noises. Grunts and hacks and wet coughs, and every so often someone made a discreet snort into a hankie. But there was money here. You could tell by their clothes and the walls of books behind glass and the high-back leather chairs.

My guide walked me over an immense Persian rug, parallel to the bookcases, past the fireplace and the sluggish members. They came one to a chair, reading newspapers, sipping Canada Dry, playing checkers, snoring. A few heads lifted to watch me; some didn't bother. Just a man, they probably thought. A young man, but still a man. I wondered if they knew that downtown in the next few weeks, a city judge would have to decide if places like this could keep women out. Maybe I was about to meet that judge, but I rather doubted it.

Their eyes followed me to a pentagonal alcove of the room, where an old man sat in a chair before a desk, speaking softly on a phone. My guide waved at him; the coot jabbed his thumb at a wooden folding chair that had been set up before him. That was for me. Only members got leather chairs. I wondered if they had assigned seats. On the old guy's lap was a copy of the *Wall Street Journal*. He waved my cards around in his hands, and I realized he was describing me to someone on the phone. When he was finished, he replaced the receiver and said, "You can go, Samuel."

"Sir, I'm supposed to wait for him."

"What did I say?"

Samuel went away, swearing sotto voce.

Haverstrom stood and watched the guy stalk out. He made a sound that sounded halfway between a chuckle and a dislodged lung. "There goes a fool, Mr. Sleet. Lost his Christmas bonus for sloppy attire and now he's been trying to kill us with kindness. Stood in here all morning lighting cigars. Didn't even take his break. Hah."

He reached up and drew a heavy accordion partition across the archway. We were alone. He said, "You check out, Mr. Sleet."

"Can I get that in writing?"

Glaring at me from behind a pair of wire-rimmed bifocals was a red-faced toad. His scalp was pink and covered with strands of white hair. His voice was a toad's voice without the summery music.

"I still have friends downtown," he continued. "A friend in the district attorney's office assures me that you are who you say you are. I'm told your late father was highly placed in the NYPD for some time, and I find you are related to this Valentine woman listed in *here*."

He slapped a palm on a fat book which lay closed on his desk. It was Bowker's American Book Trade Directory.

"You've come about Barski, I presume?"

"You know?'

"I have already received numerous antagonistic phone calls from the police. They threaten to send someone down here to interrogate me. I've told my friends downtown that I don't intend to see anyone at the moment."

"It's nice to have a choice in the matter."

Something in his throat rumbled. "Damned nuisance, having them track this to me. I don't need to get involved in murders, Mr. Sleet. It looks bad. I retired from the bench twelve years ago, but my sons are still making names for themselves."

"I just need to know if you saw Barski last Friday."

"Of course I saw him. I told the police that. They kept pushing me to tell them our business, but I told them it was private matter. Mr. Barski and I had an arrangement. He visited me once a quarter. I provided him with a list of my wants, and he tried to fulfill them by our next visit."

"Wants?" I said. "So he was your genie?"

He didn't appreciate the joke. He waited in silence for me to come around.

"Okay," I said. "I take it you mean you provided him with a *want list* of books you wanted to purchase?"

His eyes perked up. "The police are unaware of that. It hardly matters one way or another to their investigation. I've been trying to find out about this abhorrent matter all morning. Was it robbery? They won't tell me. Is anything missing from the shop? They can't say. I need to know, Mr. Sleet, and I'm willing to pay."

"Was Barski holding something for you?"

"Will you work for me, Mr. Sleet?"

"It would be nice if you answered my questions," I said.

"Answer mine and perhaps I will. Will you work for me? Yes or no?"

Tough question. Say no and he throws me out. Say yes and I'm working for a human amphibian. I said yes. He asked how much we charged for a day's work, and he slipped six fifties out of his wallet and laid them on the white tablecloth, face down, so they formed a little tent. He got out a notebook and pen. He stabbed at the money with his Mont Blanc. "Count it."

That was easy. Three hundred dollars and I still had no idea what the case was. He wrote a receipt, which I signed. He provided me with a pink carbon. Then closed his book. I stuffed the bills and receipt.

"I expect your employer to provide me with a letter of agreement at your earliest convenience," he said with a tortured smile. "Mr. Barski called me last Thursday during dinner to tell me he'd found a long-standing item on my list. An item so unusual that I'd come to regard it as a fantasy. A willow o' the wisp."

"Why don't you just say it was a book? I know it had to be. What else are you guys interested in over here?"

"Very well, a book. He said he was leaving town Friday on business and he wanted me to come down to some ... eatery in Midtown to pick it up. Rubbish. I told him off."

"Why?"

"You're a spry young fellow, Mr. Sleet. You think the world's your oyster, I'll be bound. And I'm sure it is. I am eighty-seven years old. I have an apartment next door. I rarely travel two blocks from this building. I wasn't about to go skipping downtown in the snow on the worst night of the year with every drunken lunatic loose on the street, just because he couldn't make it to me."

"Did he say *why* he was leaving town?"

"No, but it couldn't have been important. When I insisted, he did keep our original appointment for 3:00 p.m. Friday. But the damned fool was playing games. He didn't bring the book with him. I had a check for one thousand dollars ready, but he changed the terms. Now he wanted cash. I don't keep that much cash on my person or on these premises."

The image of Barski's cash-stuffed books flashed in my mind. "What's the title of the book?"

He tilted his head in the air and considered it briefly. "Let us concede for the moment that that is none of your business. The point is, I was ready to send a messenger over to the shop on Sunday. We've done it before. I send Samuel with the money, and the bookseller—whomever I'm dealing with at the moment—

gives him the book. We waited for Barski's phone call on Sunday, but never got it. I imagine he was dead by then."

"Why Sunday?"

He gave me a sick little grin. "I just wanted to make him wait. And I needed Saturday to go down and get the cash from my bank."

"Quite an inconvenience."

His mouth tensed. "It was. Now. I'm paying you for information. Find out if any books were stolen. Get the titles of the lost works, if possible, and report back to me. That's the first step. Second step is recovering the book from the estate *at the previously agreed-upon price*. I will not be chiseled by some greedy executor. I shall expect to see receipts of your reasonable expenses."

"Fine, you'll get them."

He was so smug, so content and confident in his overgrown playground. And the slicks downtown would support him all the way. Munoz would probably get in trouble for hassling him.

"You're a fine client," I said. "And so forthcoming. With your help, I should have this wrapped up in no time. What else can you tell me?"

"Just this. Mr. Barski seemed preoccupied both times I spoke to him. Wore a nose splint. The police were interested in that."

"When did he call you?"

I heard a bell chime somewhere, and footsteps padding off beyond our alcove. Lunchtime! I thought I saw Haverstrom salivating in the classic Pavlovian manner.

"Thursday. Five o'clock, right at dinnertime! Samuel had to fetch me away from my salad. Then Barski had the nerve to ask me to leave my dinner and meet him as he couldn't possibly leave his location."

"Did he say if he was waiting for someone?"

"You think I cared?"

No. He wouldn't. One last question before I either left or

choked the judge with his phone cord. "You remember the name of the restaurant?"

He rose and shunted aside the partition. The Recreation Room was empty. He walked me out to the private dining room. Behind the buffet table a man in a toque diligently lit cans of Sterno while the geezers queued, waiting for the big feed to begin. They might have been homeless men on a soup line at the Bowery Mission; only their suits set them apart from vagrants.

Haverstrom licked his chops. He led me to Table 1, closest to the buffet. He scanned the place settings and finally sat. Each table sat six, the settings marked with a folded card inscribed in gold. He sat at one marked HAVERSTROM and reached for a napkin. Probably wanted me to serve him.

He sipped a glass of water. "Look at them," he said in a whisper. "Fools. They all rush to be first and shovel it down so they can complain about gas later. Why not wait, and get a bigger portion? There's plenty to go around. Hah."

This seemed very funny to him, for some reason.

"The restaurant, Mr. Haverstrom? Did you get that?"

"What? Oh, sure ... I got that. The Six Coaches. Bit of a pricy place. Between Fifth and Sixth. If you go, watch out for the ribs. They cheat you. The menu says four, but they give you three and some gristle. But then, I haven't been there in years."

I thanked him for the advice and left. He was rubbing his hands when I left him, and I noticed that as each man sat around his table, they dug right in as he'd said, and no one said a word to him. I wondered if he'd gotten the same treatment eighty years ago on some schoolyard. It would have to add up, I thought, to make you hard and small-minded, as he was. I decided I wouldn't grow old.

"He's a charmer," I said to Samuel as I came down the stairs.

His eyelids drooped, giving him a lazy look. "Way it goes," he said.

"He wanted you to pick up something Sunday. A book. You remember the title?"

The eyes stopped moving, and stared at me hard. Seeing him up close, the folds under his eyes, the spatter of brown freckles, I realized that he looked older than he probably was. Working for tips from entitled codgers probably did a number on your collagen.

It took him two seconds to say, "No. Why? You think I'm pals with any of them?"

⚜ 7 ⚜

DEPT. OF LOST DREAMS

For a few years there, when I was bouncing around from job to job, trying to figure out what I would do with myself now that the NYPD was no longer in the cards, I actually spent a lot of time hanging around in Barski's shop bonding with a young Walter Kenning. Guess you could say he was like the brother I never had. Only three other men in the city could hold that title. One was Rawlsy, who was older and harder than I ever thought I'd be. And the other ... okay, *two* in the whole city.

Walt had come from Indiana by way of Miami, where his father had run a limo service. The man had started in trucking, had a small fleet of refrigerated ones making a run around three states. Talked about moving up in the world, someday running a class operation. The elder Mr. Kenning thought it would be fun to open a bar somewhere; a nice place to hang out, serve beer, maybe some food, attract the college crowd and the regulars.

His son didn't want to hear about it. He buried himself in his pictures and drawings, so Pop Kenning droned about his unrealized dreams to his wife, until the poor woman got sick of hearing about things that would never come to be and left. Her lawyer showered Pop with an endless stream of documents.

That left Walt with no buffer. He was stuck hearing the old man's stories, until he fled south to Florida to get an education. Lucky him, the old man relocated to be close to his boy and chase the dream of a class operation. The dream ended up being that limousine business, which employed an entourage of large-bellied ex-truckers, who thought nothing of dropping by the condo Walt shared with his father and raiding the Kenning fridge day and night.

Back then, I gather Walter had been a typical art student. He hated limos and trucks and school, too, apparently, though he'd never come out and said it. He liked only one thing about Florida: colors. Yellow sands, lavender-red sunsets, the verdant glow of the everglades from a distance. He dreamed of creating fine art but churned out images destined for tourist galleries instead.

Florida was starting to mean something, finally, until the old man's heart attack and subsequent demise. Walt was free at last, and strangely alone. For a few years he ran his father's business just to milk cash out of it and have something to do. On the side, he healed himself with paint and looked for an exit strategy. When the time was right, he sold the business, bummed around for a while, then took what was left of his money to New York.

There was art in New York, or so he'd heard. But it wasn't the same. Not really. He had no degree, no job, and apparently none of the talent galleries in this neck of the woods craved. At least Walt had a little money to help him get settled while he took some classes. And there was Milo Barski, offering to hire a student to mind the shop while he went on sales calls and shoots.

Walter entered my life around the time I was dealing with my loss. Two years into his grief, he spoke bitterly of his dad, said he didn't know if he was sorry the man was gone. *Didn't know*. That confused me. Francis had meant too much to me to be forgotten so easily and so brusquely. In Walter's view, art and, by extension, antiques were endlessly fascinating. For that reason, Milo was infinitely more fascinating than Walter's late father.

And so on the subject of parents Walter and I agreed to disagree, and he faded into the background of my life once I agreed to pick where *my* old man had left off. Walt would pop into my life when we needed a consultant on the art-related cases that occasionally wandered into my father's old agency.

"Business or pleasure?" he said.

"Unpleasurable business," I said.

We were in his office at Chatham & Shawn's Auction House and Gallery, four stories above West Fifty-Seventh Street. He was doing okay with the news of Barski's death, except for the red, puffy eyes.

"I'm sorry we haven't seen each other much," I told him.

"Aah, you know how it is," he said. "The city. The hours. It's crazy."

"Exactly!" I said.

The two of us letting each other off the hook.

"You still work for what's-his-name, the guy that looks like Tip O'Neill?" Walter said. "He's famous these days, huh? You guys must be making out okay." He sat back in his chair as if he were studying a new vase that showed up in the morning mail. He had on a red-striped, button-down shirt. Three porcelain jewelry boxes sat on his desk blotter.

"Yeah. Look, Walt, I know this is a bad day for you, but we've got to get some things cleared up. My aunt demands it, and you know I don't like getting on her bad side. Not two hours ago some guy named Dolack showed up at Barski's place expecting to buy out the store. He says *you* sent him. What's the deal?"

He clunked forward in his chair and goggled at me. He'd cut his hair thick on top, short on the sides, and let a good chunk of it hang over one of his eyes the way the handsome guys did in the cologne ads. He probably knew that.

He fidgeted, turned red, bit his lips. They parted and a puff of air escaped. "Damn," he said.

"Come on, Walt. The cops know all this. I gather they're still at the shop. They'll be coming here any minute now and they'll want answers. You may think we're all the same, but cops are not like me. You hold out on me, I just get mad, chew up the furniture, and leave. But they'll take it personally."

"I knew this would happen. Is there no privacy with these people? They kept me there forty-five minutes!"

"Consider yourself lucky. They pumped Amos for an hour after you left. Now, what gives?"

"They asked me where I was Sunday between 12:00 and 4:00 p.m.!"

"That's called an alibi. They're generally useful in murder cases. So ... what did you tell them?"

He pushed back his chair and stood up. He started pacing back and forth behind his desk. He was a tall guy, as I've said, and no dweeb under his shirt, either. He had high cheekbones and a full mouth. He'd never been a fancy dresser, but now his clothes and his attitude reminded me of the Wall Streeter I shared an apartment with, which wasn't exactly a compliment. Walt pulled off his wire-rims and rubbed his eyes a bit more. When he put his glasses on, his thick lashes flicked the glass.

This was the thing about his personality that I could never understand, or even abide. His tendency to be scared of everything. I wanted to grab him by the collar and shake him out of it. You're a tall, powerful guy. Man up!

"Yesterday was Sunday," he said. "Aw, Dante, how many people can account for what they did on a Sunday? I think I woke up at noon."

"There's a start. Were you alone?"

"Yes." He let that hang for a moment, then perked up. "I had brunch at a little cafe nearby ... the waiters could verify that ... then I came uptown, ICP had a show. I gave the police all of this.

The time, the address, all that stuff. I suppose they'll want the museum ticket, too."

"When'd you last talk to Barski?"

His eyes were wild. "You too? You're really sweating me on this stuff?"

"Yes, really."

He went behind me and closed his office door. Then punched the do not disturb button on his speakerphone. He lowered himself easily into the middle of his chair, legs slightly together, and spoke in a low voice. Milo had called him at home on New Year's Day around four o'clock to say he was leaving town. He was retiring. He'd always talked about returning to California; now he would finally do it. He needed Walt to suggest a gallery or dealer in town who'd buy him out, lock, stock and barrel. Chatham & Shawn was out; setting up an auction would take months, and they'd pay him by certified check. Barski wanted a cash buyout, or darn near close to it.

Walt whispered, "He had a thing for cash."

"An undeclared thing."

He bobbed his head.

"What's the big deal?" I said. "He wouldn't be the first person to stick it to the IRS. Is that what's got you all upset?"

"It's not that. I'm not supposed to refer people to other firms. I could lose my job. Milo's shop would be a major acquisition. I'm supposed to make a pitch for properties that large. But I couldn't. He's my friend. Or was. He didn't know the quick and dirty estate places like I do. When he called, I gave him the name of a firm on Fifth. The owner's Romanian. Blows through estates like you wouldn't believe. And he's not averse to paying a good portion of what he owes you in cash. Milo, of course, didn't trust anyone off the street. He had a price in mind, but insisted on getting a third-party appraisal. Hence Mr. Dolack."

"But why retire now? And so quickly?"

Walt said he didn't know.

I slid back in my chair. "Okay. You mean your old boss calls you and asks you to broker a deal that could end with him running off with a half million—"

He jabbed his thumb at the ceiling.

"Fine," I said, "*higher* than that, even. He's fixing to skip town with all that money in his suitcase, and you don't ask *why?*"

He gave me a blank look. Sheer innocence. "It didn't seem polite."

"Aw, come on!"

"Okay, of course I thought it sounded fishy, but I thought he was in trouble. Insurance trouble."

My turn to look dumb.

"Remember those insurance photos he used to take? The owner gets a set of prints, the insurance company gets a second, and the negatives go in the owner's safe. Milo wasn't supposed to keep any prints, but he did."

"And that's bad?"

"I don't know. I've been racking my brains trying to think of ways those relationships could go bad. On one hand, he's violating the client's privacy. Say one of his customers comes in saying he's looking for a certain type of round Empire mirror with a gold frame. Milo reviews his stash of photos and finds a former client who owns one. He tries to broker a deal."

"But that's a good thing, right? Both clients get what they want, and Milo pockets a commission."

"Right—but what if the seller doesn't report the sale to the insurance company? You see? A shady client could sell off a ton of items and then orchestrate a theft and report the whole collection stolen to the insurance company—"

"Fraud, aided and abetted by Milo Barski."

"Right. And if the payout is big enough, Milo starts to look like a liability. You don't want loose ends ..."

I chewed my bottom lip. It offered possibilities. Motives. "He was taking these photos for how long?"

"Beats me. Ages and ages. It meant a lot of travel, going to people's homes, snooping, scouting out pieces that wouldn't normally come onto the market. He loved that. He loved getting out of the shop. That's how he found a lot of his best pieces."

"Back when he used to leave you with the shop?"

"Back in the day? Sure. Usually I had morning classes, and I'd get to the shop around noon or so. Most days we'd work there together. When he had a shoot, he'd leave early in the afternoon and I'd lock up."

I rummaged in my coat and found the price tag we'd taken from Barski's apartment. "What can you tell me about this thing?"

He flipped it around in his fingers. One side read $250.00. The other, Exx.xx.

"It's your basic sales code. Think about it: what are the two most common questions a dealer like Milo gets when a person walks into their shop?"

"Gee, I don't know," I said. "'How can you live with all this junk?' Beats me."

He chuckled. "Seriously though. The first is, 'How much is this piece?' The second is, 'Will you go lower?' Haggling is part of the fun of this business. When you're haggling on the fly, a dealer wants to be able to know at a glance how much they paid for a piece originally. Knowing their hard costs helps them be as flexible as possible. They can cut to the bone to move a dead-beat item, or stand firm on a piece they sank a ton into." He pointed at the tag. "This notation? Exx.xx? That's a hundred dollars."

"What's the code?"

He hesitated. "I don't suppose there's any harm in telling you now. It has to do with music. Do you know music?"

I shook my head. "Notes, you mean? No."

"Well, Milo did, or he read it somewhere." With his right hand he wrote on a scratch pad, then tore off a page to show me.

$$E = 1$$
$$G = 2$$
$$B = 3$$
$$D = 4$$
$$F = 5$$
$$f = 6$$
$$a = 7$$
$$c = 8$$
$$e = 9$$
$$X = 0$$

"Get it? Each of the ten numbers gets an upper- or lower-case letter, based on the musical scale. X is the null figure, standing for zero. You remember grammar school music class, don't you? A smiley FACE? Every Good Boy Does Fine?"

"Deserves Fudge," I countered. After all, first-grade memories are hard to shatter.

"Whatever. Either way you say it, the letters signifying the notes are the same. And no one could figure it out. I've seen coin dealers who do the same thing. They write their code on the cardboard coin holder. Customers are getting smart these days. You can't go with your standard 'A equals 1' code anymore."

"No, you certainly can't," I said wryly. "Were the books he sold coded too?"

"I have to assume they were, but he never let me touch them. He kept a key to that cabinet behind his desk, which is what I told the police."

"What was so special about that cabinet?"

"I don't know. I could never figure it out. One time I saw him taking out those peacock feathers, and dusting them like they were gold."

"He ever mention a woman named Millicent?"

He said no. Zip on Eunice, too.

"I don't mind mentioning that the cabinet was a problem for me personally," Walt said. "If he was out of the shop and a customer wanted to look at one of the books there, it left me standing there like an idiot, going, 'Sorry, I don't have the key. Come back tomorrow.'"

"You ever see him slip money in those books?"

He looked like I'd demonstrated the arcane secrets of the shoe horn.

"Oh wow! I never saw him take cash out, but it's certainly possible. But *why*? He had a safe out back. The doors and windows were wired, we had motion detectors … the place was like Fort Knox."

"Well, that sure helped him a whole lot, didn't it?"

I remembered the alarm at Barski's apartment, and that got me thinking about the painting we'd seen hanging in his living room.

"Once upon a time," I said, "you told me you tried to give him a painting of yours, you remember? What was the story on that? He didn't want it or something?"

"Yeah, that was a nice one. He ended up picking one with the lobstermen. Why, you saw it?"

"Yeah, once," I said, hoping he wouldn't ask when or under what circumstances I'd last been in Barski's apartment. "You still have the painting he didn't want?"

"It's around." He got up, came around the desk and starting poking around the space between the two file cabinets in his office. Started pulling out canvases. Landscapes done in broad strokes, heavy on the palette knife. Weird colors, brown-green skies, red chunky people. An overgrown beach on a cloud-filled day, high grass and palm trees swaying in the wind, a tiny shack built into the side of a dune, a winding asphalt road in the sand.

"You actually keep them here in your office?"

He sighed. "You know how it goes. My apartment's small. I don't want the clutter, and I'm too attached to these to toss them out. It's not like someone's going to mistake them for a Gauguin and sell them out from under me."

After a bit, he pulled out one canvas and held it up, "Here. This one. Did it in Florida. Route 27 near the canal. I wanted to give it to him because it's always been one of my favorites. He says no, it's too depressing. Got flustered and needed to leave the shop for a bit. I could never understand it. Look at it, Dante. What's wrong with it? Why would he not want it?"

I didn't know. It was a nice piece. Black clouds over a winding road. In the foreground was an old chrome-job diner with a beat-up Ford truck parked in front of it.

"You still at it?" I asked. "Painting."

He shook his head sheepishly, but there wasn't a smile on his face. He'd worked his way through school, gotten a fine arts degree. But all that had done was qualify him to celebrate the work of artists greater than himself.

"In the end, I guess painting my own work didn't really matter that much to me," he said. "I used to blame the city. The expense. The necessity of having a real job and being gainfully employed. Now I'm getting better at shouldering the blame myself."

Downstairs on the sidewalk, icy raindrops falling on my head, I felt a jolt of recognition. Across the street, someone in a lemon-colored rain slicker lingered under the awning of a women's clothing boutique. He looked like the fisherman on the box of frozen fish sticks, decked out to battle the elements in his sou'wester.

I walked down the street, ducked into the lobby of another building. I whirled and peered at him through the glass. He was half a block behind me, marching along slowly. He had dark hair, and sharp, fast eyes. Samuel—the guy from the Grouser Club. I watched him spin around on the sidewalk as if he'd lost something. He looked in every direction, then waltzed out of my line of vision. I stepped out onto the sidewalk, hoping I could entice him to follow me farther. I tried not to make it too obvious, but I was too late. Not a fisherman in sight.

8

MR. MYSTERIOUS

The Six Coaches was a cozy but high-end basement place on Forty-Seventh Street. Red and gold canopy out front, carpeted steps to the restaurant downstairs. They sold sizzling steaks to folks who sold the sizzle on Madison Avenue. Lunchtime and the shoving was easy. I bribed a lemon-lipped maître d' for a peek at his reservation book. He tittered at my ten, but accepted my twenty. I went down a list of names crossed off in pencil, line by line, looking for Barski or any aliases that looked obvious. Nothing for Thursday, for Friday, or Saturday. Which didn't make sense. Barski told Haverstrom he was meeting someone here, so he had to have had reservations. Describing Barski to my suborned pal in the bow tie elicited nothing but a tsk. I thanked him and went to the lobby to make a phone call.

My aunt snatched up the phone on the first ring. "Book Lady," she said.

"It's me. Have the troops decamped?"

"For now, yes, but they'll be back. You cannot imagine the scope of this disaster, Dante. They found a book in Milo's garbage bin and they are raising a stink. What news?"

Over the years I've gotten good at laying out three types of reports—the quick and dirty, the good-enough-for-most-people, and a little something I called The Beatrice. My being on a payphone meant she would get nothing more than the first. I'm not made of quarters. "The trail ends here," I said in conclusion. "There's no record Barski ever met anyone in this place."

From the other end of the line came an impatient snort. "Ask around. Be pushy."

"How? I don't have his dinner date's name, do I? I love when you come up with these suggestions."

"Dante, I'm ashamed of you. Obviously you're looking for someone named Monroe."

"*Obviously*? Are you kidding?"

Bea clucked at me. "I don't know how you've come this far in this business if simple matters elude you. Goodbye."

I went back to the man at the rostrum and took another look at his book. That cost me another twenty, and got me just as far. I thought about Barski and his wine, and that got me thinking about the bar. He'd wait there if he had any waiting to do. I asked the maître d' if he remembered a gray-haired guy sitting at the bar on New Year's Day.

"Worst day of the year to ask about," he said. "And in any case, I'm not the best one to ask about the bar. Better off trying one of the bartenders." He smirked. "If you still have any cash left."

I thanked him and turned to go.

"You know," he said, throwing me a bone. "It occurs to me, you ought to come back in the evenings. That's when Munro and the others come on duty."

My tongue stuck in my throat. "What did you say?"

"Ernie Munro. The bartender?" He spelled it out for me. "He works nights, so he'd see the dinner crowd."

"Where's he now?"

"Oh. He works days in his brother's print shop. Very dirty

business … It's on Seventh down near Abingdon Square. They make these *adorable* rubber stamps. Didn't think places like that still exist. It's called Aramy or Araby, something like that. I could probably try getting you the address. Say, another twenty?"

"I think I've paid enough of your rent this month. I'll stop by in February."

His news clicked, all right. Barski gets to the Six Coaches early, waits for his man to show up, and decides to call Haverstrom over at the Club. Munro was a bartender, and if he was anything like others of his profession, he and Barski had not discussed the differences between Chippendale and Queen Anne furniture.

But how had Bea nailed his name?

I took the subway downtown. I was in my own neighborhood now and had no trouble finding the place. It was on West Street between Eleventh and Bank, a great, gray brick building called ARABLE PRINTING & GRAPHIC SUPPLY CO. The walk-up retail shop smelled of ditto fluid and hustle. A woman running six copiers behind the long counter told me to go around the building and ask at the garage entrance. She peered at me through her bifocals. "Ask nice," she warned me. "They're not supposed to let people back there."

Around the corner, burly men hustled around outside, using steel pipes to unload huge rolls of paper from a truck. A man with a runny nose said Ernie Munro was inside, two lefts and a right. Stay in the lunch area, he told me. I wasn't allowed near the presses. I went through the garage and pounded up a few dusty concrete steps. At the top of the steps I pulled open a gray, metal-sheathed door and entered a warm room filled with whirring machines. Men in dirty blue aprons looked up. Those nearby rubbed large aluminum plates with spongy gloves. A blackish film came off the plates and swirled as they rubbed. The air stunk of ink. The ground shook. More rolls of paper, drums of ink, newsprint everywhere. Forklifts zipped around like ants.

A guy waved a sponge and shouted, "Whaddaya want?"

I shouted back. He held a hand to his ear. I shouted *again*. He waved me on. I walked to a glassed-in room under a wall of high, dirty windows. Once inside, the door snicked shut and the room was silent. They had Formica-topped tables, a Coke machine, and a candy dispenser. The room was empty, except for an ink-streaked man sucking down a can of Diet Coke. As I approached, he burped bologna. "Who you looking for?"

"Ernie Munro."

The man jutted his chin at the thick plexiglass windows, which looked out over the plant. Over his left breast the name HERB was stitched in red thread. "He don't have break for another ten minutes or so."

I looked at a wall clock. Ten to one. I studied the activity on the other side of the glass with Herb the Coke-swigger. The presses closest to us were small ones, maybe the length of three Eldorados. I watched them run. The paper started egg white, webbed through a roller and shot out splattered with black ink, then squeezed through a second to catch red ink. At the end, the paper cascaded into a mechanism that cut and folded and spilled it onto a conveyor belt, transformed into neat little catalogs.

A heavy man with arms tainted in red and black grabbed some as they came off the belt, pulling them open in front of his face. I saw what looked like a colorful splash of ads depicting machine parts. The man wasn't satisfied. He tossed the pages down and ran to the first roller. He shouted to a younger man, who hopped up on a metal step and fiddled with some knobs. The heavy man went back to check if this adjustment had helped. He glanced through more catalogs, tossed them down, and started shouting about roller number two. It was a quite a routine. He shouted, the other guy hopped. And I ached just watching them. Perspiration streamed off their bodies like sweat off a horse.

At one o'clock the heavy man headed toward the lunch room. Herb drained the last of his soda and jerked his chin at me. "Here you go," he said. The men streamed in. The bathroom and the soda machine were popular attractions. I watched my man open a can of Coke and drop into a chair. He saw me and looked up. "You looking for me?"

"Yes."

"What for?"

"A man named Milo Barski. You know him?"

He was a big man, early fifties, with a fleshy face and soft eyes suggestive of a Basset Hound's. Sweat coated his forehead. In the creases of his face I spotted a few glints of gray stubble. "What is this? You a cop or something?"

I handed him one of my business cards. He took it carefully with a dirty hand and read it off. Then he jerked it at me. "Hundred-pound stock. Linen. *Nice*. So? You're a private detective. What's the problem? I don't even know the guy you're talking about."

"He's dead. Murdered."

He licked sweat off his upper lip and guzzled more soda. His lips went tight. A whistle escaped from his nose. "Who is this guy? Should I know him?"

"That's how we're playing it, huh? Someone beat him dead yesterday and I want to know why he saw you last week at the Six Coaches."

I'd gone too far. His eyes widened enough to see both of his irises. He stood and threw out his chest. "I don't know who you are, mister. But I don't have anything to tell you. I gotta get back to work. So get lost."

He shoved past me and headed for the door. I followed him into the plant. The funny thing is, he was still carrying my card. "Munro," I called after him. "The cops don't know anything about you. That could change."

He whirled around and shoved his face in mine. He was a few inches shorter than me, but that meant nothing. He gave orders, people obeyed. "Listen, punk, you stay away from me. Maybe you think I wouldn't deck you, but I would. I don't know anything about murders. I got two jobs, a wife and a kid, and I'm supposed to remember some stupid lush who talks to me at the bar? You're crazy."

He stormed off to his thundering machines. His hot breath stayed with me, hovering in front of my face. I looked at the men working the machines. Twenty or so curious eyes. Fine. Maybe I could take on Munro alone. After all, he was only 230 pounds of flesh, blood and ink. But I couldn't do it in front of his pals. They'd have me smeared, cut, folded and bundled into wedding invitations before I ever lifted a hand.

Behind the glass a big bald man hoisted his belt and rolled up his sleeves. Between two of his fingers a Coke can went pop.

Time to go.

❧ 9 ❧

EVERYTHING TOLD

T hings had calmed down by the time I got back to Fourth Avenue. The front door of Barski's shop was boarded up. Stickers attested to the fact that the premises had been sealed by order of the NYPD. And police tape was strung across the facade like the remains of an office party gone wild.

I passed under the metal Book Lady sign and walked down three wooden steps into the sugary smelling, must-filled old hole.

"I'm back!" I yelled.

The sales counter and cash register were manned by Russell, a hipster drama student who spent most of his days at the Book Lady reading *Great Scenes*, intoning his Ibsen or Chekhov or Miller, and hoping for his big break in the daytime soaps. He was ringing up a stack of books for a man in furry green earmuffs. Without looking up at me, Russell said, "They're in the back."

I walked past the counter toward the bookshelves, all six million of them. The three walls are crammed with volumes, from the creaking wooden floor to the tin-plated ceiling. Boxes of books waiting to be sifted through sat within tripping distance of the shelves. Makeshift tables made of plywood sheets stacked on wooden horses were piled with more boxes waiting for their turn. Hardcovers upon paperbacks upon magazines.

My aunt was arguing with herself near a shelf. "I am telling you I saw one here just the other day. You just have to be a little patient. It's around here somewhere."

The man in earmuffs turned. "I need to get back to work."

Bea, looking impossibly domestic in her pink apron, pulled books from a box. She moved suddenly to the right and shouted over the table, "You find anything down there?"

A gray head rose into sight behind the table. "It's not here," Amos's voice said. "You sure it was *this* table?" He caught sight of me and broke into a smile. "Hallo, Dante. Hey, your nephew's here."

Bea handed some books to Amos and abandoned him. "Keep looking," she said. She took my arm and led me away. "I have your lunch in the refrigerator. I must know everything."

We headed to the chairs in the International section, near the big globe. I plopped into the brown cloth armchair, my favorite. I resisted the temptation to rest my heels on the coffee table, which is nothing but an old, heavily shellacked door screwed onto a set of brass claw feet from an old bathtub. A fluted glass door-knob rose from the frame like a misplaced diamond. Bea rummaged in the kitchen fridge, plated my sandwich, and unrolled the waxed paper wrappings. Behind me, Giuseppe Verdi watched this operation with a bronze sneer.

She placed the sandwich in front of me with a cloth napkin and confided in a low voice, "This ignoramus collects *Reader's Digest* condensed books. I had four of the wretched things, but can't find the last. I usually just give them away, but who am I to look askance at a sale?" She dropped her voice even lower. "Who in his right mind would read one of those lobotomized texts, I ask you? Ah!" She gestured at the table. "Look. I made you a nice prosciutto and mozzarella. The baguette is fresh this morning.

French, not Italian, but I'm sure you'll find it serviceable. Just the way you like it. *Mangia*."

The way *you* like it, I thought. "Listen, I was followed today. Some guy in a raincoat tailed me from the club to Walt's office."

"What did he say when you caught him?"

"Nothing. I didn't get him."

"Pity. Shall I cut this for you, or do you prefer to treat us to an exhibit of your testosterone in action?"

I grabbed the sandwich and tore into it. The bread was thick, with a perfectly brown crisp crust. The ham, as I expected, was layered with pickled hot peppers. Bea thinks it's a sin to let a sandwich go without. I gasped. She produced a pitcher of iced tea with an etched glass. She lowered herself into the upholstered purple monstrosity that can handle her weight, and propped her soles up on the door. Verdi kept watching.

"So," she said. "*Dimmi tutto*."

This is an expression she learned from her father or grandfather, one of her family members who came from the old country. The words simply mean, "Tell me everything," and it's usually my only clue that she expects The Beatrice version—nothing held back.

I must have spoken for a good forty minutes, telling her everything. Haverstrom to Walt to Munro. She reserved her biggest sneer for the member of the Grouser Club.

"Lawyers," she said. "You know my rule."

"'First thing we do, let's suspect the lawyers.' You keep ripping off Shakespeare, he'll send *his* after you."

She raised a finger and walked me back through my story. Even though I've gotten pretty good at verbatim reports, when she hears a story she sometimes presses me for more. What was Haverstrom wearing? What did the club look like, room by room? Any noticeable smells? Could I describe the other men, the so-called Recreation Room, the dining room? What details could I give her about Walt's offices at the auction house? What did I notice about the man in the raincoat? And she insisted I write out a second copy of Barski's sales code. She reached across the table in a stretch that I thought would send her toppling out of the chair. About this phrase, she said, *Every Good Boy Deserves Fudge*. Was it a common expression?

In short, she inhaled my report the way I inhaled that sandwich. And at the end of it all, I said, "You know how I see it?"

"No. I can't wait to hear your assessment of the facts. This has been a very disturbing day and I can use the laughs."

I ignored her wisecrack. "First I figured it was a robbery, plain and simple, but now I don't know. Too many people are showing up with secrets. Barski used to carry one of those pocket datebooks. It's gone. A robber wouldn't take it. But someone who killed him for *another* reason would have. Why? Maybe they had an appointment and didn't want the cops to know? The cash in his wallet and his watch are gone, but that could have been done to make it look like a robbery. How am I doing so far?"

"I do not theorize aloud."

"Excuse me. You mind telling me how you knew Munro's name?"

She waved her hand like she was swatting away gnats. "That was nothing. You remember the books in Milo's apartment? It occurred to me that the titles of the books made some veiled reference to their contents. When Mr. Dolack showed up to buy out Milo's shop, I surmised that any cash offered in advance of the liquidation was destined to be tucked into the Sotheby's price guide. He used the books on banks and money and finance to hide cash he'd withdrawn from his accounts, or for whatever cash he had lying around. But one book, *The Era of Good Feelings*, must have referred to another transaction. 'Era of good feelings' is a term historians use to describe the administration of one American president."

"Let me guess," I said. "John Monroe."

"James."

"I was never much good at history."

"The police share your ignorance."

"Okay, genius, so it's James Monroe, and we've got an *Ernie Munro* who, judging from that empty book, was set to pay Barski some money. But ... how did you know we weren't looking for someone named Herman or Margaret or Wouk or Mitchell? We found book safes in his apartment cut out of *The Winds of War* and *Gone with the Wind*. Geez, for all we know we could have been looking for a Mr. Wynde with a Y."

"Unlikely."

"But you didn't know for sure. You just guessed."

"I rarely guess. It seemed logical that if those books were not in the suitcase, that they were no longer in play, so to speak. Perhaps they were intended for another enterprise gone wrong. Recall that one of the covers had been nearly torn off."

"Nicely reasoned. But what was Munro buying from Barski? I can't picture Munro buying chandeliers." I pitched my sandwich wrappings into a wastebasket near the sideboard. Two points.

"That is at present unknown. Can I offer you a cream puff?" she asked, gesturing over her shoulder. "Freshly filled today. I'm testing a recipe from Lo Pinto's 1948 text. I haven't decided yet if I like the consistency."

"No thanks." I rose and ducked around the corner in the direction of the bathroom. There's a sideboard there with a legendary junk drawer. I slid it out and fished around for some over-the-counter painkillers. It was early afternoon, and my leg was acting up again. I gulped two pills with iced tea and watched my aunt eat a cream puff. She bit one end, shielding the other with a hand to catch any filling that dripped out. Her lips moved around as she savored the sweet pastry and cream, her eyes focused on the ceiling. After she swallowed, she snatched up her notebook and scribbled a few lines to herself.

As soon as the notebook was back in her lap, she said, "There is at least one other mystery. The police found a book outside, discarded in Milo's garbage dumpster."

"The killer chucked it? What's the title?"

"That's the mystery. The police aren't talking."

"They're funny that way."

"The police promise to visit again. I am thrilled at the prospect, believe me."

"You said it," said another voice. It was Amos, coming over to collapse, groaning, into a chair. "I never saw such nonsense. Why waste time asking questions when they could be out looking for the killer? You should have heard these questions. 'You married, Mr. Horne?' I'm a widower. I'm wearing this ring for my health. And again with my shoe size."

"The killer had small feet," I said. "You saw the footprints."

"Is having small feet a crime?" Amos said. "But see, I showed them. I wear a *wide* shoe. Those prints were narrow." He reached to the coffee table and grabbed that morning's edition of the *New York Times*. He sat back with it on his lap, massaging his aching fingers before attempting to page through the paper.

Around us, the shop had grown silent. The *Reader's Digest* fetishist had departed with only three volumes after considerable whining, and Russell the acting student had curled up on his stool with his book. Amos tried reading, but soon dropped the paper. "I can't believe he's gone. We were *just* talking to him last week, and he's gone. I don't think I can get used to that." He looked at me. "Your aunt's not going to play chess with me. I need someone I can beat. That's the thing about Milo. When he loses, it's just a game to him. I remember one time when Elaine was still alive, we went to see her cousin over at Maimonides Hospital. Gall bladder, nothing serious. And I said to Elaine, 'Let's go see Milo. He lives nearby.' Well, we went. I wasn't expecting much but we got him on a good day. He was the most *gracious* host. Wine and cheese, crackers, ham, everything you could imagine. Put some records on the Victrola and danced with

Elaine. 'You're such a gentleman, Mr. Barski,' Elaine says, and Milo says, 'I don't get many visitors.' And then, as we're pulling on our coats and heading out, I see him cleaning up and pouring our leftover wine back into the bottle ..."

Amos rocked in his chair and slapped his knee. "How could a person be that way—both generous *and* cheap?" He chuckled until his eyes grew moist. "Bea! Do you think his murder was"— he paused, almost afraid to say what he was thinking—"you know ... mob-related?"

This was one of Amos's longtime theories. He attributed organized crime to every perceived facet of the city's decline, from people forgetting to pick up after their dogs, to the price of socks at Macy's, and to the slow, inevitable decline of their own beloved Book Row.

Bea threw her head back and scoffed, "Mobs? Mobsters do not ransack bookshelves."

She got up and snatched a legal pad off the sideboard and flipped through it as she returned to her chair. She was in the process of compiling her spring catalog, and there were countless little details to get right about the best and brightest of the rare and used books—mostly of a culinary nature—that she hoped to sell to her longtime customers. "Honestly, Amos, your slavish attention to the day's news is transforming you into a paranoiac." She plopped back into her chair, waving the yellow pad over her head. "As a bookman, you ought to know better! Haven't you learned the oldest lesson in the business?"

"And what is that, tell me?"

"Read books, man! Not news!"

Frankly, I don't know how she could read, write, cook, or taste-test anything today. "Well, Dante?" she said, scowling up at me. "Go to work. Emory must be pulling up the carpet. And *you*," she said, snorting at Amos. "Stop reading that ridiculous newspaper!"

❧ 10 ❧

THE REST OF THE FAMILY

The Emory Bray Agency rents a suite in a flashy building just off Times Square, not far from Schubert Alley. We're a minute from Sardi's, the legendary Broadway eatery, which is probably not saying much since we're also four minutes from a place that sells plastic vomit and Richard Nixon masks all year round.

Across the street is Nathan's, Bray's favorite place to slum and suck down the dozen-clam special. There's also the Bun & Bun for breakfast (and lunch), and the old Bond Clothes building, whose faded red-blue facade is one of Manhattan's most venerated eyesores. Bray likes to tell visitors that Times Square is "about" movie theaters. This is true. From the window of my father's old office I can see the Loew's, which currently is playing two Oscar contenders six times a day, back to back, for six dollars apiece. Three blocks north, closer to the Port Authority, you can catch a XXX-rated film on your lunchbreak for two bucks.

In our front office, Melinda was evaluating her Sensuality Quotient with a self-test in *Cosmo*. She didn't bother to hide the magazine when I came in. Too obvious. For that you could lose three points on the old SQ.

"Anyone in?" I asked, and was told Bray was "in conference" with his No. 1, Rothman. I knocked on Bray's door and entered. He was behind his desk, leaning back in his chair so his gut popped into sight. Both of his thumbs were tucked under his belt as if he were trying to stretch a few more inches out of the leather. He needed those inches.

"Where have you been?"

"I take it you've missed me?"

He was a heavy man with broad shoulders, a hard paunch, and flabby face. Over the years his features have thickened, leaving a frenetic subway map of broken capillaries coursing under his lumpy nose and cheeks. His hair has gone from blond to white to yellow. His clothes rarely fit him well. But why should he care? He was once a cop and later my father's business partner. People paid him to solve their problems—business problems, marital problems, legal problems, take your pick—not pose for *GQ*. "You have got a lot of nerve walking out of here the way you did this morning."

I stepped to his desk and produced the thick wad of Haverstrom's money and placed it in a stack on his desk.

He shut up.

"Now," I said. "Would you like to talk or would you like to listen?"

In a chair in front of Bray's desk, Imelda Rothman made polite noises before finding her voice. "Emory, I think we want to hear this."

Sensible. But then, I always kind of respected Rothman, our CFO. She's a smart lady, a good dresser, and an even better listener. Unlike Bray, she has learned how to properly brush her teeth. Her tanned face wore a smattering of brown freckles, and her hair probably cost my weekly salary. Today she wore a blue suit with fine pinstripes and a white blouse tied at the collar. She cleared her throat, primly crossing her legs in expectation of a good story.

I told them the quick and dirty version, everything except our somewhat illegal visit to Barski's apartment. Rothman liked what she heard. "It looks *good*, Em," she told Bray when I finished speaking. "We've got a client. A reputable one, and the job's a cinch. We find what the gentleman wants, make sure it finds its way to him at the disposition of the estate, and collect our fee. No big deal."

"Who says it's a big deal?" Emory said. "I don't like our people running out of here to deal with family problems." He looked at me. "Is that battle-axe staying out of this mess?"

He was referring to my Aunt Beatrice. "She's promised she will," I lied.

"Nuts. I hate that woman. She lies like a rug." He wiped his mouth a bit. Just thinking about Aunt Bea makes him foam at the mouth. "Why run the risk of irritating the cops all over again? We had enough of that last summer. They'll catch that killer when he tries to pawn a piece he swiped from the shop. You watch. They'll get him. We don't need to stick our noses into it."

I'd watch, all right. Bray wouldn't. The death of Barski was not something worth occupying his time. Emory Bray liked his cases the way he liked his meals, his Broadway shows, and, dare I say it, his women—big, gaudy, and simple.

Of course, they didn't always work out that way. The walls of his office were decorated with his diploma and awards and all his grip-and-grin photos. Bray with the mayor. Bray with a phalanx of Girl Scouts. Bray and clients happy to go on the record. Lately, his prized possession was a framed page of the *New York Tab*. It showed him carrying Annie Coltharp out of the warehouse last year, his gun drawn, the girl clinging to his neck and weeping. In screaming block letters the headline read:

BIG DICK RESCUES CHILD!
"I want my mommy," cries girl, age 5

74

Mr. and Mrs. Coltharp hired him, er, *us*, to assist the cops and feds when the girl went missing. Bray made the ransom drop, and he was the first one into the warehouse in Jersey where the girl was held, so the papers made him the hero. It was great for business, but it was Aunt Bea who later noticed that the guy who made the ransom demand had a very particular accent. Rawlsy, who works with us, played the recording for her because he thought it sounded hinky. She looked at us and said, "He's bilingual. Probably French-Canadian. Didn't Mr. Coltharp tell you he hired his chauffeur on a business trip to Quebec?"

Yep—the girl's own father set the whole thing up for the insurance money. We leaned on the chauffeur and his cousin, who did the job. They cracked and gave us Coltharp. But Aunt Bea's contribution never made the papers. So in the eyes of the world, Bray was the genius. Which is good, because splashy stories like that bring business in the door. There was no percentage in publicizing Aunt Bea's efforts, even if she would allow it. The only people who write big checks to booksellers are weirdo collectors.

Bray tilted back in his chair, a signal that he was finished talking. I headed for the door.

"Might be good publicity if this Haverstrom fellow is famous or well connected," Rothman said suddenly. "Could steer clients our way." She eyed us both. "Proceed carefully, gentlemen. *Judiciously.*"

Gotta love Bray and Rothman. My father left me a pair of gems.

I left through the bathroom that connects Bray's office with my father's. I stripped off my coat and blazer and sat on the couch. I left the lights off. In the gray afternoon light I watched drizzle fall in Times Square. Far away the Chrysler Building looked dismal. The gargoyles needed a good bath.

I tried thinking about Barski but it was too depressing. I looked at the empty desk and listened to the traffic on the street

JOSEPH D'AGNESE

below. Rush hour approached. Soon, all over the city men and women would be fleeing toward buses and trains and subways, heading to the kids in the suburbs and outer boroughs. There was a chipping noise at the window. Great—the rain had shifted to snow. My leg ached. I could take either an aspirin or a nap. I opted for a nap. The couch was closer.

But then Simon Rawls walked in, carrying a Burberry trench coat over his arm. "Something wrong with the lights?"

"I was about to snooze."

"Well, bag that and listen up." He dropped the raincoat on the floor and went to the dinette to get himself a drink. He wore a greenish Harris tweed and a loosened tie. He was a thin man in his early thirties with light-brown hair slicked back, thinning at the temples. Nervous blue eyes roved in a forever moist complexion. A handsome man, one of my best buddies, but what woman would want to cuddle a fish face?

Drink in hand, Rawlsy headed for the couch. "That paper you gave me?" he said without preamble. "The *Sun-Chronicle*? Defunct. Died in the sixties. By then Barski was no longer on staff. Guy I know at the *LA Times* gave me the number of a friend who's doing a book on the demise of the paper."

"You called him?"

He twisted his mouth. "We're talking me here, Dan. Okay, so … guy says Barski joined the paper after the war. Shot regular news stuff, but he liked rich folks, so they gave him the gossip section, society stuff. And before you know it, he's freelancing for slicks."

"The magazines I gave you?"

"Right. They all check out. The writer says Barski was a hit. Women loved him. Men loved him. Poodles loved him. Went to parties and stuff."

"So what happened? If he was so great, why wasn't he shooting for *Town & Country* today? Why was he selling junk—er, *antiques*, in New York?"

76

"That part's hazy. The writer seemed to think Barski was fired. Possibly over his drinking?"

"Wait," I said. "I'm sensing a logical fallacy. You're saying a *newspaper* fired an employee for *drinking*?"

"I know!" Rawlsy laughed, hoisting his own afternoon cocktail. "It's not like journalism is a respectable profession like the rarefied air of the private investigations racket. I gather that after his dismissal he went freelance a hundred percent. Then Barski's brother died around that time, so Merry Milo took over the family business."

"Interesting path to Bea's door."

"Anyway, the writer's surprised Barski's dead. Starts interviewing me, like *I* know what's going on." He giggled, which is a chore for any former law student, but he managed it nicely. "Maybe I bought Barski a place in history. You want a cool, refreshing beverage, my good man?"

He headed for the bottles once again.

"No thanks. Anything else?"

"That's it. Oh. Called the National Archives in St. Louis. Told them I was a reporter doing an obit, so one of the archivists pulled his old records. Barski's from the LA area originally, spent two and a half years in the Army Air Corps. Caught a bullet in the buns in France. Purple Heart. They sent him home. He spent the rest of the war shooting planes in Washington."

"*Shooting* planes?"

"With a camera. Pretty little propaganda shots."

"Any family?"

"So far just the brother."

"What about that Millicent woman?"

"Nothing. I called the bank, they can't talk. There's no Mauro in the Allentown directory, and about ten or eleven Eversmans. That one will take time."

I mulled it over. "You always do a good job, but miss the

important thing. Why'd he leave California? Why come out here, even with a business to come back to?"

"Beats me. I just get the pieces. You fit 'em together."

He finished assembling his drink and returned to the couch. "Tell you what I did, though. I got a friend of mine, he's a paralegal in LA? I had him do some checking for me. Barski never applied for a marriage license in the state of California. That's definite. He might have skipped to Las Vegas. They do that out there. My friend's also checking the papers for the names, see if any banns were posted."

"Great. And you got the stuff on Walt and Amos?"

"Oh yes," he said. He loosened his tie and sank into the couch. "Actually, I've got more on Kenning." He flung some sheets of legal-sized paper at me. "Do I know this guy?"

"You should. He helped me stick you in a cab enough times." I read the sheet on Walt. Rawlsy had gotten everything I knew and a little bit more. I learned Walt's father's name was Walter, Sr. That didn't bring the dad into focus any clearer. The sheet Rawlsy had on Amos was pretty skimpy; it told me the man had closed his bookshop five years ago, ran around doing appraisals and working out of his apartment on the West Side these days, raised tropical fish, that his daughter Cheryl had had a baby boy in May. "The cops were quizzing him about serving in DC during the war, just like Barski," I said. "You don't have that down here."

He waved at the bookshelf. "Figured you could look that up yourself. Third shelf."

I rose and scanned my dad's old etagere. He'd had a nifty setup there. A big TV with cable service and a link to the closed-circuit camera system that runs through our conference rooms and a lot of our offices. I also still had a ton of my father's old books.

I selected the *Who's Who* that Rawlsy had marked with a Post-It and returned to my desk, flipping through the H's.

HORNE, AMOS BILLINGS: educator, grammarian, bookman: b. August 4, 1920, Baltimore, Md.; non-grad., Washington College, Chesteron, Md., 1938-1942; Sgt., U.S. Army, 1942-1944; English instructor. Swain Prep School, Dundalk, Md., 1944-1947; m. Elaine Bowers (b. 1923, d. 1980) Sept. 1946; 2 daughters, Christine Elaine, Cheryl Anne; proprietor, Horne's Rare Book Service, Baltimore, 1950-1953, and New York, 1953-1982; author. *Why Can't You Write It Right?* (1951, Dodd, Mead), *Speak Your Mind, But Say It Right* (1953, Dodd, Mead), *Think, Speak & Write Your Way Through High School* (1959, Prentice Hall), reissued as *Think, Speak & Write Your Way Through College* (1978, Prentice Hall); member, Antiquarian Booksellers Association of America.

"And yet he's the last person you'd ask to correct anything you've written," I said aloud when I was done.

Rawlsy stirred. "Mmm-hmm. That book of his is still selling. And I suppose it'll keep on selling as long as people stay dumb. So ... are we actually getting paid for this case, or is this another one of those things we do for your aunt?"

"It's off the clock, if that's what you're asking."

"Thought so. You need anything else from me?"

I shook my head. As I put the book back, an image popped into my head of Amos and Milo playing chess in the shop, stacking the captured pieces into a green ceramic soup tureen in the shape of a cabbage. Always seemed strange to me, that habit. Suddenly it didn't seem so strange. *Cabbages and kings.* I remembered the end table I'd seen in Milo's apartment, cluttered with metallic animals. *A brass menagerie.* The cast-iron piggy bank hiding on a shelf behind a mother-of-pearl jewelry box. *Pearls before swine.* And now I knew another: *Every good boy deserves fudge.*

Was there some reason behind these whimsical references to literature and music? Was that just the way his mind worked? Or were they the sort of mnemonic devices a man employed to stave off senility?

The intercom buzzed me out of my reverie, and Melinda was cooing in her brutal Bronx accent, "Dante? There's a lady here to see you? A Ms. Pozzle of the Homicide Tax Force? You want to see her?"

"Do I have a choice?" I said into the phone. To Rawlsy I said, "Well, shoot. *Her.*"

"You want I should go?"

"I might need your gift for improvisational embroidering of facts ... Lieutenant! How are we?"

Abby Posluszny stalked in without waiting for me to answer her knock. She wore a beige raincoat, a black felt hat, and black dress shoes with galoshes. She was only five-eight, and as lean as a swizzle stick. Her elastic lips were already revving, pulling and stretching away on her round face. I had the impression she was about to spit at me.

She had her speech prepared. "Dante," she spewed. "Get your hat and coat. You're coming with me. And I don't want to hear any excuses."

"Why?"

"None of this *why* nonsense. Today you failed to identify yourself as a licensed PI when questioned by my men at a crime scene. You proceeded to disobey a direct police order to await further questioning. You were out all day, so I can only assume you and your aunt are already interfering with this case. Am I right?"

"That depends. I was there this morning as an ordinary citizen to offer moral support to my aunt, whose dear friend was untimely offed. Furthermore, since I wasn't on the case and Munoz didn't ask me to state my occupation, I wasn't obliged to tell him. Further, I think if you check with the uniforms at the scene, I *did* show my license as I entered the shop. I'm not aware of any law that requires me to show my license to *everyone* at the scene of a crime. I have always relied on the fine communication skills of your officers, working together as a team."

"He specifically asked if your father had been a cop."

I cocked my head quizzically. "Actually, he asked if he knew the name. There's a difference. See? My memory's quite good, Abby. We can play this all day if you like. I could even give you a transcript. I'm surprised Munoz never heard of the great Francis Xavier Sleet. How quickly we forget, huh?"

"Where did you and your aunt go this morning?"

"The Abbondanza Bakery on Mulberry Street. We bought pastries."

"For two hours?"

"There was a line," I said. "Also, we couldn't decide what Detective Munoz would like. Aunt Bea thought he was a cannoli man. But I pegged *Birk* as the cannoli man. I see Munoz as more of a coffee and cruller type. What do you think?"

Posluszny pulled on her gloves. "Your coat, your hat."

"Will I need a toothbrush?"

"Move."

❧ 11 ❧

TRAGEDY TIMES TWO

A sour-faced patrolman drove while Posluszny studied her nails and spoke in an annoyed voice. We were stuck in rush hour. I had a horrible vision of spending the night with them in that Ford cruiser.

"It's like this," Abby said. "I've got an old bookseller that's friends with your aunt, and a yuppie who worked for the dead guy. They're so scared I believe them. I have a material witness who turns out to be a retired judge. Munoz asks him nicely to talk and he clams up. Then I get a call from the Chief of Detectives telling me to lay off, the judge knows nothing. That chaps me, people telling me how to do my job."

"But ma'am," I said, "earlier today Detective Munoz displayed his acumen by labeling the case murder in the commission of a felony. So why the long face?"

"That's before he visited the dead guy's apartment."

"Oh? What was the apartment like?"

"None of your business."

So. They'd found the money, but since she hadn't mentioned Munro, I could assume that they hadn't nailed the significance of the books in Barski's suitcase.

Score: Us, 2. Cops, zip.

She reached into the front seat of the police cruiser and sat back with a couple of sealed evidence bags.

She handed me the first bag.

"Birk heard some noise out behind Barski's shop today. When he went out to check, he saw a kid—probably a teen—run down the block sucking on a slice of pizza. Somehow Birk thought to check the dumpster. He found *that*. A private outfit picks up the garbage Tuesdays and Thursdays, so everything Barski threw in it is still there. So far that's all we found of interest."

It wasn't such a bad find. Through the plastic I saw two one-dollar stamps stuck to the upper right-hand corner of a nine-by-twelve, padded manila envelope. The postmark read Saturday, Jan. 3. Barski's name and the address of his shop had been typed on a square white sticker and affixed to the center. In the upper left-hand corner, where there should have been a return address, someone had handwritten the initials, R.Q.

"You found it open like this?" I said. "The tape and staples undone?"

"Right," she said, proffering the second bag. "These were inside. Plenty of smudges, but no prints we can use."

I peered through the plastic. It was an old hardcover book in blue-black cloth covers. The pages were brown and the spine read: *An American Tragedy, Dreiser,* and further down, *Vol. 1,* followed by the name of the publisher, *Boni & Liveright.* No dust jacket. My heart thumped wildly. The book missing from Barski's suitcase!

She slipped me the third and final bag, which contained a small index card. "Read it," Abby said.

The note on the card had been typed on the same machine as the mailing label. A fairly new machine, even strokes, probably an electric.

Jan. 1

Mr. Barski:

I have examined the enclosed volume and find the signature to be fraudulent. While the book itself is a sixth printing of the rare first edition, the signature bears no resemblance to extant examples of Dreiser's handwriting. In addition, the writing appears have been done with a felt tip marker of a type that was non-existent in 1925 or at any period during Dreiser's lifetime. I sincerely hope you did not pay good money for this edition. If you'll permit, I suggest you remove the offending flyleaf and sell the book as a reading copy. Perhaps you can recoup some of your losses. As always, I am happy to be of service.

R.Q.

I whistled. Poor guy. Barski had gotten suckered by someone, and decided to throw the book out. "Who's R.Q.?" I said.

"No clue. I'm guessing your aunt has some kind of directory on the trade that we can use."

"So you've shown this to Bea?"

Abby reached for the bag. "Not yet. To be honest, I don't really want your aunt involved in this one, but I don't have much choice. Books are her area of expertise. My hands are tied."

"She's usually helpful, Abby."

Her lips curled. She turned stiffly and looked me straight in the eye. Her glance was filled with a lot of things—pity, compassion, respect, quiet rage. Basically, everything a guy like me has come to expect from a longtime family friend. "Listen, Dante. I know you hate talking about Francis, but let's just get it out. Your father was one of the most decent men I ever knew. He gave me chances to prove myself at a time when most of the bosses still thought women had no right to be on the force. I *loved* the man. But it's a different world. I can't keep making excuses for you and your aunt. I've known the woman longer than I've known you. She used to tell your father how to run his cases. She thinks she's Perry Mason and Sherlock Holmes all wrapped up in a big manicotti shell. Well, she's *not*. As long as she insists on being a pain in the keister, I feel very comfortable exploiting her. But it ends at the books. After that, it's my case. All I'm asking is that you keep her in check. Understood?"

What choice did I have? She was asking so nicely I couldn't refuse. "Understood," I said.

They had an assembly line of sorts going on at Milo's shop when we arrived. Detective Munoz was picking books off the floor, checking them against one of the marble-covered notebooks they must have gotten from Barski's apartment, and then passing the volume to Bea, who grumbled and rolled her eyes and scoured them, inside and out, for anything unusual. Between the theatrics, she answered the lieutenant's questions.

For a while Abby and I watched them work. I wondered what the lieutenant thought they would find in those books. Money? More fake autographs? As the sky grew dark and the snow began dumping outside, I pitched in on the theory that it would help get us all home quicker. Lights played with the odd shapes in the cramped shop, and I felt like a kid again, wandering through its aisles, touching, exploring, pretending.

By seven o'clock we finished the books. Abby announced she would send a team—and another qualified expert—tomorrow to finish poring through the antiques.

There was one more job to do before the night ended for us. And as we rocketed out to Brooklyn and Barski's apartment, Detective Munoz dreaming of the overtime he was going to rack up on this case, we mulled over the lone clue we'd come up with.

Our analysis of the books in Milo's shop had come up one book short. If it wasn't a dead end, it looked like Barski may have lost his life over something called *The Curious Mr. Tarrant*, by C. Daly King. The notebook told us he'd paid $150 for it only last Monday.

"I've never seen a copy," Bea told Abby as they huddled in

the backseat of the police cruiser. "But I believe it holds the record as the single rarest mystery title of the twentieth century."

"How much is really worth?" Abby wanted to know.

"I'll need more time to make that determination. But I can assure you right now that it's worth far more than a mere $150."

"Gimme a ballpark," Abby pressed. "Five hundred?"

My aunt just rocked her head back against the car seat and chuckled.

The kitchen in Brooklyn still smelled of bacon grease.

"What do you mean, organization?" the lieutenant was saying.

"Nothing tells as much about a man as the books he reads," Bea said, waiting for Abby to flip on the lights. "And, I would add, the way in which he organizes them. Many people simply don't organize them at all. They toss everything on the shelves haphazardly and assume that they'll be able to find what they want when they need to."

"Like you," I tossed in.

She glared at me. "But methodical people," she went on, "organize their volumes methodically. Milo was just that sort of man. He warded off the chaos of the world by the sheer force of ritual."

Abby draped her coat over the back of a kitchen chair and tossed her hat and gloves on the table. Snowflakes on her sleeves melted onto the floor. "Not to get picky, what good's it gonna do me to know how the guy organized his books?"

Together, the four of us walked down the corridor to Barski's living room. Through the windows I saw blinking Christmas lights of neighbors' apartments across the yard. The room was very still and silent, and I sensed the need then to have something happening, a kettle boiling in the kitchen, the TV or stereo blasting, anything to drown out the grave silence of a dead man's home.

"The killer broke the glass on *each* door of the breakfront," Bea was saying, "so he obviously didn't know exactly where Milo kept the object he wanted. But if you're after a book written by Jane Austen, why break the glass on *all* the doors when the As are all kept on the top shelf?"

"But that's only if the books are arranged alphabetically," Abby said.

"Exactly!" Aunt Bea said.

"Give the lady a free case of Turtle Wax," I barked cheerfully.

Bea stepped up to Barski's wall unit and scanned the titles. "Ah ... and see, these *aren't* in alphabetical order ... Dante, can you get the light, please? Excellent ... let's see ... no, no, they aren't categorized by subject either ... He's got fiction tossed in with self-help."

Munoz sniggered in the doorway. "How about the Dewey Decimal System, lady? You try that?"

"Ah, clever man you have, Lieutenant. No, Detective. Dewey organized by subject, I'm afraid. It must be something else, then ... Dante, is your notebook out? Good. Take this down and we'll see if it has any rhyme or reason ... ready?" She took the lieutenant's hand, and balancing herself like a gargantuan acrobat, she stood on the living room armchair and began to read off titles, right to left, from the top shelf.

"Let's go, then ... *The Gentlemen from Indianapolis*, *Vanity Fair*. *The Consul's File*. *August Folly*. *The Brandon*s ... He's got quite of a few of hers, doesn't he? And they're all together, too ... Well, then it's most likely arranged by author surname, then ... Dante? New page, please ... ready? Good. Booth *Tarkington* ... *Thackeray*, William Makepeace ... *Theroux*, Paul ... you see the pattern? Keep going ... *Thirkell*, Angela ... Goodness, he must have them all! Thirkell, Thirkell, Thirkell ... Ah! D.M. What's next? *Thomas* ... *Dylan* Thomas ... Oh, he's got Thurber. I'm frankly surprised that he'd go in for such light humor. And Tolstoy! Hah. Like I believe he actually read *War and Peace*! Trevanian ... Trollope ... Heavens, when will the Ts end? Ah! Finally something delicious—Twain, Twain, Twain, *Twain*."

"This gonna take all night?" Munoz grumbled.

I kept writing furiously, following Bea down a bizarre alphabetical arrangement: the Hs came next. Hailey and Hamsun and Hardy and Harte and Hawthorne, Heller and Hemingway, O. Henry and Hersey. Then a string of George Eliot's works. My aunt took Abby's hand and lumbered off the armchair to continue scanning the bookshelves. On she went, book by book, shelf by shelf. Even before she was calling out Quarles and Quincy, crouched on her haunches at the lower recesses of the bookshelf, I had it figured out. The letters running down the notebook page tipped me off.

T ... H ... E ...

Barski had arranged these books to spell the word *THE*.

"Maybe it's a rhyme," I said aloud, recalling the thought I had earlier that day, about Milo's apparent penchant for literary or musical allusions. "It's one of his mnemonic devices, Bea! Like *Every good boy deserves fudge!*"

"What's he saying?" Munoz demanded.

"Shush," Abby said.

"Yes, you're right," Bea nodded from the top of the armchair. "They form a sentence, don't they?"

She tapped the ceramic Royal Doulton figurines between the stacks of books. "And these little figures are the punctuation separating the words ... Read them off, Dante. Just the letters of the author surnames."

I held the notebook to catch the dismal light from the etched-glass ceiling lamp over our heads.

"Daffiest thing I've ever heard of," Abby was saying. "I mean, it's got to have every letter of the alphabet or it doesn't work. What sentence has all twenty-six letters?"

"A pangram," my aunt said. "Only this one has been modified to be a *perfect* pangram."

Whatever she'd just said was Greek to me and the good officer. But all I had to do to make sense of it was hold up my notebook for all of us to see.

"This one," I said. "This sentence right here."

The quick brown fox jumps over lazy dog.

A LITTLE AFTER EIGHT, I WALKED MY AUNT BACK TO the building in SoHo where she lived. She took my arm to keep herself from sliding in the slush blanketing Prince Street.

"What's to doubt?" I was saying. "You saw the postmark. It was mailed Monday."

"Postmarks mean nothing. Go to any post office, any day of the week, and you'll find discarded envelopes, *open* discarded envelopes, with postmarks, lying in the trash."

I looked at her puffing face. Snowflakes collected in the brim of her eggplant-colored woolen hat. "You know what I think? Your crazy pride won't let you admit that Milo would ask someone else to appraise that book before you. So you're coming up with insane scenarios."

"I have never heard him mention this Mr. R.Q."

"So he doesn't exist? Be real."

We came to the big brick building where she lived. The ground floor was wholly devoted to retail space. For as long as I'd known her, the space had been taken up by a dumpy discount shoe store. But that enterprise had recently packed up and fled to the outer boroughs. Something else was moving in. From the looks of the fixtures the contractors were installing, it was something expensive. That was New York for you. The rent was always spiraling upward. The city forever changing.

I frankly didn't know how long Bea would be able to hang on to her tiny little piece of Book Row on Fourth Avenue. But she would never lose the incredible loft space that she'd lived in all these years. I don't know the full story of how she locked it down. My mother, God rest her, once told me the space had belonged to an artist lover of Bea's, and when things went horribly, horribly wrong—death or extradition, I can't pretend to know—she lucked out.

"Why don't you come up for dinner?" she said. "It's been a perfectly miserable day. You deserve a hot meal."

"Are you cooking?"

"Of course! I was thinking of a quick orecchiette with sliced sausage and steamed broccoli rabe, all tossed in garlic and olive oil."

"Sounds delicious, but no. I'm tired."

"You're a good nephew." She leaned in and gave me a peck on the cheek. "Patient with your elder relations. *Buona sera.*"

When I got to the warehouse on Cornelia Street, I ignored the old lift and trudged up four flights. I opened the door, and the shrill sound of bamboo flutes hit my ears. The apartment was dimly lit, except for the kitchen. My roomie's quad speakers were shaking with Japanese trills. Our living/dining area was decked out for a romantic dinner for two. A two-inch high table was set with incense and candles and chopsticks. Two pairs of kimonos sat on the floor, folded and waiting.

The Finance Man was in the kitchen, slicing a strip steak into chunks and chuckling with a young woman. Both of them were still dressed in their business attire. He wore a denim apron over his light blue Oxford shirt and rep tie. She was blond, with flawless teeth, and wore a dark blue suit over a very similar light blue Oxford shirt and rep tie. Reeboks on her feet. He munched water chestnuts. She sipped white wine like she had it for breakfast every morning.

"Oh hi! You're home," Trey said, pushing back his red-brown hornrims. "Your boss called twice in fifteen minutes. Sounds angry. You're just in time. Dante Sleet, meet Betsey Townsend-Myers."

"Nice to meet you!" she said, offering a hand.

I said likewise.

"We're doing *homemade* Chinese," Trey said.

I could have pointed out that Japanese music clashed with the Chinese theming. But I figured I'd save my critiques for a day without murder.

"*Heeeeeyyyyy*—you're welcome to join us," Trey said awkwardly, his voice telling me I was not under any circumstances to accept. "There's plenty of food. I've been telling Betz all about you. She's been *dying* to meet you."

Translation: Private investigators make trendy roommates.

"Lovely offer," I conceded, "but I wouldn't want to intrude."

"It's no bother," he prattled on. "We're just grabbing a bite and catching a late movie. I just wanted Betz to see my Stella."

"It's totally amazing," Betz said, cocking a hip. "Don't you think so?"

Trey was proud of his Stella. It hung on the wall over his bed. To me it looked like a strip of the old West Side Highway after a three-car collision on a Saturday night. To him it was a cultural aphrodisiac.

"Wow," she said. "That is so cool. I've never met someone like you."

"A roommate or a PI?"

Chuckles all around. I yanked open cabinets. I found some aspirin and washed them down with tap water. Then I collected my leftover boxes of Chinese takeout out of the fridge and embarked on my own brand of culinary legerdemain, with our microwave lending critical assistance.

Betsey asked, rather on cue, I thought, "Do you have to carry a gun?"

"Well, I'm licensed to carry the biggest one allowable in the tri-state area." I paused. "Would you like to see it?"

She shuddered. "I don't care for guns. They're kind of—what, Trey?—archaic?"

The roomie dumped vegetables into his hot wok. Sesame-oil-scented steam blossomed into his face. "Deadly? Pathetically macho?"

"Have a pleasant evening," I said, disappearing to my room.

We had a good-sized one-bedroom-turned-two but it was mostly his furniture, his paintings, his subscription to *Architectural Digest*. Because I answered the ad he'd placed in the *Voice*, I now paid half the rent to confine most of my belongings to a snug drywall bedroom the landlord had thrown together. In that bedroom now, I knocked my phone receiver off the hook. Let Bray deal with that.

I put on some Charlie Parker to relax. When I finished eating, I sat on my bed with my baseball mitt and bounced a rubber ball off the wall a few times to help me think. Trouble was, I didn't want to think.

Parker filled the room with his plaintive notes. After a while I rolled over and slept, but my dreams were *crazy*. Insane, Technicolor productions starring Milo Barski, Bray, my parents, and Aunt Bea. I awoke close to midnight, my leg throbbing. I heard amorous sounds coming through the drywall. I racked up another two points for the Stella and fell back to sleep.

❧ 12 ☙

PURPLE GIRL

Come morning I found a girl with purple hair sitting in the Barcelona chair in our living room. She paged languorously through one of Trey's interior decorating magazines. She'd made herself right at home, too; tossed her long vintage-shop tweed coat over the couch and kicked off her black high-top sneakers with orange laces. Underneath, she wore a shiny gold waiter's jacket with rolled-up sleeves. Her T-shirt, which proclaimed ELVIS LIVES, was fluorescent pink, and her tapered jeans were soft enough to have gone fifteen rounds in a rock tumbler.

Her hair, I noticed when I drew closer, was only *half* purple. The rest was a perfectly acceptable chestnut color. From her left ear hung a plastic orange stegosaurus. A tiny one, not one of those dreary, life-sized ones you've heard so much about it. She was maybe eighteen, definitely petite and pretty. In all, a very neat-looking package of good looks, bangles and purple dye. And she showed no sign of leaving.

"Oh, you're awake," she said. "Trey said you'd be up late. He's kind of weird. You guys split this place?"

I felt a little uncomfortable, since I was wearing a beat-up police academy T-shirt and a pair of boxers. But I managed to find my voice. "Split? Yeah, two ways."

"I'm thinking of getting a place like this with a couple of my friends. What's it cost you?"

"Too much. Look, miss—"

"No really. How much?"

I told her.

She whistled. She had wonderful brown eyes with greenish flecks; she fixed them on an enormous framed photo on the wall. A big red-blond athlete on the field, swinging a baseball bat and swearing his lungs out. His two sisters rooting in the background. Erin's gift to me before going off to law school and out of my life.

"Here I am sitting here," she said, "trying to picture what you look like, and all the time, there you were, on the wall." She laughed, waving a slender hand with orange fingernails. "I keep forgetting I only talked to Trey and Betz. They're weird. Very corporate. You think she wore braces?"

"I'd rather not know. May I ask: Who the heck are you?"

"Kathleen. But I prefer *Leena*. I've been trying to get the 'rents to call me that, but forget it. See, it's my father. He came home all crazy last night, kept reading the papers about that old guy that got killed Sunday. The antiques guy?"

"Barski? This is about Barski?"

"That's what *I'm* trying to figure out. You think Dad tells me these things? Anyway, I was supposed to be asleep but I wasn't. He was in my sister's room and he never goes in there. He's just sitting on the bed, having himself a good cry, which is like the first time I ever saw him do that, you know? Finally he gets up and tosses this card out and goes to bed. I fished it out of the trash and that's why I'm here."

"Card? What card?"

Her orange nails went into her jacket pocket and came up

with a crumpled business card. *My* business card. Smeared with black and red ink.

"Munro!" I slumped into a back-breaking chair across from her. My shower could wait. "You're Ernie Munro's daughter."

"Duh. See, I thought if this news is bad enough to make Dad cry, then I better check it out. He'd never tell Mom. Thinks he's too macho, which is childish but a lot of guys are like that, especially dads. Anyway, I didn't want to wait for business hours. Your phone was busy, so I came right over." Well, sure—I'd left it off the hook. "I looked you up in the book. There's only one Dante Sleet."

"Imagine that! And all this time I thought I was throwing out other people's bills."

Her eyes flashed. "You like to make jokes. You think you're funny. Don't get me wrong. You *are*. Just not in the way you think."

"Then it's wise that I've resisted the impulse to do open mic nights. So, uh, yesterday your Dad nearly broke me over his knee. You think he knows something about Barski's death?"

She shrugged and closed the magazine. She tucked her feet under her a bit more and gripped them with her hands. Argyles wriggled on her feet. "I know nothing about this dead antiques guy. I thought Dad had talked to you about my sister."

"What about your sister?"

"Well, she always wanted to sing. She had a pretty good voice in high school. Mom had her take voice lessons, play the piano. Only, her senior year she starts singing with the Dipsticks. I know —pretty stupid name. But she liked one of the guys. He played the guitar and he dumped her when they graduated. She wanted to study voice in college, but they sent her to a Catholic school. All girls. Nuns and everything. I mean, we're not even Catholic. Not really. I think they thought it would straighten her out."

"Who's *they*? Your mother and father?"

"Who else? My mom was definitely in on it. She talks to saints. Alison did her voice classes and she hooks up with Tony and Andy in Newport. Naturally Tony's like loaded and he's got a record company and Andy's looking for someone to sing backup on his new album. I didn't talk to Alison back then. She was like a major pain. But it turns out she really liked this guy."

"Tony or Andy?"

"*Tony*," she said, her voice rising with impatience.

"And Alison's your sister?"

"Yesss. Aren't you listening?"

"I'm trying, believe me."

"So anyway, she bags school sophomore year and comes home and she's dating this Tony guy. Dad goes totally out of control. Calls her a bunch of terrible names, and throws her out. You believe it?"

I could believe Ernie Munro doing anything, including beating the heck out of the Bronx Zoo's polar bears. "Mom freaked. Cried for days. Alison moves in with this Tony guy and comes back to get her clothes. Told Mom she was really leaving. That's it. Mail came from school. Was she was coming back or what? Dad trashed it all. Went through the whole disowning ritual. Yelled at me when I tried picking it out. But Alison stuck to her guns. Never came back." She paused to catch her breath. She needed it by then, her eyes growing moist. "I mean, who would've figured she'd *really* never come back?"

I leaned closer. "Leena?" I said. "Yesterday your father said he had a wife and *a* kid. He was angry, but a man doesn't forget he's got two daughters when he losing his cool. What gives?"

Her face went red in all the wrong places. Her eyes dropped to the floor. "What do you think I'm trying to tell you? She's dead. They called it an accident. We think she was murdered."

"THAT'S ALL WE HAVE ON HER," THE INTERN SAID.

I put down the newspaper clippings I was reading and took the next file. Right on top was the paper's front page from Labor Day two years ago. The headline read:

SINGER DIES IN LONG ISLAND ACCIDENT
Wild Weekend Bash Ends in Horror

Under that was a publicity shot of Alison Munro and a tagline promising photos inside. I started reading. Leena had sketched out the story in my apartment, and now I had the black-and-white confirmation that she'd done a good job.

I learned that during the last summer of her life, Alison and her friends had spent much of the summer at a Hamptons beach house owned by the family of her boyfriend, one Anthony J. Crowell, 36, described as president and producer of something called Zephyr Productions. On the night of Sunday, September 2, Alison Munro, 21, had drunk heavily and fought with two other party guests, Jennifer Redmond, 24, and Rosita Starr, 18. The fight had been physical; Alison caught a few slaps and dealt a few, too. After allegedly striking Starr, Alison swore at Crowell and drove off in a car she'd rented for the weekend.

Alison drove six miles and proceeded to get blitzed at the bar of a trendy, Victorian-style inn in the vicinity that was known for its nightlife. At midnight, when the bartender refused to serve her, she left swearing but returned in a few minutes, complaining that she'd locked herself out of her vehicle. A bartender offered her a wire hanger and asked if he could help. She swore at him and stormed out. It wasn't until six o'clock that morning that hotel management found her rental Nissan, with its doors locked, its keys in the ignition, and the wire hanger on the ground. They notified police. At 10:00 a.m., a couple walking their dog on the beach discovered Alison's body on the sand only blocks from the inn. She'd been dead for hours. Suffered a massive head trauma. The police questioned Crowell's houseguests and anyone who attended the party, as well as other summer residents along that stretch of beach, and came up with nothing.

The article mentioned that Alison had left college a year earlier and had later recorded a "widely heard" album and a few singles with "up-and-coming" star Andrew Kassinopoulos, a.k.a. Andy Kay, 24.

And that was it. All that remained were questions. How did Alison get from the inn's parking lot to the beach? Where had she actually died? Police suspected foul play. Traces of moss or mildew were found on the body and head wound, suggesting she might have been killed in nearby woods and moved after death. But police couldn't nail down the precise sequence of events since that morning's falling tide might have washed away blood, her purse, a murder weapon, or any other helpful clues. Had she met someone in the parking lot of the inn? Had she fallen or been struck? The leads dried up and the cops shelved the case. Alison Munro would have been twenty-four years old come May of this year.

And now somehow her death was linked to Milo Barski's. I thought I had the faintest inkling of a link. In Barski's suitcase we'd found copies of *The Winds of War* and *Gone with the Wind*, two books that had been cut to serve as book safes. As it happens, the book safes had been empty, hinting that perhaps he was expecting to fill them with cash. Alison had done session work for *Zephyr* Productions. A zephyr was another name for *wind*. There had to be a connection, but I had no idea what it was.

I got up and carried the files over to the mousy young woman who minded the file room. I wondered what crimes she'd committed in college to be banished to the morgue of the *New York Tab*. As I stuffed my notebook in my pocket, she asked, "When's the story running?"

"Can't tell yet. I've got leads to chase down, hunches to play. Always play your hunches."

Only *Tab* reporters allowed, she'd told me earlier, and I fired back that I was a friend of the publisher's and offered to have her call him directly. She shrank from that task, and I was in.

"Will it really be in *People*?" she asked.

Poor thing. Keen-witted she wasn't. If you told her the word gullible wasn't in the dictionary, she'd believe it.

"Yep. Hundred words or two pictures, whichever comes first."

Back in the newsroom, Bernie Housknecht perched on the tip of his chair, gazing into a green computer screen, a man in love with his prose. Around him, madness raged in the newsroom of the *Tab*. Phones rang, editors barked, photographers swaggered. But Bernie Housknecht was far off in fruitcake heaven, the realm of sicko killers, religious wackos, alien visitors, and babies who cry rocks.

He punched in a period and looked at me. He was the most latently fat man I knew. His pink, unlined face had a compact roundness to it. Watching him talk, you had the feeling that if he nicked himself shaving he'd drown in a sea of flub. As for the rest of him, you knew it was there, but where? Immaculately dressed and sweet-smelling, he hid his shape well under a crisp yellow Oxford and tie. And he spoke in a voice a tad more masculine than Truman Capote's.

"Did you talk to the gossip columnist?" I asked.

"Things I do for you. Liddell says Crowell's company is bush league, but knowing Liddell he's pissed they don't invite him to their parties. Theoretically, Crowell knows his stuff. Played in a band once, shilled albums for a big outfit for three or four years. He managed a few hotshots some years ago. Their singles hit Top 40 and they dumped him, so he finds this guy with the hair."

"Andy Kay."

"That's the genius. This time, Crowell's smart. Locks him in a contract, so Kay can't walk. Only, he's not walking 'cause no one wants him."

"How's Crowell's company staying afloat?"

He scratched the back of his head with a pinkie, then

smoothed down his thick black hair. "Crowell's got daddy money to play with. That's all Liddell knows. He doesn't think much of Kay's records. You want a name? Luzetta Trevilliam. Former employee. Liddell tried to interview her when she left but she blew him off. Used to be Zephyr's business manager."

I jotted down the number he gave me.

"That's it," he said. "You want more, talk to Liddell yourself. I'm way over time here."

"You're a pal, Bernie. You'll hear from Mr. Bray if we get a break on this."

"Great. I love when people remember their friends. Now scoot. I'm busy."

"What're you working on?"

His eyes brightened. "Amazing story. Some eighty-two-year-old coot went nuts in the Bronx, carved up the family. Cops found bizarre markings on the wall. They think they were all in a cult together, and that Grandpa had a little ... uh ... doctrinal disagreement with his daughter. You want the headline we're going with?"

"Please, no."

He smiled with pleasure. "PSYCHO GRAMPS HACKS VOODOO MOM. It's gold."

"You're a sick pup, Bernie."

The subway got me downtown. The cops had finished checking Milo's shop. The place was sealed up and empty, a single cruiser parked outside. Next door my Aunt Bea was busy shelving books while Amos scanned newspapers. Book Lady & Friends had only one customer: a crook-necked guy zealously stuffing books into a cardboard box like a moocher swiping canapes at a banquet.

"They find anything?" I said.

From the couch in the back, Amos piped up, "Goose eggs."

I inspected the fridge's contents. Fresh lemonade and apple turnovers. I helped myself.

Amos waved his unlit pipe at me. "Then they had John Henry down here," he said. "Had Milo's safe open in twenty seconds. Knocked off the combination lock with a sledgehammer and shoved a crowbar in the hole. If they can crack them so fast, why call them safes? What's so safe about that? It's a misnomer."

"Amos, I can truthfully say I've never considered that in all my years of life."

My aunt stalked to her armchair. She wore a shapeless purple dress that matched the color of her cowboy boots. "Guess what they found inside the safe? A hundred fifty in a cash drawer, plus a selection of estate jewelry that he put out every morning. The highlights were the insurance photos. All neatly tucked away in manila envelopes. Lieutenant Posluszny said she'd check the images with the various insurance companies." She eyed the remains of my apple turnover with desire. "Where were you?"

"Out learning about *another* murder."

Her brows shot up.

I handed her a bag from Tower Records containing two albums and two 45s. She pulled out an album and studied it thoughtfully. On the cover of the LP, a bare-chested man stood before a set of triple windows, a dark-haired girl—who I now recognized as Alison Munro—peeked around the mirror.

"That's Milo's photo," she said. "The one we found in his apartment."

"Ta-da."

She flipped it over. The words had swum in my head all the way from the record store. *Produced by Anthony J. Crowell for Zephyr Productions. Engineered & Mixed by Van Nilsson. Background Vocals by Alison Munro, Rosita Starr.* A few other names, a drummer, bassist, keyboardist, then: *Jacket design by Marilyn Su. Photos by M. Barski.*

"The girl's related to the bartender?"

"His daughter. She's dead. And her sister wants me to prove it was murder."

She looked briefly at the 45s. One was the single, "Visitor to

Hard Times," from the *Hard Times* album. She went back to the LP. A photo on the back showed a short-haired Andy Kay hitchhiking on a Jersey highway at dawn.

"Methinks the fellow is styling himself after the Springsteen boy," she said.

"He's not a boy anymore."

"He'll always be to me."

I told her everything the girl in the record store had told me. Kay had released *Hard Times* shortly after Springsteen's *Born in the U.S.A.* Jingoistic rock was in, but not for Andy Kay; the album went nowhere. So Andy ripped his jeans, got out his anarchy flag, slapped on some eyeshadow and let his hair grow out. Out came "Jagged Beings" from *Spitting Image*; it hit the bottom of the charts and stayed there, but at least it made the charts. Alison had had a solo bit on that one. The other single was "Baby's Got a Flaming Heart," from an album Kay was supposed to have released last November.

"You saw the name?" my aunt said. "Zephyr? Like the *wind?*"

"I'm way ahead of you. I hate to say it, guys, but it doesn't look good for Milo. I'm beginning to think those book safes Barski made were intended for *collections.*"

Amos gawked at me. "What book safes?"

I ignored him. "Bea, he had something on someone and was bleeding them."

"Stop," Bea said, holding up a hand. "It's pointless to make assumptions at this stage."

"Come on, Bea. It looked funny from the beginning. I think this is the sad truth."

"We don't know for certain, and until then, we do not slander the dead in my shop. *Capisce?*"

I zipped it. She wet her lips and tried again. "Zephyr's address is not far. I'll get my coat."

I watched her slip around the corner to the coatrack. "Since when do you make house calls?"

She pulled on a lavender number and matching woolen hat. She looked like a ripe fig on legs. "This will be an experience!" she said. "Amos, mind the shop. I'm going off to see how they make rock 'n' roll."

"It's almost twenty blocks," I said. "We can take the subway."

She grimaced. In general, mass transportation sickened her. Hurtling through a graffiti-spattered sewer was too close to her vision of hell to permit even a short ride. We would walk. And I would talk.

"You want the long version or the short?" I said.

We stepped onto the sidewalk and caught a face full of cold rain.

She unfolded her ducky umbrella. "The twenty-block version."

❧ 13 ❧

ZEPHYR

The Olmsted shared a grimy block on Broadway with a welfare hotel, and I had to wonder how people told the difference. In its lobby were a meager candy and newspaper stand, a bored security guard, and plenty of imitation marble paneling. I figured the paneling did the trick.

We rode a gum-strewn elevator to the seventh floor and followed signs. A water fountain. Two bathrooms. A bank of phone booths. Then came a pair of glass-paned doors.

The reception area shook with hard rock music flowing from six speakers. The walls and furniture were azure, and the shag carpet was so thick and blue I thought I'd slipped into someone's indoor pool. Before us loomed a desk as round as a barn silo. Behind it danced a sharp-faced young woman wearing a bulky turquoise-and-gray sweater and something resembling black thermal underwear. She waved a stapler as she danced, swaying and gyrating, occasionally collating some papers and stapling them without breaking stride. A swell show.

Bea folded her hands on the counter and waited. The girl looked up at last, mouthed "Oh" with her lips and lowered the volume on the stereo behind her. Lowered it, I should say, just a tad. The noise was still absolutely deafening. She shouted, "If you have a demo, just leave it on the shelf. We'll call you." She returned to her dancing.

Bea looked at me, her lips white. "What is a demo?"

"We're not musicians!" I shouted.

"You here about the job?"

"Business manager?" I said, thinking of the woman who'd left that very post.

"No. Marketing director."

I shook my head. Eyes now filling with curiosity, the young woman killed the sound. My eardrums sighed with relief. Bea had a finger in both ears. "My dear girl, we want to see Mr. Crowell," my aunt said. "It's quite important and regards Milo Barski who, as you may know, was bludgeoned to death on Sunday. Please inform Mr. Crowell of our presence."

The receptionist hesitated. She probably didn't get many visitors who wanted to discuss bludgeonings. And she was equally unaccustomed to imperious grand dames like my aunt, who gave orders like the queen ordering tea. So she took down our names and scurried off as fast as anyone wearing long johns in public possibly can.

We snooped as we waited. A plastic nameplate on the desk read JENNIFER REDMOND. Witness No. 1. On a low table, a small Sony TV set played a music video in which a shirtless jerk with a mane of black hair screamed his lungs out in some city-bred art director's conception of a garage in the sticks: spotless, with a rowing scull lashed to the ceiling.

My aunt studied wall posters and framed magazine articles about hairy-headed, lipsticked-and-rouged stars wearing shimmering costume jewelry. Then she checked out the female performers as well.

"What is this"—she struggled for the right word —"flummery?"

"Metal," I said. "Metal is in right now. You may have heard."

"Pathetic," she declared. "You listen to these people?"

"No. But someone does, or they wouldn't be here. Most artists with indie labels are utter unknowns, unless they're really good."

"Their obscurity is a blessing for us all." She whirled around. "Ah—hello."

Jennifer Redmond returned, leading a thin man behind her. A smoking cigarette dangled from his lips. "*Hiiii*," he said, "I'm Tony Crowell." He threw out his right palm as if to shake Bea's hand. But at the last second, he seemed to change his mind. He whipped the cigarette out of his mouth and rested it in an ashtray on Jennifer Redmond's desk. Then he threw out his hand again and smiled like the record plugger he was. "How you doing?"

"Fine, under the circumstances ..." my aunt said, shaking hands and making the introductions.

Crowell beamed till it hurt. He wore jeans, a black shirt with French cuffs, and a white leather tie as thin as a strand of fettuccine. His black hair was parted in the middle and feathered back in a longish style I hadn't seen since the seventies. The wrinkles around his eyes and cheeks told me he was fast approaching forty and hated himself for it. "What's this about Milo Barski?"

"Mr. Crowell, you may not know—"

"Call me Tony."

"Very well ... *Tony*. Milo was killed this weekend."

"I know. I saw something about it in the papers. A real shame. He did some good work for us. Shot a couple of our album covers. They catch the guy who did it?"

"Not yet. I was a friend of his, and now his executor. His estate is quite a mess, as you can imagine, and I thought you wouldn't mind answering a few questions?"

He cleared his throat and stared at the floor. "I really ought to refer you to our attorney, but ... um, if it's quick ... What do you need to know, exactly?"

"Oh, the usual ... who, what, when ... How else can I make sense of his records?"

The smile faded. Crowell patted his chest, came up with a pack of Winstons, plucked one out and popped it into his mouth without lighting it. "You know, Miss—I'm sorry—Valentino?"

"*Ms.*," Aunt Beatrice corrected him. "And the Valentino name expelled its last breath nearly a century ago on the shores of Ellis Island. *Valentine.* Like the embarrassing annual celebration of expensive, unnecessary displays of affection."

"Um, right, *Ms.* Valentine," Crowell said. "It's just that ... well, you might be after information that could be considered proprietary."

"Of course," my aunt said with a strange bow. "I understand perfectly. I mean, why tell us when you must tell the police eventually, either at my behest or the order of a surrogate judge? Good day, Mr. Crowell."

Something akin to fear swept across the man's face. "Police? Judges? Hey, look, maybe we can take care of this right away, huh?" He sucked at his unlit cigarette and extended his arm. Aunt Bea took it.

As we headed down a hallway filled with framed album covers, he said, "Now ... just what do you need to know?"

He led us to a cramped studio fitted with a large plexiglass window and a mixing console. A curly haired blond giant fooled with the board, talking to a man on the other side of the glass. I had no trouble recognizing the man in the booth as Andy Kay.

Crowell explained that they were rehearsing, not recording. A short woman with heavy makeup and red-brown hair perched in a chair near the blond guy. Crowell told her to get up. She said a few words that turned Bea white, then wandered off with the slow sway of a go-go dancer.

Bea lowered herself into the chair and looked around and small-talked. My, my, such complicated technology. She watched Andy Kay, his kinky dark hair in headphones, sing into the mic.

JOSEPH D'AGNESE

He faltered a few times and gave up. "Hey," he called, his voice suddenly bathed in static. "What's going on? Is it family day or something?"

"Yeah—what *is* the deal?" the sound guy said, eyeing Bea. He had tousled hair that would never need combing and pale blue eyes. He rested a huge arm on his chinos and stared at his boss. "This a huge distraction, Tony."

"Van, please. Ms. Valentine's come about Milo Barski. You remember Mr. Barski, don't you?"

Andy Kay must have heard us through his headsets. "The hippie photographer guy?"

By now a ring of cigarette smoke encircled Crowell's head. He fed them Bea's story and the Latina lounging in the doorway let out another expletive. "I can't believe it," she said. "Guy gets killed on top of the way we treated him."

"We treated him well," Crowell snapped. "You have a problem, Rosie? We treated him pretty darn nice. He got his money."

"Sure," Rosie said. "Probably after a year of calling."

"That's enough," Crowell said. He beamed at Bea. "We weren't doing that well back then. There may have been a few delays in accounting. You can understand. But he got paid in full, believe me."

"Milo was an antiques dealer, Mr. Crowell," Bea said. "He took photos of antiques. As far as we know he hadn't photographed a human being in twenty years. How did he end up freelancing here?"

Again, the smile. "You know how it is, Ms. Valentine. *Bea.* It's all who you know, right? One hand washes the other. My mother's an artist. My parents have an extensive collection of pieces that they were anxious to have insured. And that's it, really. Friend of a friend, so to speak. Milo was willing to make a few extra dollars, so he took the shots."

"He was cheap," Rosie piped.

Crowell glared at her. "I said that's enough."

"He was weird, is what he was," Kay said into his microphone. The base of his nostrils was impossibly wide, and he had skin as pocked as a chicken's. On looks alone I thought he had great future as a musician.

The next words out of my aunt's mouth nearly gave me the sweats. "Barski's will makes a small bequest to one Alison Munro," she said. "A Zephyr employee. Is she here?"

They looked stunned. Eyes roved, fell on others, or else looked away. Nilsson spoke first. "She was a session singer here for a while. Really sweet girl. But ... ah ... she's dead."

"That's right," Crowell said with a croak. "She was eager and willing, so we put her to work. Our relationship didn't last long before ... before it happened."

"How did she die?" Bea persisted.

Crowell's lips moved like those of a politician stalling for time. Andy Kay beat him to it. His voice filled the control room. "Accident," he said.

"That's right," Crowell said. "Look, it's an old story, frankly. She was despondent, I guess you could say. We had a business dispute. She wanted a crack at her own album, but she wasn't ready. She slapped some of us around. Fought with Rosie here. One thing led to another, and she—like we said—went and had an accident."

Bea clucked and clapped her hands twice, very slowly. All eyes were drawn to that bizarre gesture. "This is amusing. Mr. Crowell. You say you fought over business. As if she were a mere employee?"

"Well, she was."

"And yet the newspapers say you were her lover."

"Oh, geez!" Crowell said.

The rest happened quickly. I was keeping my eyes on Crowell, but Bea said later I should have been watching Andy Kay in the sound booth. Anyway, for what it's worth, Rosita Starr tittered in the doorway.

"That's enough!" Crowell snapped, his voice so loud that Rosita flinched.

From the sound booth, Kay's voice boomed, "Hey! You can't talk to her like that!"

Rosita stalked out. Crowell went after her, squeezing past me, his ears turning red. I didn't bother looking down the hall. I had no trouble hearing the slap and her gasp. Kay tore off his headphones and flew out of the booth into the hallway. "Nice going, Tony," I heard him tell his producer.

"You can go to hell, too," I heard Crowell say.

And then he appeared in the doorway, face red, nostrils flaring. He looked down at Bea, who was still sitting in front of the board. "We're done, lady. You can both take a walk. You have any more questions, you can talk to my lawyer."

Bea was unruffled, her brow serene, her eyes watching him like a hawk. "May I have your attorney's name, Mr. Crowell?"

"We're fresh out of attorneys at the moment," Crowell said. "But don't worry. When I get one, he'll be all over you."

Downstairs in the lobby, we found Kay leaning against the fake marble, his knee up, his hands beating out a tune on his ripped jeans. He wore a flannel shirt over a black T-shirt. The T-shirt bore a picture of a cracked wineglass and the words, *Is it live …or is it Memorex?*

"You guys are hilarious," he said. "A lot of guts. You think he's gonna take that lying down?" Kay's eyes looked moist and bloodshot. "You know who he is?"

My aunt jutted her chin at him. "No, Mr. Kay, I don't. Please illuminate me."

I took two steps toward the candy stand, where Rosita Starr was paying for some smokes. Her hair was a frizzy mess, and with the added strands from her red angora turtleneck, she positively shimmered in fuzz. Her hips were cocked in a tight leather skirt. She tore open her Pall Malls and was blowing smoke in seconds. What was up with this place? Everyone was a chimney. "You and the old lady," she said. "You real cowboys."

I could make out the welts of three, possibly four, fingers on her right cheek. "You okay?" I said.

She was taken aback by my concern. Her eyes shyly raked the floor. "I'll be okay."

"What happened between Tony and Alison, Rosie?"

"You got eyes? He dumped her. He likes dumping people. I should know."

"That's what you and she fought about that night? Not her career?"

"That's right. She was getting on my case about me and Tony fooling around behind her back. But he and I never got it on. It was all just flirty-flirty up until that night. When she didn't come back to the party, Tony was all upset. One thing led to another, and, well, I spent the night with him." Her eyes got serious. "That was the first time. I should have known better. I was an idiot. Me and Alison, we shoulda saved our breath and fought over something that really mattered. Like contracts." She jerked her chin over my shoulders at Kay, who was still speaking to Bea. It was a scenario I thought I'd never see—the book lady of Book Row immersed in conversation with a heavy metal hunkasaurus.

"He's a star, man," Rosie told me. "Could really go places. But he's still here. Why? Can't go. Locked in for two more albums and crap royalties. Tony's stealing us blind, man."

"*Us*? You too?"

"Yeah. I'm gonna be a star. That's why I changed my name. Starr with two r's, get it? See, me and Andy, we got a thing now." She sucked at her cigarette as if it were a candy cane. "Your friend, Mr. Barski? Nice old man. You know he once shot Grace Kelly? He was cute. He said I was real pretty."

Bea appeared at my side and took my arm. "Farewell, Miss Starr. If you'll permit me, you should hire an attorney immediately."

"I don't have the money for that," Starr said.

"There are lawyers who would jump at the chance to take a workplace assault case. They'd work *pro bono*—"

The woman held up a hand. "Lady, what did I say? No lawyers. I can't afford to get bogged down. I'm playing past him. We all are."

Bea nodded, drinking in Starr's words. "Very well. But may I say that no woman should ever pay a price for speaking her mind."

"Yeah, right?" Rosie said, staring up at my aunt through suddenly watery eyes.

"Farewell, my dear."

We turned to go. As we left, I heard Andy Kay say, "Come 'ere, babe," and move in to grab Starr's waist. Their lips moved together and it got messy, a teased-out tangle of hair and makeup. Rosie's hand rested on Kay's hip, cigarette ash trickling to the lobby floor.

Bea snorted and stormed off in the direction of the revolving door. "Let's go," she hissed. "I detest being made an involuntary voyeur."

❧ 14 ❧

TOAD IN A HOLE

The Grouser Club's dining room steward approached me. "Sir," he said, "as a rule, we don't allow, ah … non-*members* upstairs."

He was being careful to avoid saying *women*.

"It's okay," I said. "I cleared it with Samuel."

"Yes," he continued. "I'm well aware of that. But that allowance is under that condition—"

"What?" I said. "That she *behave* herself?"

I was probably too short with him, but it had been a troubling morning thus far. The thought of another man bulldozing Bea did not sit well with me. Not because these men were rude, but because the poor wretches had no idea who they were dealing with. The steward stiffened and changed tack. "Is there something I can help her with? Has the lady lost something?"

Yeah, I thought. Her mind.

Only that could explain why my aunt was wandering in and out of the tables in the private dining room. Lunch had ended minutes earlier. Haverstrom was waiting for us in the Recreation Room. And Bea was doing her impression of a bloodhound chasing a scent.

JOSEPH D'AGNESE

I watched her inspect the remains of people's lunches. She hit table No. 1, Haverstrom's, then inspected table No. 7 behind it. Something caught her attention. An unused place setting. She lifted the name card in that spot, read it, and slipped it back onto the table.

"Have fun?" I said when she returned to me.

"This is *work*, not fun. It helps that men of this sort are creatures of habit. Mr. Haverstrom sits at table No. 1 in the six o'clock position. Let us imagine that Milo calls him during dinner and this Samuel person brings him the message *out here in front of all these other men.*"

"Uh-huh. You think one of the other codgers overheard them?"

"Precisely. Only one man can do that, and he sits at 12 o'clock, No. 7. He was absent from the great midday meal today. Shall we?"

In the Recreation Room, the men were still in their seats, a day older, a day ranker. Even those who seemed asleep opened their eyes as we passed and watched us through rheumy lids. One guy froze and watched as my aunt sallied across the Persian rug in the middle of the room.

Haverstrom was whooping it up in his alcove, which is to say he sat in his seat, a glowing cigar in his manicured hands. Samuel stood over him, holding a lighter. The old man watched us approach, his eyes flitting slowly up and down, taking us in, measuring us. Two stiff-backed chairs from the dining room awaited us.

Haverstrom glanced at his watch. "What took you so long? We finished eating ten minutes ago. Oh, never mind." His eyes went straight to mine. "I've been trying all morning to reach you. Don't you ever go in?"

"I've been out working. For you."

He could not resist. "And what have you learned?"

Aunt Bea cleared her throat and threw out her chin. "My

name is Bea Valentine," she announced firmly. Haverstrom gawked, craning his head to look up at her the way tourists gaze at the Statue of Liberty. He shot to his feet and extended a hand. "Ah, the bookseller. Pleasure. I'm proud to say that I know of your work, madam. The bibliographies on early nineteenth-century cookery and household management are the most recent, I take it. The succotash paper, I'm told, was well received at your talk at the Grolier Club. Who knew that recipe had appeared so early in a cookbook? I was not in attendance because I have no interest in that specialty, but I respect the scholarship."

"That is all we can ask," she said graciously.

I sat. My aunt gave her chair a withering look. Samuel gleaned something in her glance and dashed off. He returned moments later with a more suitable upholstered armchair, which he slid behind her. My aunt lowered herself into it and peered at Haverstrom over the top of her purse.

"Now," he said, "what have you learned?"

Behind us, Samuel drew the partition across the alcove.

I opened my mouth, but Bea beat me to it. "A book is missing from Barski's shop," she said. *"The Curious Mr. Tarrant."*

Haverstrom choked on his cigar. We waited for him to recover. He lowered the cigar to the ashtray and grumbled, "I knew it. It's gone! Someone stole it!"

"What's so important about it?" I asked.

Haverstrom sputtered, "Timing! Timing is everything. If I don't get that book by the thirty-first, I'm out. It's a bet, you see? We started it five years ago. Every year we have a contest, keeps us occupied. Coin collectors do it, the stamp fanatics, and us. The bibliophiles."

"You couldn't settle for a softball game?"

He shifted his irritated glance to Bea. "But it's gotten out of hand. Either I get all my annual wants or I'm going to have to write a very large check to someone else's charity. It's me against the American Lit cretins. No one collects what I do."

My aunt said, "You collect mystery fiction?"

In response, Haverstrom cranked his legs into service and reached across the desk for a small box from which he gingerly extracted a book. Without a word he passed it to Bea, who opened it gently, turning the pages with her right hand. The pages were the color of toast. She reached the title page. *And Then There Were None*, by Agatha Christie.

"That came to hand yesterday," Haverstrom snorted proudly. "First American edition. I'm having a cover made for the dust jacket. But look inside. The signature …"

I stretched to peer over Bea's purple enshrouded shoulder. On the dedication page was a fountain pen scrawl saluting someone on their birthday. I expected to see Dame Agatha's signature, but instead I saw the name *Barry Fitzgerald*.

"Who?" I said.

"The actor," Haverstrom replied. "He played the judge in the 1945 film version of the book. Bought it from a dealer this week. I've got a couple of good ones, some with signatures, some without. God knows what my sons will do with them when I pass, but that's the perennial dilemma, isn't it? Can't take it with you."

"It's not my area of expertise," Bea piped up, "but I venture to say that *Tarrant* is worth considerably more than a thousand dollars."

"It's worth the price we agreed upon!" Haverstrom scoffed. "If you ask me, Barski was too desperate to hold out for more." Looking at me, he said, "It's one of the rarest in detective fiction. The author was an American, but his book was published in England in 1935. Probably couldn't get it published here. Your friend Barski bought it off a fool who didn't know what he had. We agreed on a thousand and I'm not going higher … oh, but what's the difference? You haven't recovered it, have you?"

"Never say never," I said. "Incidentally, my employer will be contacting you with an agreement and arrange for a more sizable retainer."

His mouth crinkled. "You'll get it. You'll get more, too, as long as you get that damned book."

"I'm afraid you'll have to face the fact that you've lost your wager already," my aunt said. "Even if the book were in hand, you'd have to wait for the disposition of the estate to take possession, and only if we can find supporting documentation of your agreement with Milo. As you well know, the executor's chief obligation is to realize the highest possible price for the heirs."

"Ah, yes," Haverstrom said. "And who is the executor? Have you met him?"

"She sits before you."

He glowered. "Of course she is. Well, you'll not get a penny more. A handshake deal is a deal nonetheless."

"An unverifiable deal," my aunt said.

His eyes softened. His chin nearly quivered. "Madam, I implore you as a fellow book lover. We're *all* book lovers here, most of us. We love to touch them and feel them and own them … I can't blame anyone for stealing it. If I were desperate, I'd do the same." He caught himself, added hastily, "That was not an admission of anything."

"No," Bea said. "Have you ever bought books from someone with the initials R.Q.?"

"What? *Initials*?" He mulled it over, but I could tell from his vacant look that he couldn't help us. "No … don't think so. Why?"

"And no one with those initials is a member of this club?"

"Inquire with Samuel. My instinct is no. Why? Is this person believed to be the culprit?"

Bea raised a finger in thought. "Tell me, you didn't ask Milo to find you a first edition copy of *An American Tragedy*?"

"That old thing? Why? I told you, I collect mysteries of the traditional sort. That book is something one of the others might collect."

"Like Mr. Balsam, perhaps?"

Color came to his cheeks and shot to his ears. "Adrian Balsam, here in the club? That fool. A Faulkner freak."

"A competitor of yours, is he?"

"Of course. His late wife was a longtime patron of the hospital foundations. Damned if I'm going to write a check to put their name on a new wing! I haven't seen him around lately."

"Describe him," I said, and then bit my tongue as he proceeded to describe a man very much like himself. Old and gray and bespectacled.

"How is Balsam involved?" Haverstrom asked. "Is he missing something from Barski's shop too?"

It was a curious assumption to make. His eyes were free of deceit; I decided he wasn't putting us on.

"Goodbye," my aunt said coldly.

At the bottom of the stairs, Bea stopped at Samuel's rostrum.

"Took long enough," the guy said.

"You haven't seen Mr. Balsam, have you, Samuel?" Aunt Bea said.

His eyes flitted to me, then back. "Not for a while. Probably down with a cold. Can't blame him with all this weather."

"Oh yes," I said with a mock shudder. "The weather. It's frightful, isn't it? Better keep your rain slicker handy, Sammy-boy."

We slipped away before he could react to my dig. Outside, Bea straightened her hat and unfurled her umbrella. "What gems we are meeting."

"Haverstrom's a book freak," I said. "You know the type. What did you expect?"

She tsked. She stopped cold on the sidewalk corner, watching a street vendor burn pretzels over a gassy flame. The air was filled with the acrid smell of black crust and melting salt. "He's a repulsive toad," she said. "I caution you against tainting me with the same brush."

The light changed and we started across the avenue.

"Do you think Balsam's involved somehow?"

"Dante, my dear, you know me. Anything I'm thinking right now is mere supposition. I observe everything in the meantime. Samuel follows you to Walter's office. On whose instruction? Haverstrom's? Balsam's? His own?"

"So what do we do?"

"We? *I'm* returning to the warmth of the shop and the comforts of a delightful minestrone. *You* have the man's money. Earn it."

❧ 15 ❧

MAN WITH A SCAM

About Leena there isn't much to tell. In school she'd been a quiet one, hung out at lunchtime in the cafeteria reading classic gothic lit, three or four a week, sometimes, and no one noticed. Blew her classmates away on the Regents and suddenly her teachers were taking credit for it. She finished high school a year ahead, before her guidance counselors took notice and helped her plan for college. Her parents thought that this time around, for *this* daughter, maybe a nearby school would do. Live at home, commute to class, lots of kids did it. What they didn't say, or what Leena suspected, was that they'd blown their college nest egg on sending her sister to schools that were expected to straighten Alison out.

Leena told me this with a hint of sarcasm in her voice, and I wondered what that final year in high school had been like. Her sister dead, her parents in a fog. Conversations ending when she entered rooms, friends not knowing what to say and so saying nothing. Appallingly quiet dinners.

At first she thought she'd like to study fashion design. The 'rents loved that; the Fashion Institute was right there in midtown. Then Leena talked about fashion *marketing*, and that was still okay. But then she'd stopped talking altogether, and got herself a job painting T-shirts in a vintage clothing shop in the Village. She wanted time off from the relentless pursuit of knowledge, and felt that she could *always* go to school. Strangely, Ernie Munro didn't fight her decision. Maybe he was feeling like an overworked dad who wasn't looking forward to tuition payments. Or maybe he longed to take time off, too.

"Looks difficult," I said, watching her make a shirt.

"Couldn't be easier," Leena told me.

It looked messy. She wore a paint-spattered smock as she dragged the paint over the screen with a squeegee. For some reason her intense focus made her look good. Small nose, slight body, like the photos I'd seen of Alison. The resemblance had been close. It surprised me to find Ernie Munro's face hidden in hers, softened and elegant and made beautiful.

When she was done with the squeegee, she lifted the screen off the shirt, revealing the shape of a grinning, sassy parrot. She slid the wet shirt down the counter and did a few more.

"You came," she said as she worked.

Loud music pulsed through the speakers of the shop, sailing out over racks of fur stoles, reconditioned trench coats, cases of costume jewelry, wide silk ties, tons of hats. Trilbys. Derbies. Borsalinos. Fedoras.

"I came to return this," I said, handing her a roll of bills. I hadn't counted it. When she'd given it to me that morning, she'd said it contained a hundred dollars. For a hundred dollars you couldn't get my father's partner, the great Emory Bray, to lift his giant hams out of his chair.

"Don't you want the case?"

"Sure," I said. "But someone with bucks wants an answer to a different problem, and I have a hunch that the two cases are linked."

Her eyes crinkled, smiling. "Coo-ol!"

"The only thing is, can you get your father to talk to me?"

"Not about my sister. Her he won't talk about."

"I need him to sign a release of sorts. He's never collected books, has he? Antiques?"

"Nooo. Are you crazy? *My* dad? But you know, I have an idea."

She quickly sketched it out. It sounded good to me, and on my way out the door, I cocked a finger at the plastic object dangling from her ear. "I never said. Love the stegosaurus."

"Triceratops. See you at six."

On the way out I bumped into a man who was trying on a low-waisted pink jumper. This is why I love the Village. Why I love the crazy mix of people in New York City. By six p.m. the two of us were uptown, immersed in a far more conservative crowd, waiting at one of the high-top tables in the lounge of the steakhouse where Leena's father worked.

"I'll be right over," Munro said. "I got a few minutes before the rush."

A more upscale crowd than the lunch bunch packed the Six Coaches, and Munro, now dressed in a frilly white shirt, a black vest, pants and tie, made sure they stayed reasonably snockered. In contrast to the sweaty, ink-stained man I'd met at the print shop, this incarnation was scrubbed pink, with thin brown hair swept back on his head, glistening with water. He worked the bar with a younger man, the two of them rolling back and forth like sailors on the deck of a ship. His thick hands flew, doing a million things at once; shoving pint glasses under beer taps, grabbing money, punching the cash register. He caught the cash drawer with his belly, popped it back with a thrust of his belt, doled out the change and drinks, and pocketed his tip with the same quick swipe he used to wipe the bar.

For the second time in twenty-four hours I felt tired watching him. I wondered what he did on weekends. He didn't seem capable of relaxing. He had to move, work, hustle.

"You people don't give up, do you?" he said when he came

over. He sounded mad, but he had a beer and a Coke for us. He slid the beer in front of me.

"I'll have a vodka sour," Leena said.

"You'll have a Coke," he said without looking at her. Patting his thin hair down with the palm of his hand, he looked at me and said, "She says I should trust you. Gimme one good reason why."

I tasted my beer and set it down. "The police haven't bothered you, have they?"

He shook his head.

"You know why?" I continued, taking my best shot. "Because they haven't figured out the connection between you and Barski, and they're unlikely to do so. I wouldn't even be here if I didn't happen to have a genius in the family. So, you're safe. *Talk to me.* Your daughter and an old family friend of ours is dead. It's stretching matters to assume they're connected, but we're never going to know for sure unless we talk. How does that sound?"

He was silent. He could have been thinking about the cops or gauging the level of beer in my glass. His arm went up and touched Leena, sort of rested there across her shoulders. "What the old guy told me had nothing to do with him getting killed. Only now? With him dead and all? It'll look bad if I come out with it."

Leena leaned over, her shoulder meeting his chest. "Please, Pop. Don't make this harder. Can't you just tell him?"

"Aw, nuts," he puffed. "I know all about you private investigators. I tried hiring some myself a while ago. You people get paid for keeping your mouths shut. So shut up about this. Barski was going to sell me something, proof about who killed my daughter."

"How would he know?" I said.

"He says he was there the night it happened. Was staying over on the island, visiting clients. Saw the whole thing. The bum took pictures, too. Now he wanted money for them. I should have wrung his neck, offering to sell me something he should have turned over to the authorities years ago. I should have gone right to the cops. But no. I sat there and talked price."

Wow. Aunt Bea had fought me on this. She didn't want me speaking ill of the dead. But now the truth was out. Big shock: Barski was a heel. I couldn't say I was surprised. Images flicked across my mind. The books in his suitcase, crammed with cash. Lists of dates and money amounts. "Even if he had something that damning," I said, "he had to know that their discovery now would mean questions for *him*."

I could tell from Munro's face that he disagreed. "Way he talked, he was banking on being long gone. He had to get out of town and he needed cash. Kept quiet all this time 'cause he was afraid. Now he was *more* afraid."

Leena wiped droplets off her Coke glass. "What happened to Alison, Dad? Did he say?"

"Aw, Kath ... you think he's gonna come out and tell me, just like that? Gave me bits of it, just enough to convince me that he had the goods. He said he saw her come back to the party that night, get out of a little blue sports car. An MG. She was intoxicated, he tells me. Like I don't know ..." He rested his thick hands on the table and hung his head over them like a man praying.

"I have to say, it does sound far-fetched," I said. "Most guys I know that age hate being out past nine or ten, let alone midnight."

"What do you want from me, mister? That's what he told me. Every detail. What she wore. The way she looked. The MG. How would he know such things if he wasn't a hundred percent there?"

"How much did he want?" Leena pressed.

Her father avoided looking her in the eye. "Ten large."

His daughter slapped the table, rocking our drinks. "Ten *thousand* dollars?"

"I—I talked him down to five," the heavy man said, his lips making a dismal, smacking sound.

"Oh. My. Gosh." Leena said. "You were actually going to do it?"

"He had the goods!"

"Okay, mister, I don't ever want to hear you tell me how I'm wasting money on clothes when I should be saving for college. Here you are, blowing my whole college fund on a crook!"

Great. I was stuck in the middle of a family argument. I could have stayed on Fourth Avenue if I wanted one of my own. I noticed the eyes of some of the other patrons shift over to our table.

"Since when do you want to go to college?" Munro said. "That's not what you've been telling me and your mother."

Leena shook her head, the dinosaur bouncing vigorously. "You don't get me. You never have."

"What's to get? You paint your hair all these different colors. You run around with Village weirdos in those stupid outfits. You want to go to college? College kids don't have stupid giraffes in their ears."

Triceratops, I thought. Mesozoic.

I raised a hand to intercede. If I didn't, we'd be here all night. "Can we get back to the central issue, please? Mr. Munro—did you or did you not pay him the money?"

"I was supposed to Monday. Yesterday. I needed time to close one of our bank CDs. I brought the cash to work yesterday and kept it in my locker. I didn't know he was dead till you showed up at the print shop."

"Was Barski bringing the photos *here*?"

"That's right. Said he'd be waiting when I came on duty. When I heard he was dead, I just kept it on me all night and hid it at home. You believe it? Riding the subway to Brooklyn with five thousand, cash? I could have gotten mugged."

His daughter was incensed. Her flushed face was obvious even in the dim light of the lounge. She kept her eyes locked on her glass. When she spoke, her voice oozed with sarcasm. "Oh, Daddy, you are *soooo* smart. Instead of playing ball with the sleazebag, did it occur to you to just call the cops on him?"

"And have him run off, change his story? You're real bright, lady. You think so little of your old man. Don't worry ... I had it all figured out. First: Lock down the evidence. Second: Call the cops on him. Third: Get our money back. What am I, an idiot? Did I figure he would go get himself killed?" His eyes shifted to the bar. "Look, I gotta go. I can't waste time like this."

"You're not exactly feeling sorry about him being killed, are you?" I said.

He glowered at me. "Am I supposed to? I think it's a damn shame, all right? A real *tragedy*. That's what he told me. 'Losing a daughter is a horrible *tragedy*.' Bum. He could have saved her. He could have acted. He could have done something. Look, Kathy, honey, you can't tell your mother about this. She'd flip. Let's just keep this between you and me, okay?"

I was expecting another smart remark from her, but instead she touched her father's cheek. I thought I saw the man's eyes soften. "You are too much, Dad."

It was a sweet moment, which I hesitated to break up. I needed the time to think, anyway. My mind was already sifting through a series of compelling clues. Munro's use of the word "tragedy" had me thinking of the book the cops had found in Barski's dumpster. *An American Tragedy*, by Dreiser.

Was Milo intending to present that book to Munro, with the evidence neatly tucked into it? That didn't sound right. The Dreiser the cops found didn't have photos in it. It had not been retrofitted like the ones in Barski's apartment to resemble a book safe. And I didn't think eight-by-ten glossies would fit in a book-sized keepsake anyway.

But still, I couldn't get that notion out of my head. Tragedy. *Tragedy*.

Barski was desperate for cash. When Munro couldn't come with up the full amount, maybe Barski decided to play a dangerous game and collect money from *both* sides of that tragedy. Five thousand from the dead girl's father, and possibly more from the murderer himself?

The idea was so tantalizing I could not wait to get to a payphone to give my aunt the quick and dirty version. It made a kind of sense, didn't it? Whoever killed Alison Munro killed Barski.

Who said you couldn't have two geniuses in the family?

There was just one more thing I needed to pull off tonight before I made my report to Aunt Bea. I did it about an hour later when Leena and I arrived at her parents' home in Brooklyn.

Her mother came to the door carrying a string of Christmas lights. Mrs. Munro was a petite woman in a floral print dress. Brown-haired like her daughters, with a worried look that could disappear without a trace. Her eyes went from Leena to me and back again, locking on Leena and cutting me out of her vision as if hoping I'd disappear.

"You must be running late," she said to Leena. "I called the store. They said you'd left hours ago …" She tried to smile. "You should have called if you had a date."

I felt honored. Most mothers did not want me anywhere near their daughters. I let Leena do the talking. I'd prepped her on the subway to Bensonhurst.

"We stopped to see Dad," she said, stepping into the house. The wooden floors were varnished and shone yellow in the vestibule light. She took off her tweed coat and hung it. I kept mine. "This is Dante."

The woman looked me up and down frankly. She smiled more when she reached my tie and jacket. I guessed I was an improvement over others her daughter had brought home. My hair was reddish, my own color, and my ears were unpierced. "You have to excuse me," she said. "I was taking down the tree.

We should have done it earlier, but I like to wait till the New Year."

"My aunt does that."

She gave a little laugh. This was more than she had expected. Imagine! Her daughter's date had an aunt with a Christmas tree. What a world.

"Why don't you come sit and have something to drink. Coffee, hot chocolate? Kathleen, I have dinner warm in the oven. Don't tell me you ate."

"Mom, he's staying like a minute."

She led her daughter to the kitchen and their voices faded. I entered the living room. Satin-covered balls lay on a coffee table before a couch with yellow pillows. Six or seven plastic Christmas tree branches rested near a big empty cardboard box. In front of the bay window stood a bare, five-foot stick, painted green and screwed into a red and green base, Christmas detritus scattered around it. I saw tiny plastic elves, three Christmas stockings with names glittering in gold, assorted sheep, shepherds, wise men, and a big hollow-looking angel, her mouth open wide in song, looming tall over a phalanx of toy soldiers.

Over the scent of Christmas candles, I smelled pork chops. Her mother was asking, "Did your father sound okay," and Leena was saying, "Sure, why?" And then the woman lowered her voice and uttered a whisper that was just as loud as her speaking voice, something about *lots of money* and *sock drawer* and *doesn't want me to know.*

Leena laughed nervously. "I don't know about *that.* But Mom? Dante's a detective. Dad wants him to look in Alison's room. He signed a release."

"More detectives? What is this? He's not touching her room. Where is he? How could you let him just—Never mind, I'll tell him."

She nabbed me at the foot of the stairs.

"You stop this second, you hear me? I don't know anything

about this. My husband didn't tell me about this. The police have been all over that room. There's *nothing* there. Nothing."

"Sometimes you miss things," I said.

"What's to miss? It's a room. We bought it all at the JC Penney. My sister made the drapes. There's nothing important up there." She searched her daughter's face. "Why's your father starting this all over again? Hmm?" Finding no satisfaction in her daughter's eyes, she darted into the kitchen. "I'm calling him right now. Where's that number?"

Leena and I cleared the steps in nothing flat. I saw three bedrooms, a bathroom and linen closet. She led me to the room with the closed door.

It was a little girl's room. Canopied bed with a pink coverlet and pillows. White rolltop desk. White chest of drawers with gold trim. A porcelain ballerina lamp. No posters, just framed frothy prints of dancers in tights, doing their routines. The room felt stuffy. Leena sat on the pink bed. I went to the desk. The larger drawers were empty except for some Bic pens. In the thin drawer over the chair I found a cherry-flavored Chap Stick, some paper clips and a pile of concert ticket stubs. I picked through these, hoping to find mention of Zephyr Productions. Nothing.

The wastebasket was empty, so I attacked the bureau next. Naturally Alison would have taken her favorite clothes, leaving the ugliest stuff behind. I found a woolen coat, a rabbit fur jacket, and some dresses that would have only pleased her mother.

"It stinks in here," Leena said. Her voice had an odd quality, a shade lower, a shade slower. "You notice?"

"Mmm-hmm."

"I used to be afraid to come in here. Silly, huh?"

Good, I thought. Let's all be afraid. Afraid of rooms. Afraid of reporting murders. Everyone afraid.

I went to a low bookcase and poked among the high school classics. *The Catcher in the Rye* was there, along with *Wuthering Heights*. Knickknacks too. A copper Statue of Liberty, two bucks on the Circle Line. A glass ball containing a red-nosed reindeer and fake snowflakes. A fragrant cedar wood box with the words, *A Souvenir of Wildwood, N.J.* I poked some more and found some college textbooks. I found a few religious books, a bunch of music sheets inked up by an arranger, a workbook for learning to play the piano, and a copy of *Think, Speak & Write Your Way Through College* by one Amos Horne. I smiled as I flipped through it. She'd never touched it.

Between the books I found a small decorative stationery box, full of letters and mail addressed to Alison. A postcard from Aunt Patricia extolling the virtues of Montreal. A notice that Alison's subscription to *Rolling Stone* was near death. A letter addressed *To the Parents of Alison Munro.* The stationery told me she'd gone to Magnificat College, Newport, Rhode Island. The postmark said it had been mailed in the December before Alison had left college.

I read it. Someone named Sister Michael Marie was "pained, shocked, troubled, and saddened" to hear of Alison's decision to leave Magnificat, especially since Alison "surprised" everyone with her "her comeback and unswerving dedication to her studies" in the last year ...

It was not the sort of mail a young woman would keep. It was mail a mother might carefully preserve, unwilling to discard any memory of her lost child.

I waded through more nun talk before replacing the mail. Leena lay face down on her sister's bed, staring at a photo on the night table. A smiling man in a T-shirt held a girl of three or four on his shoulders. The years had robbed Munro of his hair and smile.

A cardboard box at the side of the desk caught my eye. I bent to open it. There were record albums on top. *Billy Joel, The Beatles, Springsteen.*

Leena said, "That's the stuff she had with her at the beach house. Dad gave the clothes away."

I nodded. I was flipping quickly through a photo album,

seeing pictures of the two sisters and their family and a small white mutt that appeared and disappeared in the span of a few summer photos. I flipped to the last page of the album and something fell out.

I whistled.

"What is it?" Leena said.

"Oh, nothing," I said. "Just a peacock feather."

BATTERED AND SLICED

"Hey, you!"

"Who, me?" I said.

"Naw," said the rent-a-cop. "The other guy. Sign the book, bud."

He was a sickly man, gone gray, still working and still used to throwing around the weight he once had. He shoved the book across his desk and I wrote in my name, Zephyr's, and the time, 7:20 p.m.

The guard had a little radio plugged in behind his counter, and I heard Robert Goulet singing "If Ever I Would Leave You." The Olmsted's lobby was empty, the newsstand locked up for the night. The guard said goodnight and went back to his post. I rode the elevator up.

Common sense told me recording sessions ran late. On the seventh floor I met Zephyr's receptionist, Jennifer Redmond, waiting for the elevator. She had her bulky sweater in her arms and her hand on her hips.

"You," she said.

"Me. I'm here with olive branches. Is Tony in?"

"They're in his office, but I don't know if he wants to see you."

"That makes two of us."

At Jennifer's desk silo, I merrily banged out the theme to *Camelot* with my hands. I heard a voice yell, "What?" and then Van Nilsson, the recording engineer, was there, looming at the side of the desk like a big, blond ape waiting for a bus. "You again?"

"No one's happy to see me tonight. I need to see Tony."

His lips soured. "Why? Never mind. It's none of my business. This way."

I followed him through winding corridors filled with staid, empty offices. I made a crack about them remodeling and when would the rest of the staff move back in? That got a chuckle out of him, and he returned with a conspiratorial crack about low record sales.

After we'd walked halfway to Ypsilanti and back, we came to an unmarked door, through which he ushered me with a flourish. Company president Tony Crowell sat at a desk, just hanging up the phone. Van Nilsson came in after me and stood at the door like an MP.

"You were told to stay out," Crowell said, waving a smoking cigarette butt at me. He wore sunglasses in his hair, an angry grin on his lips. I tried smiling like that, but couldn't. It hurt.

I reached for my wallet. "You deserve the truth," I said, and proceeded to lie to his face. "I'm a PI. It was a mistake to bring Barski's executor here with me. I should have realized that she had an axe to grind." I handed them each my card. I resumed my patter before they could think. "I'm sorry about the hassle. The dead guy's attorney wanted me to talk to Barski's past business associates. I just thought I should get down here tonight before you considered consulting counsel."

I was kissing his butt. Crowell liked that. He studied my fancy card and let his fingers rove over the lettering. "You know?" he said, still grinning. "That's exactly what I was going to do. Call my freaking lawyers."

"May we just speak off the record? I'm sure that you'll find what I have to say utterly absorbing."

He threw a hand up, as if to say, hey, was it his fault he was so busy? "I'm real tied up over here right now. I have calls to make to the coast, some radio DJ's coming by ... can it wait? Van, keep him company. Give me about an hour, huh?"

I followed Van out the door and considered tying a string to his wrist so I wouldn't get lost. He brooded on his way out. "What is this, anyway? None of us knew the old guy, now he leaves Allie money. Weird."

His words threw me. I had to struggle to remember the little white lie Aunt Bea had told them earlier today. This is why one should always be completely honest in all one's dealings. Lies are absolutely delicious, but they're hell on your brain.

"What's weird?" I said. "Old guys fall for young women all the time."

Van stopped short in the hall. Ran his fingers through his white-blond hair and ended in a scratch. "It wasn't like that with her," he said. "She was like ... pure, you know? Sweet ..."

Looking at him, seeing the way his eyes looked just then, I felt I had hit a nerve. Can't explain it, but I knew it was there—that goofy, teddy bear look you sometimes find in guys like him. I pushed it.

"Angelic?" I said.

"You making fun of me?"

"Did you have a thing for her, Van?"

His arms swung up and shoved me hard into the wall. I braced myself, crouching, arms loose, readying for a follow-up blow that never came.

The anger in his eyes extinguished itself and he was just a big lug again. "How about you lay off, please, huh?" We had reached the front reception area. He jerked a finger at Jennifer's silo. "You better wait here," he said. "I have work to do."

"Thanks," I said. And when he turned to go, I added, "Hey, I'm sorry, Van. I didn't know."

He tilted his head like a puppy. "Cynicism is really unpleasant, you know that? Guys like you, the cops, you got me all wrong. I never went *near* that girl. I never touched that girl, you hear me? She was a really sweet person. She deserved better than what she got …"

He stood nervously swinging his arms and pushing up the sleeves of his pastel-colored shirt. Behind his eyes, his brain was thinking. Hard.

"Look … I have work … but—you wanna come back to the studio?"

The lights were still on in the control room. The top of the channel board was covered with a tarp. He grabbed a broom and swept. His lips were pressed shut, but his unspoken words hung in the air.

"I get the feeling you liked her," I said.

His head bobbed, the thick curls shaking. "She was all right. Didn't know any better. Didn't know what this business was like. The games you have to play … Tony, he comes on like a charmer, makes you think he loves you …" He shook his head. "You call that love? I mean, what's love?"

"Exactly, Van. What's love," I said, deadpan. "That's the question humans have asked themselves for centuries, isn't it?"

Keep him talking.

"She had a good voice, but she shouldn't have wasted it here."

"You remember much about that party? The night she died?"

"You ask stupid questions for a lawyer's snitch. She's dead. Why keep harping on it?"

"It's been two years. People remember things."

He set the broom down and fussed with a briefcase that sat on one of the chairs. "The cops were harping on me 'cause I spent a lot of time at the door, watching for her. I was *worried* about her. When she left, she made a big production of it to let everyone know she was mad. Made everyone move their cars. I was gonna go after her, but I was afraid of how it would look. She was Tony's girl. Or was."

"Van, you didn't see her come back?"

He shook his head.

"Understandable," I said. "It's a party. A lot of action. People drinking."

He looked offended. "I don't drink, mister."

"Yeah, right. Cops believe that?"

You never know what's going to enrage a teddy bear. He whirled around and shoved me hard into the door. I chopped at his arm. He took me with a quick jab to the chin. I lashed out at him with both fists, and he just swatted them away and threw his arms around my neck.

I fell as a dead man falls, onto a nice hard bed of nothing. I don't know how long I was out, but I woke with an aching arm, my fluttering eyelids trying to focus on the white ceiling above me. Needles raced up my left arm. I sat up, groaning, and my jaw started pounding for attention.

I was on a couch made of white leather, too soft and too expensive for an office. I looked around the room. Saw a nice sound system on some shelves with pottery and some shiny red flowers. A dizzying abstract painting hung on the wall on my right. A block of white marble sat at my feet, buried in the shag as if it had skidded to a stop there. Beyond the windows of the apartment, the city glowed in the darkness.

I heard glass tinkling. Van stood behind me at a kitchen counter pouring himself a glass of milk. He saw me moving and reached for a second glass.

"Welcome to Never-Never-Land," he said. I held my head in my hands. I considered taking it off completely and getting a new one, but the available ones probably wouldn't fit. "You choked me out. Cut off my air and put me to sleep."

He came around the counter and handed me the milk. I took a sip and put it down on the marble.

"I'm real sorry," he said. "I'm trying to work on that? When I was a kid the counselor called it impulsive."

"Well, you're an adult now, and I call it insane. Where are we?"

"Tony's place. Eleventh floor. Nice, huh?"

"You dragged me in the elevator and up here to apologize?"

He stepped back. One of the control room chairs sat on the other side of the marble block, looking like it didn't belong. Van plopped into it with his glass of milk, and spun it around.

"Wheeled," he said. "It was Tony's idea. Some radio jock was coming over. Tony told me to get rid of you. Look, I'm really sorry," he said again.

"You know," I said, massaging my neck, "maybe Zephyr doesn't have a money problem. Zephyr has a violence problem. Where'd you learn to do that?"

"Upstate, I guess. Buffalo, New York. I was a champion wrestler three years. They said it was playing dirty. See, they didn't understand, either. I'm impulsive. I never got a scholarship."

"Poor you."

"You ever wrestle?"

"Nope."

"Aw, come on, guy like you? What're you, six-two, six-three?"

"Yes," I said. "I weigh two-ten, I crochet, and in my spare time I work for world peace. I look great in a bathing suit, too. Is Tony still downstairs?"

I watched him drain his glass and wipe off his milk mustache. "Yep." He walked over to the kitchen and washed the glass in the sink. "He'll be up after his meeting. He wants to apologize, too."

"I'll just go down."

"No, you have to stay."

"What's going on, big powwow?"

"DJs are a big deal."

"He pay them off?"

He shrugged, wanting to play dumb but thought better of it. "Payola makes the vinyl go 'round, right?"

I asked where the bathroom was, and he gestured. He started to say something about waiting, no, *stopping*, but by then I had stepped into the bedroom to discover a young woman in a towel drying her hair in front of a mirror. She yelped when I came in.

Jennifer, the receptionist.

"You again!" she screeched. "Get out of here!"

"It's funny, isn't it?" I said. "Where you are, there I am fated to be. Don't worry. I'm just using the bathroom."

Droplets of water trickled down the glass doors of the shower. She'd hung a fresh set of towels on the doors, and lined up a pair of men's slippers just outside the tub. She was neat but she didn't do mirrors. I raised my hand and wiped a circle in its clouded center and studied my face. My neck was red but I thought it would clear. I had a good bruise under my chin, though, from his first tap. Nice and swollen. I'd need ice. I ran some water and doused myself. I dried with one of Crowell's expensive cream-colored towels. I checked the cabinet. No aspirin.

Jennifer was standing outside the door, dressed now in a plush white robe with gold letters over the breast pocket that read *TC*. It reached her ankles. Behind her, the bed was turned down, the pillows fluffed and waiting.

"Been seeing each other long?"

"Are you better now?" she said.

"Yes."

"Then get the hell out!"

She slammed the bedroom door after me. Van chided me as I

collected ice from the freezer and made myself a pack using the fluffy hand towel I'd stolen from the bathroom.

"You shouldn't use those," Van said. "They're Egyptian."

I clapped the pack to my chin. "I'll bet they are. You know, if this whole record thing doesn't pan out, Tony should sell fancy linen. He can call it Crowell's Towels."

His jaw dropped. "Dude—that is an *amazing* concept."

"I know," I said. "I'm just that good."

I was done with these people. I stalked out to the elevator and was gone before he could ratchet his mouth shut. On the seventh floor I found the doors unlocked and the lights on. I stopped at the silo and tapped out a little tune on the bell.

Strangely, there was a newly lit cigarette burning in the ashtray on Jennifer's desk. When no one answered, I headed down the hall, carefully retracing my steps from a few hours ago. A sliver of light escaped from under Crowell's door. I pounded it. No answer.

"Tony?" I called. "Can we get this over with, please?"

No answer.

I pushed the door in. He sat behind the desk, arms dangling over the armrests, a fresh cigarette burning a hole in the carpet under his fingers. His head was tossed back as if listening to a demo tape, his sunglasses perched on his nose, which looked strange. Broken, in other words, as of three minutes ago. His face was battered, his lips cut. Blood soaked his shirt and tie. And a brown-handled kitchen knife was buried in his chest.

TOOK ME FOREVER TO GET MY AUNT BEATRICE TO answer the phone and accept the charges. "It's me," I said. "Call me back Down Here."

I fed her the number of the payphone outside the homicide squad room and hung up. She called me right back.

"Why are you There?"

"Tony bought it. Someone stuck him, then beat him badly. Or the other way around, maybe. They've got Nilsson and Jennifer and I'm up next, and I'm still figuring on what story to hand them."

"You? You were there?"

"It's a long story. The short of it is that the fine gendarmes of the NYPD now know that we were at Zephyr today, feeding them a line of malarkey about Barski and Alison Munro. The whole thing stinks. Some genius got the idea of calling Abby Posluszny and she's on her way down. You know she doesn't like having her poker game interrupted."

For a long while I heard nothing but the infuriated whistling of nostrils. I imagined her reclining in elegant comfort in that huge loft of hers, the city arrayed in all its splendor outside her arched, cast-iron windows. At this hour she was probably in her custom-made pajamas, under the blankets, nose in a book.

"This I do not believe," Bea said. "You never should have gone back there! The jig is up."

"Mayhaps," I said. "But I wouldn't have wanted to miss this. It's quite a party. We have two deputy DAs fighting over it, and three lawyers dressed in this year's Christian Dior pulling for the Crowell family. They're calling for death by thumbscrew."

"You are daft. Are you all right?"

"Not really. Nilsson and I had words."

She grunted. "Who threw the first blow?"

"There was only the one—his," I said. "Here's the catch: I was out cold on a couch while he and Jennifer were in the apartment in separate rooms. I think she could've gotten out of the apartment without him knowing it, but then again, I was seeing angels most of the time I was there. But anyone could've done it. The place isn't exactly a fortress. They have a guard downstairs, but all you do after hours is sign a book and you're in."

"They have names?"

"From the book? Yeah, but they're all accounted for. The

guard says no one came in between eight and nine, when I called down."

"Why eight?"

"That's when Tony apparently got a call from someone saying they were heading over. A disc jockey."

"Man or woman?"

"Van didn't see the person. Tony made him leave. With me, I might add."

She snorted. "This ... this is insufferable! Insupportable!"

"It is that."

"And when does this guard come on duty?"

"At six."

"After rush hour. Of course. Anyone could have entered then and hidden in the building. Yes ... hid in the bathrooms and made a call from a payphone on one of the floors ... oh, Dante, why do you do this to me?"

"I seem to recall you doing this to *me*. Which reminds me, they'll probably want to see you."

"Now? It's almost bedtime. I am reading D'Annunzio."

"Abby won't care if you're reading Wambaugh."

"I won't answer!" she snapped at me. "I'm indisposed. Do you need a liar?" This was her favorite way of referring to the city's fine demographic of legal representatives. "Shall I call Mr. Rawls?"

"It's not that bad," I said.

"Yet," she muttered, and then we rang off.

I gave them a good story, heavy on the truth, with a few dashes of hyperbole, and leaving out things like the name of my client and the deal Barski had made with Munro. I could tell they didn't like it, but when it's after midnight you'll take what you can get. Abby was downright unpleasant.

When it was all over, I splurged on a cab to SoHo and rode the cage-like elevator up to Aunt Bea's apartment, where she treated to me to crusty bread, soft creamy butter, and what remained of her homemade minestrone soup. I sat dunking and slurping away at her kitchen island, copper pots dangling over my head, and unfurled my story. The whole story. The Aunt Beatrice version. Every little bit of it, the way she liked it.

Above and in between the bookshelves, the old brick walls were decorated with a million little pieces of framed art hung cheek by jowl in a crazy, uneven mosaic. She'd bought each of those pictures in every city in the world she'd ever traveled to. Watercolors, charcoal and pencil sketches, oils—every one of them created by street artists, all of them costing just a few bucks, and all small enough to stuff in her suitcase for the flight home. This was what they amounted to, a lifetime of memories.

She sat in the purple velvet armchair, afghan draped around her, and listened. As she did, she stroked the peacock feather I'd filched from Alison Munro's bedroom.

"You're sure about the cigarettes? Winstons?"

"Yeah—but I don't see that it matters any."

Her lips pursed. "This is your gift, Dante. You see *everything*. Give you a room and your mind takes it all in, but does it understand? Sadly, no."

"I am not in the mood for this," I said. I slid the bowl and cutlery into the dishwasher, and came around to the couch. She started fussing about getting me sheets and blankets, but I waved her off. I seem to recall her laying the afghan over me, but by the time the fabric hit my shoulders I was out.

🏵 17 🏵

COMMODORE

The next morning, as we rode out of the hallowed Borough after planting Barski in a neat plot in Green-Wood Cemetery, Bea had her lips together in a pout of disdain, a look any accidental reader of the *New York Tab* will understand. In her lap and on the front seat of the Crown Victoria she had all of the city's newspapers—the *Slimes*, the *Snooze*, and the *Gross*, as she was fond of calling them. But her greatest irritation was reserved for the fourth and last.

"I don't hate *all* journalists," she said, "just those whose work gets into print."

"Bad?" I said.

"I can only say that the *Scab* has covered Mr. Crowell's murder in its usual distinctive style."

I focused on driving. It was only a little after nine, but we had risen at six to congregate at eight—along with Amos Horne, Walter Kenning, and the extended family of Mrs. Gutierrez—for the short, sweet, snowy ceremony.

Bea cycled through each of the papers as I drove. That fink writer, Bernie Housknecht, had pieced together my questions to him and had concocted a story that was a masterpiece of *Tab* journalism. The headline was a beaut. It would have people every-where plunking down quarters, if only to figure out what it meant.

ROCK PLAYBOY SLAIN
Cops probe sex link!

The front page had a small head shot of Tony Crowell and a huge blown-up photo of Rosita Starr in sunglasses and a bikini. The blurbs did little to explain her presence, but promised more "hot pix" inside. The center foldout was splashed with photos of Crowell as a boy in a private school uniform, his parents' Upper East Side townhome, the house on the cusp of the Hamptons, covers of some of the albums he'd produced, and more photos of girls in bikinis. One of them was Alison Munro.

The story, if you could call it that, described the death of "party rocker" Tony Crowell, son of the late investment banker, Arnold Crowell. The story trumpeted the fact that Tony Crowell had been "linked romantically" with several of his former artists, one of whom had died mysteriously two years ago. Was there a link?

My aunt laughed. "Ah!" she said, "Behold—the blessed liars sing."

She proceeded to do one of my least favorite things: read the news aloud to me.

"Attorneys for Mrs. Carla Crowell decried what they called 'this vicious and cowardly attack on one of the music industry's most visionary producers.' They demanded 'swift and speedy apprehension of the perpetrator of this heinous act.' How about that, Dante? Swift *and* speedy!"

"Does visionary mean no one could figure out what the hell he was doing?"

The Crowell family offered no reward, but had retained the

services of the "powerhouse" private investigator Emory Bray to assist police in their investigation.

"Dante, listen: While Bray could not be reached for comment, Imelda Q. Rothman, his associate, said late Tuesday, 'The Bray Agency stands ready to assist the family and local law enforcement in any way possible. If I were the killer, I'd be quaking in my boots knowing that Mr. Bray's keen mind and extensive resources were being brought to bear on the problem.'"

"Please let it end," I said.

"It gets better. Or worse, rather."

The mother of the dead girl, Alison Munro, refused comment. The police had no comment, either. They were questioning witnesses, following leads, and of course, probing the ever-tantalizing sex link.

"What a mess," I said. "Just what Leena's family needs."

"There's no mention of Milo," my aunt said. "Once again Mr. Housknecht misses the crucial point."

"Maybe that link wasn't sexy enough for him?"

On her instruction, I pointed the Crown Vic east to Long Island. After a long, miserable slog through bumper to bumper traffic, we left the sprawl of the city behind and were zipping down a highway that looked like countless others in the nation.

Each summer pale city dwellers flocked to Long Island's south shore, lugging gallons of zinc cream, bushels of bestsellers, and the hottest fashions. Prices soared. Rosé wine was guzzled by the tanker. And sweet, languorous summer memories were made, provided you had the cash.

When we turned off the highway, we found a sleepy residential village whose biggest activity that morning was the snow plows chugging up and down Main. I bought a map at a coffee shop where townies dawdled over decaf, and then we headed a quarter of a mile out of town toward the ocean.

It was practically impossible to see the house from the road because in that part of town almost all the houses were hidden from view by tall, stone walls, iron gates, quaint but still off-putting white fencing, and tons of thick vegetation. Through the gates I could see a two-story, modern chockablock structure. A spiral staircase just to the right of the front door led to the second-story deck.

I U-turned and headed back to the beach. The road ended in sand. On our left was a shuttered snack bar and permit office with outdoor showers and restrooms. A sprawling, empty parking lot on my right strongly cautioned me against leaving my vehicle here without the proper permits. I watched drifts of snow blow across this abandoned tundra for a few minutes, hesitating.

"Oh for heaven's sake, park it!" Bea snapped.

"The signs say—"

"We're at the beach in January. We might as well be on the face of the moon."

She was out of the car before I got the keys out of the ignition. She had dressed in her funeral finery—a long, black coat with some kind of fur collar, and a wide-brimmed hat with pale gray feathers and a black veil. But now, as I came around the corner of the car, she had the back door open and was squeezing her feet into sturdy hikers and switching the feathered number for a furry cap with ear flaps. She looked like the most elegant person to ever traipse across Siberia.

"We're doing this?" I said.

"Just a short walk," she said. "I missed my morning constitutional, so this shall have to suffice."

The wind was brutal. Whipped so hard off the ocean that we raised our voices to be heard above it. She marched along the sand with the plucky confidence of the birds surrounding us. Her head erect. Beak into the wind. Ruffled, but determined.

Most of the houses facing the water were the kind covered in cedar shakes and looking as if they'd been designed to house all branches of a particular family tree, down to the trunks and roots. The Crowell house was distinctly modern, all cubes, glass and powdered steel railings. On the other side of it were a line of trees, and beyond that, a construction site, and a fancy white building and a marina.

"The yacht club," I said, pointing. "We could have lunch there. We're certainly dressed for it."

"Hmmph," she said.

Amid the trees to the left of the Crowell house, a bunch of men in down jackets and hard hats picked around the square-shaped forms of building foundations. It looked like a war zone; rubble and planking and pipes stuck out everywhere, and the ground was heaped with mounds of frozen dirt.

Gulls swooped overhead, cawing pitifully. They were freezing their tails off. So was I.

My aunt was in her favorite position—arms akimbo. She studied the back of the Crowell house. Her eyes flitted to the spiral staircase, second-story deck and railing, and then down to the teak wood deck. The pool was covered with a thick tarp. I had no problem imagining an insane party in progress on both levels of that house.

Two years ago, if Barski was to be believed, Alison Munro had left this part in the dead of night, alone and unhappy. She was found dead on the beach the next morning, six miles from this site, in the direction of the city. If you believed Milo Barski's story, she had actually returned here that night. She had gotten past the high stone walls and fences, past the thick vegetation that was supposed to keep out the riff-raff, and then ... what?

Aunt Bea dug her hands into her pockets and headed closer to the house.

"Okay," I called after her. "I don't think it's a good idea to go snooping. You wanted to see, so we came, we saw, we froze our butts. Time to head back."

But she was too far to hear me. She was standing on a narrow boardwalk built into the sand to the left of the Crowell house. It was the walkway residents of these fancy houses used to access the beach. It looked as if the planking had been there forever, but had recently been commandeered by the construction firm working next door.

No trespassing, the signs said, warning us of danger, possible falling objects, and the necessity of wearing hard hats in this vicinity. People certainly seemed to like signs out this way.

My aunt ignored them all. She marched up the boardwalk to get a better look at the Crowell house.

By the time I reached her, she was scowling and speaking into the wind. "She wouldn't have needed her keys anyway. One, it's unlikely she had keys to the house. It wasn't hers. She was Mr. Crowell's guest. Two, the other guests would have let her in. All she had to do was ring the bell."

In moments like this I had to wonder how much my aunt remembered about being young and crazy. "It was a party weekend at the beach, Bea," I said. "There would have been a *ton* of people. A house is never more open than when a party's raging. I'm not sure why you're obsessing on her getting inside the house. They were probably going till five in the morning."

"No," she said. "Unlikely. The sound ordinance in this municipality is quite strict. Crowell would have grown up knowing that, and heeding that dictum to avoid censure from his parents' neighbors and from the local police. It's just ... oh heavens, I don't know why it still vexes me. And *this*," she said with a sour expression, waving her left hand toward the construction zone, "this whole mess would have not have been in progress at the time, so that idea is out."

"What idea?"

"Nothing."

"Come on, tell me."

"Yeah, lady, tell us."

We both turned. Standing behind Bea on the wooden walkway was a guy in his twenties who looked about six-six, minus the snow underfoot. He had shoulders from here to Sag Harbor and wore a camel-colored woolen coat with leather toggles. I decided I could take him, but it would hurt. Once I got that neat calculation out of the way, he was just another pink-faced kid with a crewcut who happened to have an unpleasant bulge under his left armpit.

"You guys are trespassing."

My aunt smiled and waved a hand. "No worries, young man," she said. "We got lost."

"Bull. You were just in town asking directions here."

Which brings me to Reason No. 1 why you should not visit fancypants beach towns. The locals are snitches.

He jerked a thumb over his shoulder. "Let's go. Mr. DiGaetano wants to talk to you."

"I'm afraid we have a prior engagement in the city," my aunt said. "Perhaps some other time."

"Lady, I wasn't asking."

He led us up the walkway to the construction site. There were a lot of trees and a pond-in-progress where ducks had already taken up residence, paddling and dunking themselves in what amounted to a frigid puddle. As we passed the Crowell house on our right, Bea slowed to peer through the trees. Shade darkened the gray stucco and deck, leaving it streaked with mildew just beyond the spiral staircase. The woods consisted of pines and tall hollies, mostly, and what we could see of the house through the branches was nothing but the south side of the structure. There was just one window on that side of the house. It was on the ground level, and from our angle I caught a glimpse of a sink and toilet in that room.

"Keep it moving, lady," our own personal thug said. "It's just ahead."

On our left, it looked as if the workmen were building about a half dozen structures, markedly smaller in size than the homes of the Crowell family and their neighbors.

Our guide graciously opened the door of a blue Jeep that was parked on the gravel outside an on-site trailer office. A man in a hard hat sat at the wheel, drinking out of a soup thermos. When he saw us getting in, he screwed on the cap and started the engine.

The ride was quick, silent, and aromatic. No one spoke. As we bounced over gravel to the country club next door, I became aware of a damp odor that reminded me of dogs coming in out of the rain. Silly me, I thought it was the driver. But no. It was our pal in the toggled-up overcoat. He was well-dressed but stinking. Sweat dripped down his temples.

Minutes later we were in some guy's office off the main lobby of the yacht club. Our friend's boss waved him away. "Good work. Now get back to your weights," he told the thug. "Or maybe take a shower or something."

"They might be trouble," our chaperone said, rocking on the balls of his feet.

"What did I just say?" his boss said. "There's no trouble here. We're just conversing."

The big sweaty guy stared his master down, took his time leaving, and lumbered out of the office.

Our host gestured at a plate of sandwiches on his desk. "I took the liberty of ordering lunch," Nick DiGaetano said.

He was surrounded by relics of the sea. Two harpoons were crossed over the mantlepiece, over an old portrait of a stiff-lipped sea captain, his face covered with a fine lattice of cracks in the paint and glaze. On the wall near his desk a red-cheeked maiden gazed down primly from an ornate, gilded frame. Ships sailed in bottles on the tiny shelves beside instruments of polished brass. Barometers, compasses, sextants. A ship's wheel stood to the right of the door we had entered, looking immovable and heavy as any ballast had ever been. The furniture was Early American and lately polished, and gave off an odor of spray-can lemons.

Our host sat behind his desk, spearing fried things on a wide platter with a tiny fork. He was a heavy man in his late fifties and wore a double-breasted jacket with gold metallic buttons and gold piping. Epaulets rode his shoulders, but their insignia matched no navy I was aware of. His rough, fleshy face had a worn look about it, and the thin black mustache under his nose might have been sketched in with a grease pencil. On his head a muskrat had curled up and died, pompadour-style. I wondered how much he'd paid for it.

"I know who you are, so there's no need for any of the usual niceties," he said. "I pay my lawyers good money to keep up with what's going on around me. You two are related. Beatrice Valentino and Dante Sleet."

"Valentine," my aunt said in a clipped voice.

Her nostrils were flaring. Not a good sign.

"Whatever," the man said. "Valentino, Valentine, Valentina—I know all the variants. Makes no difference to me. We're all paisans, right? Have a seat. Take the wingback, Mrs. Valentine."

"Ms."

"That's all real leather. Cost me a good dollar."

"I prefer to stand."

"Suit yourself. Dante, you want a bite? I'd offer you the calamari, but it's an addiction with me." He dipped a round ball of battered goop into a dish of cocktail sauce and gulped it merrily. "My people, they came from Naples, Ms. Valentine. How about yourself?"

"If I had known we were going to compare pedigrees, I might have brought my documents," my aunt said. "Mr. DiGaetano, I demand you let us go. Your man has abducted us for a trivial infraction and with threat of violence."

He laughed, his teeth chewing on purplish tentacles. "You people make me laugh. You're the ones trespassing. By all rights I should call the cops and press charges, but I'm not. I want to talk to you myself, see if we can't settle this on our own. See, I don't need trouble around here. I'm trying to do a good thing for these people, but they don't see it."

"Enlighten me."

"I have real estate interests the town's been fighting for years. The highfalutin' families out this way had it good for a long time. Townies and them, no outsiders. But the shore's changing. City folks need a place to go in the summers. It's the inevitable march of progress. Took me forever to get my needs met, then that girl had to go die out there. Held up my work for months. Any little thing makes the town council skittish. It's a game with these people. Now we have another unfortunate circumstance—"

"Tony Crowell's murder," I said.

"The kid's well known out here. The family's been here since it was all potato farms and fishermen. We had a news crew this morning. Now you guys show up. I know why you're here. The widow hired this Bray guy to help find who killed her son. You should be confining yourself to those matters. See? This has nothing to do with me. Harassing me, bringing media scrutiny to our peaceful stretch of the beach, is most unwelcome."

My aunt shifted her weight. "Have you spoke to the Crowell woman, Mr. DiGaetano?"

"As a matter of fact, I've been trying all day to call and offer my condolences. She's in seclusion. I can't blame her. We are acquainted, if you must know. I built their house. Built all of them on this stretch, from here to the municipal lot. The summer people look down their noses at old Nick DiGaetano. Funny thing is, I probably have more in common with Tony than she or her husband ever did. So he likes to party. Have his friends over. I get that. Not once did I or any one of my employees call the cops on him. I'm peaceful that way. What happens in these houses out this way is not my business. Including murder."

"Who said Miss Munro was murdered?" my aunt said.

He picked a bit of batter from his teeth. "Isn't that what the papers are saying? 'Sex *link*.' They think there's some connection with his death and the girl's. You see? That can be very bad for me. I have six condo buildings I need to finish by April. Phase 3 of our Renaissance Estates project. If anyone asks, you could make it clear to these people that I am nothing but a sympathetic party—"

"Who trains local kids to pack heat," I said.

"Rudy's chief of security here. He's completely licensed. How else can he do his job? He's a good kid, like a nephew to me. And, I might add, a perfect example of the good I've done for this town. Employing their kids. Helping them out. Rudy's good, but he's loose upstairs. His brother and him used to be on the football team here. Alfie was real bright, but his family had no clout. Who do you think got him into Princeton? Who made the necessary introductions?" He jabbed the tiny fork at his lapels. "Me. Good old Uncle Nick. Ask anybody. They'll tell you. Ask 'em what school Alfie Vranin goes to."

He looked at my aunt, his eyes seeming to plead with hers. Aunt Bea looked either bored or disgusted. Either reaction was warranted.

"Hey, Ms. Valentine, maybe you can understand. I came from nothing. I worked construction all my life. I developed this beach, took it from nothing but weeds and seashells to a premier destination. I expect what I deserve—honor, respect, courtesy."

"And who honors the dead, Mr. DiGaetano?"

"Who honors who?"

"The dead," Bea said. "Alison and Milo and Tony Crowell."

I didn't think throwing Barski into the mix was wise, but it shows where my aunt's mind was.

Confused by the reference, DiGaetano's eyes shot to me. "Young man, you were hired to do a job. But you're looking in the wrong place. I wish you'd go tell that to your boss." For some reason, his face looked incredibly sad just then. He seemed to sense it. He willed his eyes to perk up and his voice hit a higher pitch. "Look, er, Ms. Valentine, you know what they call me? *Commodore*. That's a guy who runs a fleet of ships. Forty years ago

I didn't have two cents in my pocket and now I'm a Commodore. This a great country or what?"

They drove us back to the beach parking lot, where I was delighted to find a bright orange citation clipped to our windshield. A twenty-five-dollar fine. Fantastic. A police cruiser was parked just outside the lot, engine idling.

When I got in the Crown Vic, Bea had the window rolled down. She said nothing, but I knew she was letting the cold air wash away the stink of fried food and deceit.

"You know this word, *paisano?*"

"Who doesn't?"

"From the word *paese*, meaning small town. It implies kinship. And that is one thing I do not wish to share with that man."

"You amaze me sometimes," I said.

"How so?"

"In there. Just now. You actually stood up for Barski. For Tony Crowell, even."

"No, I didn't. I know you think so. I may not have liked them, but I detest murder even more. You mistake me. I stood up for truth. That is all." She peered at her watch. "And now, sadly, I'm actually peckish. And we are hours from Fourth Avenue."

"We can grab sandwiches in town."

"Indeed," she said. "Although I imagine the fried fish at some roadhouse might be exceptional and appropriate."

There was just one problem with our neat little plan. As we rolled out of the parking lot, the cop in the cruiser flashed his lights and sounded his siren. The patrolman leaned out the window and waved at me.

"Can you follow me downtown, sir?"

18

MAIDENS AND CRONES

Police Chief Welty made us wait forty minutes. We sat on uncomfortable plastic chairs in the drafty lobby of the police station while a desk sergeant fielded calls. The whole time he dispatched three officers. One on foot to the hardware store to break up a fight in the snow shovel aisle, and two to roust some kids playing on some dunes that were being restored. In all, a big day for crime in the little town of Rockport, Long Island.

The chief, when we met him, sat on the edge of his desk, reading the morning *Tab* and sipping something out of a white mug with brown letters spelling HENRY. He waved us in with a sweeping, enthusiastic gesture.

"Gosh, I'm real sorry to keep you folks waiting out there like that, but the phone's been ringing all morning." He bobbed his head up and down in *whatcha-gonna-do?* fashion. He was a round-faced man with a soft jaw and thick black hair. His eyes were so wide and luminous that they didn't seem to have eyelids. He wore a blue wool blazer, brown khakis, and a loosened dark tie. He pumped our hands good and hard, treating us like old school chums he'd just discovered out back cleaning his pool.

"Gosh, I have some awful news to break to you folks," he said. "Lieutenant Posluszny sends her worst. I gather she's a real tough lady. She threatens to have your investigator licenses pulled. *Oops*, that would be a little difficult in your case, wouldn't it, Ms. Valentine? You don't have one. You're just a busybody up in everybody's business, aren't you?"

"I often wonder if I am Lieutenant Posluszny's favorite topic of conversation," Bea said.

Welty roared and slapped his knee. He looked thirtyish, but had to be fifty or so, judging from the date on the SUNY-Stony Brook diploma hanging on the wall behind him. "Well, she did talk quite a bit about you. But we're not here to discuss the good people of the NYPD, are we? We have our own little issues right here. Like Mr. DiGaetano, who regards himself as a philanthropist and hero to our year-rounds."

"Locals, you mean?" I said.

He evinced an *aw shucks* look with his eyebrows. "Go ahead. You can say it. We're townies. And we used to be proud of that, but the town's changing. We're right on the edge of the fancy shore towns, and it was only time before we got sucked into their glamour. And guess who's leading the charge?"

"The Commodore?"

"Don't get me wrong. I know you and your Mr. Bray get top dollar back in the city. Folks who have the bucks to spend think they need the hand-holding us cops can't provide. But if you and your Mr. Bray—or even the good lieutenant—can help me nail the bum, I'll dance in the back end of a horse outfit at our next Halloween Ball. Uncle Nick's a slimeball. So maybe he does rough up trespassers. Maybe he burns little old ladies out of their homes. *Maybe*. But you won't get him on the Crowell thing. And he didn't kill Alison Munro."

"Off the record, who did?" Aunt Bea said.

"On or off the record, ma'am, I just don't know. The ME ruled it accidental because we couldn't say otherwise. But I'm frankly delighted young Tony's death is giving us all cause to revisit those events. I don't like passing bad news on to parents. I have two daughters myself."

The wood-and-fabric armchair in which my aunt sat was absurdly small for her hips, and she kept twisting in it to make herself comfortable. "Any guesses about what *did* happen to Ms. Munro, Chief?" she said.

He rocked back in his chair. "Could have been anything. Maybe she accepted a ride from someone she shouldn't have, and changed her mind at the last second. A fall out of a speeding car would have done it. Or … our shoreline is mostly sand but you'll find stretches of rock here and there where they're rebuilding the dunes. That could have done it, too. As it was, she had enough alcohol in her system to lose her balance just about anywhere."

"So you can't say—"

"You go with what you can prove, ma'am, and I couldn't prove much. There are still plenty of things I can't answer. Did someone pick her up at the inn? If it was a Good Samaritan, why haven't they come forward? If they weren't on the up-and-up, then, well, maybe that's our answer right there. One of our patrolmen stopped by around 10:30 p.m. to remind Mr. Crowell about the noise curfew. They moved the party inside. Some of the guests left. Others—mostly the ones staying at the house—kept on rocking. One of our guys went back thirty minutes later to tell them the music was still too loud. Ha! They had just pulled the curtains shut all over the house, thinking that would deaden the sound. Anyway, the fellow working the door said no one new arrived after ten p.m., and Mr. Crowell and his inner circle never left the premises. They all alibied each other. I believed the man at the door. He's a teetotaler."

Van Nilsson, I thought. The sound engineer who'd squeezed me to sleep.

"So what's that leave, folks? Not much. We talked to everyone, the houseguests *and* the partygoers. Even the caterers and their servers making the rounds with the crab cakes. But in the end, you know what? It all added up to a dead end. Poor girl was dying six miles away."

"It appalls me," Bea said, "that everyone in that inner circle, as you say, refers to her death as an accident. It sounded far too brutal to be an accident."

"Accidents are still tragedies, ma'am."

My aunt cocked her chin. "You are most astute, Chief. I commend you."

"Thanks, but it doesn't do me much good. That's exactly what I told the reporters, but that doesn't make good copy for the newspapers."

"I don't suppose DiGaetano or Rudy were in the area of the inn that night?" I said.

He shook his head. "Nice try. I wish he was. They were both at some yacht club function that ran at least until midnight. You know, you go back forty years and all this stretch of beach was owned by one old woman. A Mrs. Hallquist. Family went way back. She fancied herself a naturalist. That just means she let the dunes do what they wanted. Lived in a rambling old pile out on the beach. Developers had been after her to sell for *years*. She always turned them down. Then one day her house went up in smoke. Fire inspector said her furnace blew from soot, and those guys usually know their stuff. But it always galled me that the person who swept in and bought the entire tract of land was none other than the fellow who ran the heating and cooling business that serviced her boiler."

"The Commodore?"

I could tell that he wanted to smile, but the memory was too painful. "I was just a rookie on the force back then. But we all thought it was suspicious. He built that whole stretch on the land he got. The Crowell house. The other Shingle-styles. The marina. The club. You talk to him, he brought style to a dinky little piece of the shore. I know you have larger concerns, Mr. Sleet. I just figured your high and mighty Mr. Bray ought to know."

I thought it was funny that everyone I'd met this morning wanted in some way to convey a message to the great and powerful Mr. Bray, and that most likely the big schlub was sitting in his office hoping Rawlsy and Rothman and I were doing the heavy lifting so he didn't have to.

"You should visit us in the summer sometime," the chief said. "Every year we're caught up in a culture war between us townies and the summer people. Things are always changing because the town council's all volunteers and very fearful of scaring off the money that pours in every summer. We have what you call an indecision problem. We want a beach, but we want the state to fix our erosion problems. We like tourists, but we don't like the traffic and their rude, big-city manners. But the one constant is, people know Uncle Nicky is the man who gets things done."

"He got the Vranin boy into Princeton," I chimed in.

"Alfie Vranin got *himself* into Princeton. But if you listen to Nicky, there's no end of good he's done for the community. Let's see, he got the Grotten girl into nursing school. He arranged for the Nifongs to get a loan for their gas station. The list goes on. Some true, some hyperbole. So if Nicky wants to build his condos and charge rent to the summer people, who will stand in his way? Just don't get the media coming out here and telling people our gracious town is an unsafe place for sweet young women and little old ladies."

My aunt grimaced as she rose delicately from her chair. "Well, Chief," she said. "You have been most helpful, and I thank you for reminding me of something I often shudder to remember."

He looked up, fascinated. "Which is what, ma'am?"

"That the world would rather patronize maidens and crones than be genuinely kind to them. Good day, sir."

✣ 19 ✣

TWO WHO TALKED

"I can't believe he's dead," Marilyn Su said. "You know he still owes me fifteen hundred bucks? I don't suppose I could get it now? Nah, I already took it as a tax write-off. Can you get the lights?"

The switch was right behind me, under a poster of Chaplin's Little Tramp. Pleasant company for a darkened room.

The art director had met Tony Crowell at a party in the East Village, and now wished she hadn't. She'd designed three Zephyr albums, including Andy Kay's.

"And you know what sucks is I can't take it to small claims court, and it's not worth getting a lawyer for, so what do I do? Eat it, I guess."

"Bon appétit."

She was a thin, pretty woman with Asian features, long, dark hair, and a vibe that said she didn't take guff from anyone. I'll bet she grew up in a house full of brothers. She adjusted her Mets cap and flung a Kodachrome slide on the light table. When she bent to peer through a loupe, her legs stretched and I caught a glimpse of lace under a fuzzy worn patch in her jeans, right at the hip.

MURDER ON BOOK ROW

I'd gotten her name out of the library, out of Adsense's Creative Services Directory. Her day job was designing for a group of teeny bopper magazines, but she offered reasonable rates for freelance work. The magazine company's Madison Avenue address had not prepared me for the cluttered mess I found fifty-four flights above the street. Her office walls were covered with pin-ups and postcards of movie stars. Marilyn Monroe leered at me from a bulletin board, and Bogart, lounging on the back of the door, tried to bum a cigarette off me. A spray of colored pencils stuck into the drop ceiling, and a mobile of pink-and-green fish dangled over Su's designing board.

She herself was a mishmash of design. The ball cap, the jeans, and the slightly visible panties were all offset by a form-fitting lavender T-shirt that bore the silhouette of a ballerina on its back, and a message that read, "I'd rather be dancing."

"Who did it, a girl?" she asked. "Jealous boyfriend or something? Did you see the newspaper spread—pardon the pun—on him and his entourage? Bet you anything a word person laid that thing out. The photos were run *so* huge, grainy as hell. So bad!"

She popped a slide of some metal rock star into her projector and flipped it on. Instantly the wall was alive with Man Eats Snake.

"Did you know Alison Munro?"

"Oh, hey, yeah. You heard about her? That was lousy. She was real classic. Like a young Audrey Hepburn. You know the way she did her hair? Kind of short, with the kerchief and all? So pretty. She and Tony had something going for about five minutes."

"You met her when, at the photo shoot?"

"Right, right," she nodded, fiddling with the projector to shrink the metal guy down to cover size. Then she tacked a piece of tracing paper to the opposite wall, right over the projection. "I came up with the designs for all those covers. I was going to get a friend of mine to shoot them, right? I mean, he's got a studio and all? And Tony calls and goes, 'Don't worry, I got a guy who'll work cheap and we can shoot it at the recording studio.' I should have known the moment he asked me to bring my own backdrops that the check would get lost in the mail."

She stopped, lit herself a Marlboro, glugged some of her bottled water, and got back to her tracing. She blocked out a rough outline of the image in pencil with her left hand, the cigarette balanced between the delicate fingers of her right. "So I get to the shoot, and they've tricked out one of those empty offices with props and stuff. The camera's all set up, and it turns out that their photog is basically George Burns. Well, not really. More like a late John Huston. You know, with the grumpy face and bristly beard and all?"

"Milo Barski?"

"*Riiiiight!* Exactly. That is so funny. You knew. Wow. I was totally prepared to hate him, but he impressed me. Totally classic. Professional, courteous, the whole bit. This deep, grumpy voice …"

She started to contort her face to imitate him—

"He's dead," I said, cutting off the impression.

She looked like I'd just suggested running big grainy photos on the sides of buildings. "I can't believe it! Wow! That is too freaky. So, like, everyone's dead now? Tony, Alison, *and* Mr. Barski. I guess I shouldn't be surprised. What was it, heart attack?"

"Murder."

Her Marlboro shed ash at an astounding rate. "Whoa! You are blowing my mind today, guy. You investigating that one, too?"

"Maybe. So keep chatting."

"Well, geez, now I don't know what to say. I mean, we talked a little while, not long. Alison monopolized him the whole time."

"How so?"

Her lips locked on the cigarette and sucked away. "Well, geez, I don't know what was going on there."

"Well, geez Louise indeed," I said. "Was she *flirting* with him or *conning* him, or what? Use your words."

"Hmm … let me think. He mentioned that he ran this antiques shop downtown and she kept bringing it up all through the shoot. Asked him all kinds of stuff. What's he sell. What's it go for. Did he have any help? Was it cheap stuff, or top of the line. You know, real nitty gritty, like she cared."

"This went on all day?"

"Well, most of the first day. We shot all those stars in one weekend. Alison, she was there all three days on account of Tony. But she kept talking to this guy. We sent out for lunch, and they sat down and ate together. Sunday night we're going down in the elevator with him and his equipment and she's tagging along and she goes, 'So when will you know?' And *he* goes, 'Later this week. Don't worry, I won't forget.' Now what the heck do you think that was all about?"

"Were you the only one who heard them speaking?"

"It was only the three of us in the elevator. By then I was sort of liking the dude. Classic types are my hobby. Real class went out of style with the old-timers, you know. Did you know he shot Brando and Marilyn?"

I stretched my lower lip two feet, thinking.

"So what's it all mean, Mr. Private Eye?" she said.

"Beats me."

"Maybe she wanted to buy something nice for her parents? That's what I figured then."

It's what I figured, too. But still, I would have given anything to know the full course of their conversation.

"When did all this happen? Do you recall the month or year?"

"It was the summer before she died."

I pulled my ear next. It didn't help. I had one question I couldn't resist asking. "Forgive me for asking, but there's no other way to do it other than blurting it out. Did Tony hit on you when you first met?"

She smiled devilishly. "Are you hitting on me by asking that question?"

I didn't know what to say. Luckily, she let me off the hook with a wave of her hand. "I'm just messing with you. Answer: Of course. Answer to the question you didn't ask: No, I don't date jerks. I pegged him for one the second I met him. I don't know why other women don't."

"Thanks a lot. You know, you're a real gem, Marilyn."

"Back at ya, kid. You know, I always wanted to be a private eye."

"That makes one of us," I said.

"Aw, come on! It must be great. It's totally classic. You ever see *The Maltese Falcon*? When he tells her off at the end?"

"I don't watch much TV."

She walked me to the elevator, punctuating her speech with her cigarette: "You. Have. Got. To. See. It!"

LUZETTA TREVILLIAM HAD TOLD HIM SO.

And although Zephyr's former business manager had little time to waste with me—it was getting close to five and she was heading out to her sister's in Maplewood, New Jersey—she did feel it was worth telling me so, too. She led me to the break room of the accounting firm where she worked, and lowered her voice as she spilled the beans. The air in the vicinity of the microwave smelled of someone's cheesy afternoon soup.

"You predicted Tony's death?"

She nodded her square chin down into three folds, which hid the clover-shaped collar of her blouse. Her beautiful cinnamon-colored lips formed a kiss. "I told him so. I'm not clairvoyant or anything, Mr. Sleet. I'm not talking that way. But I told him one of those people would come after him if he kept cheating them like that."

"Zephyr had money problems?" I said. "I'm shocked!"

She allowed herself a demure smile. She was a black woman, big and tall even while seated. Her hair was pulled back in a reserved bun. Her dark-blue suit was faintly pinstriped, and she wore a school ring on her right hand. She looked fiftyish and motherly, and I wouldn't have wanted her to get a glimpse of my checkbook.

"Money problems? Mr. Sleet, if I didn't chase him every month we wouldn't've had a roof over our heads. I gave him checks, he'd shove them in his drawer. That's not responsible financial behavior, now is it?"

It sounded like a good tactic to me, but I said no.

"Finally I couldn't take it anymore, I just quit. We had people calling all the time asking for their money. Session musicians, second engineers, artists … Lord! I kept telling him he had to pay them and the utilities, but he was very snippy."

"But he had money," I said. "Family money. Plenty of it. Why cheat people?"

"Family money's irrelevant here. What the man spent in his personal life has nothing to do with the business side. You understand that, right? I'm the comptroller. I'm looking at the books and it's clear from the start we had a cash flow problem. The money was coming in, just not when we needed it. And he was a *child*, plain and simple. No responsibility. Week I left, the publicity manager left too. I said, 'Mr. Crowell, looks like you'll be writing your checks and your own press releases from now on.'"

"I gather he was," I said. "Neither of those positions was ever filled."

She got a kick out of that. The sweet joy of vindication that is the only pleasure an I-told-you-so'er ever gets. "Incredible. We had that big old suite, all these empty offices with nobody in them, and I used to tell him, 'Mr. Crowell, we could move and save all this rent money.' But he laughed. Said someday he'd own the whole building. 'Zephyr Records is making it big, Luzetta. You watch.'"

"What was he spending money on?"

She gazed at me shyly. "Oh, Mr. Sleet. You must know. It's in all the papers. Once he figured out that entertainment could be considered a tax-deductible expense, the boy just went to town. You should have seen those party expenses. He rented out a discotheque when they released *Hard Times,* and that disc went nowhere. We blew through freelancers like crazy. Because he never paid them, he was obliged to keep looking for new people. It was a vicious cycle."

"Did he stiff Milo Barski?"

Her eyes puckered. "Mr. Barski? That funny white man? Seem to remember he had a lawyer friend call to complain, but nothing ever came of it. We owed Mr. Barski a thousand, maybe fifteen hundred, something like that? Tony probably sent him only a few hundred because that's all we had in the account. Oh my! Sweet little Mr. Barski. What a name to bring up. You know him? What's he up to?"

"He's dead."

Her hand went to her breast. "Aw, what a shame! Oh well, people die sometimes. And he was old."

This was true. "How did the place survive between the infusions of cash?"

"Bridge loans, mostly. From his father. That's what made the books so complicated. He didn't like stiffing his family. Didn't like letting them see what an irresponsible child he was. That's the problem with him, if you ask me. That family of his came up a couple of times to visit. His mother and sister. His father one time, God rest his soul, poor man. Very sickly."

"What were they like?"

"Father was very gracious," she said slowly, making up her mind to dispense with the niceties first. "I offered him coffee and cake and he says, 'Don't go to any trouble,' and I said, 'No trouble, Mr. Crowell, a pleasure.' He tried to do for himself, but he couldn't on account of being so ill. The daughter, she was sweet, helped me bring some extra chairs to Mr. Crowell's office."

"What about the mother?"

She shuddered. "This goes no further, okay? She rubbed me the wrong way, acting like a queen or something. I think that's where Tony got it. When the poor gentleman passed, Mrs. Crowell was calling the shots. He wouldn't ask her for money, so he had to get it from somewhere else."

"Where?"

"His uncle."

"His *uncle?*"

"Chubby white man, bad toupee. Used to stop by nights once in a while in the company of this big tall white boy. They'd sit around in Tony's office, wasting time. Man gave Tony cash."

"Did Tony have you log it in the books?"

"Sometimes." She paused. "Not all the time. He said they were private loans. My, he could have gotten better interest on a credit card!"

I kicked back my chair. I'd heard enough.

"Did I say something wrong, Mr. Sleet? You leaving? Don't you want to finish your coffee?"

❧ 20 ❧

LEGEND IN HIS OWN MIND

T he Federal Express envelope Rawlsy left on my father's desk contained two Xeroxes from the *Los Angeles Sun-Chronicle*, dated the second week of June, 1962.

NORTH HOLLYWOOD—Two persons were injured early Saturday morning in a two-car collision on Laurel Canyon Boulevard.

Police said Eunice K. Mauro, 32, a hairdresser from West Hollywood, suffered serious head injuries when her late-model Dodge failed to negotiate a turn in the road, and struck an oncoming Ford truck driven by Albert Holm Dumbroski, 54, of Glendale.

Police said Dumbroski was treated for cuts and released. Mauro was listed in critical condition. Police spokesman Evan Werner said the area's heavy rainfall in the last two days may have contributed to the accident ...

Two more paragraphs of nothing followed. The second clipping had run two days later in the news brief section, noting that

Eunice had been released and sent in stable condition to her parents' home in Allentown, Pennsylvania.

I picked up the phone and dialed a number which, years ago, used to mean a free ride home. Today it meant *agita*.

"Munoz," said Munoz.

"Lieutenant Posluszny, please."

"Hold on ... Who's this?"

"Well ... *me*."

"Who me?"

"Sleet me."

"You bum! Didn't we tell you two not to leave town?"

"I seem to recall some ranting of that nature, yes."

"Then what were you two doing out on Long Island this morning?"

"Finding a good beach spot. I've heard it's best to book early for the summer. Is the lieutenant there?"

"Not to you, she isn't. You know we don't make requests like that for our health. So far this week, we've questioned you regarding two deaths. *Two*. You found one corpse, your aunt the other. Pretty suspicious, wouldn't you say?"

"What can I say? Murder runs in the family."

"Like hell, pal. Like hell."

"Gosh, you know, all this chiding has taught me a lesson, Detective. I just know that I'll never do it again. Can I talk to Abby now?"

"What for?"

"I wish to make an inquiry, if you must know."

"What inquiry?"

"Who is Eunice K. Mauro?"

"None of your business."

His response spoke volumes. It told me that they had found the mysterious peacock woman's name among Barski's personal effects and had already run the lead down.

"Do you even know, Detective?"

"Of course. I made the calls myself."

"Wouldn't happen to have that number handy, would you?"

"That's police business. I'm a cop. You're not. You couldn't even hack the academy."

There was some truth to his remark, but not much. In any case, it was a sore subject with me. A period of my life I don't care to remember.

"That is a very hurtful remark, Detective. At least tell me what she's got to do with Barski."

"Nothing but a motive, pal, plain and simple. Your aunt's pal was blackmailing someone. Now we know why."

This did not come as a shock. In fact, it felt like something I'd always known was in the cards. A man who was willing to sell proof of Alison's murder to her father would absolutely stoop to blackmail. "How about a hint?" I said. "Pretty please?"

Click!

I made a mental note to stop by the fish market someday soon and pick up a nice trout, flounder, or sea bass, and have it mailed parcel post to one Luis Munoz, Detective, Third Grade. I thought it would give his workplace atmosphere. At least for a few days.

Maniacal reveries aside, I typed out a quick memo to Rawlsy, urging him to stay on the Grouse hunt. My aunt had urged us to locate and interview a club member named Adrian Balsam, but Rawlsy had not been able to turn him up on two visits to the man's doorman building on the Upper West Side. Phone calls to the gentleman's apartment went unanswered, and there had been no further sign of him at the Grouser Club. It was a mystery—or Balsam had pocketed a couple of rolls of quarters and zipped down to Atlantic City for a few days. Besides these few instructions, I left Rawlsy numbers for Leena and her dad. In case of developments, he was to report to Bea.

I sealed it up in an envelope emblazoned with the Bray Agency logo, wrote MILK MONEY on it, stepped next door to the operatives' room and slid it under Rawlsy's blotter. When I left the room, I saw legendary detective Emory Bray hovering over Melinda as she tidied her desk. She had a long trip out to Astoria, and always got ready early. Her *Cosmo* poked out of her handbag.

Bray's yellow mop of hair swiveled to me. He rocked back and forth on his brown wingtips and pointed to his office. "You! In my office!"

"Why?" I said.

"Where have you been? We've got four investigators running around on cases on your say-so alone. I have receipts for three hundred dollars' worth of photo equipment sitting on my desk. I've gotten calls all day from lawyers threatening to sue my butt. Reporters keep calling me for comment on a case I haven't been briefed on. My freaking picture's in the newspaper! And the only one who knows what's going on is *you*. And where are you?"

"At the beach."

"The beach, my *tuchas*. Get in my office."

"You shouldn't speak like this in front of Melinda."

She waved a hand. "Oh, I've heard worse, honey."

"I want a full report. Pronto. You don't go home till I know what's going on. You hear me?"

Like a bell. His neck cords were popping and his face was so red I thought some of his more prominent nasal capillaries would burst. "I'm sorry," I said, hoping I sounded contrite. "I was wrong to keep you out of it. You deserve to know the whole story. Just let me get my notebook, and I'll be right in."

"I have a reputation in this city," he droned on. "A tradition of excellence. It must be upheld."

"Absolutely," I said.

"Darn right," he thundered. He tucked in his voluminous shirt-ends and tugged up his waistline. He did some more authoritative rocking, stormed into his office, and slammed the door.

I stepped into my father's office, snatched up my notebook, hat and coat, and peeked out the door. Melinda had left.

I heard the sound of ice clinking in a rocks glass. It emanated from Bray's office next door. His post-work drink. Good.

I sailed out the door of our office suite and didn't look back.

🎇 21 🎇

A LIFE TOUCHED

llentown was a city trying to look classy in the middle of snowbound farmland. A city of wood-front tenements and state liquor stores and circular motor inns standing tall against the landscape like huge pancake stacks. At eight at night all was frozen and deserted; the hotspot was the main strip downtown where cops kept kids in jacked-up chrome machines from drag racing up the one-way street. In the window of Hess's department store I thought I saw a mannequin yawn.

I parked on one of their numbered streets and walked to a small neon-lit bar and grill that promised forty-six different beers on tap. One step inside and I smelled at least thirty-four of them. Three wizened gents whose pants rode high on their torsos sat at the bar, picking at a few crumbled pretzels. They watched two ESPN broadcasters haggle over the Super Bowl.

Their heads swiveled as I entered and became the main attraction. I ordered a burger and a beer from a lean man in an apron behind the counter. I asked if they had a phone.

"It's in the back. They upped it. Costs you a quarter now."

"I'll remember that."

The booth stood in the shadows between two restrooms. It

was an old wood and glass enclosure, its windows gray with finger smudges. On the door of the ladies room hung a poster of the St. Pauli girl in all her airbrushed glory.

I got out the Allentown directory and went to work. I found no listings for Eunice K. Mauro, or any other kind of Mauro. I got lucky with Eversman, which was the other surname we had found mentioned in Barski's last will and testament. There were seven Eversmans in Allentown and more in places with names like Wescosville, Emmaus, and Macungie. I dug out a bunch of quarters and started dialing.

Macungie came up big. The home of one Eversman, Ralph W. Probably Wilbur. Ralph sounded like I'd interrupted his viewing of *Wheel of Fortune*.

"Is Millicent there?" I said over the jangling and applause on the other end of the line.

"No. Went to see her sister. Who's this?"

"Her sister Eunice?"

"That's right. Who *is* this?"

Sometimes it's just that easy.

"That is so funny! I thought Eunice lived with *you*, Ralph!"

"Whaddaya talking about? The woman's been at Valley Nursing for years. Hey, you mind telling me who the heck you—"

I hung up. The book told me Lehigh Valley Nursing had an address on Hamilton Boulevard. Back at the bar, brown onions slithered out from under my hamburger bun. I sipped the beer first. Good, as always.

My bar companions watched me closely. I watched them back. One wore a pork pie hat on the back of his head. The others looked as if they expected me to whip out a machete and hack the place to Kibbles & Bits. Maybe they didn't get many strangers in Allentown. Or maybe I had picked the wrong bar. Either way, the air was heavy with curiosity. Pork Pie took a sip of beer, lapped at his lips with his tongue, and let it stay there as if he might need it later.

"You guys know how to get to Hamilton Boulevard?"

Instantly I got four different sets of directions.

"WAIT HERE," I SAID TO MILLIE EVERSMAN. "I'LL GET you a tissue."

I left her on the orange and blue couch and went to the main desk of the nursing home. A teenager in the white coat dragged himself away from the TV and rummaged in the drawers for some Kleenex. If he moved any slower, the cleaning ladies would sweep around him and call it a night. I decided that there was altogether too much television watching going on in the Commonwealth of Pennsylvania. Down the hall, in the recreation room, a bunch of men and women in wheelchairs watched Tom Selleck beat up a hairy-chested man on the hood of his Ferrari. All in a day's work.

"Got 'em," the teenager said.

I presented the small plastic pack to Mrs. Eversman. She was a brown-haired woman in her fifties wearing a double-knit pantsuit of sedate green and a blouse of smoky blue. She dabbed her eyes with a tissue. "I don't know why I did that. I've told her story so many times already. Didn't the police tell you?"

"Not really. We're not speaking, I'm afraid."

"Oh." She took a few deep breaths and stopped shaking. Her hand snapped up a few more tissues and stowed them away in her purse, which sat on her lap. "The officer said his executor's people would be in touch."

"Here I am."

"What a mess." She clapped her hand to her mouth. "I can just imagine the paperwork. We could sure use the money. Last month they moved her up to a higher care level. More pills and bills, Ralph says. She gets a little money from Medicaid and the insurance. The rest we pay."

"When did you last speak to Barski?"

"I called him only last month to ask if he could see his way to maybe sending some more."

"Wait. You *admit* you demanded money from him?"

Her face changed. "What do you mean, *demand*? I asked. Nicely. I explained how we needed more. I knew he had it. Ralph gave me an argument about calling him. We haven't talked to him in years. The money just came like clockwork."

"Every month?"

She stopped her dabbing and frowned. "That policeman sure didn't tell you a thing, did he? Mr. Barski has been sending money to my sister's fund every month for the past twenty-five years."

Something dropped in my stomach. It didn't bounce back. My mind reeled back to the money orders I'd found in Barski's apartment. All of them had been made out to The E.K. Mauro Trust Fund. Barski had been sending this family $200 to $500 a month.

"He's been paying since her accident?" I said. "But why? Was it his fault?"

"Who can say? Accidents are accidents, right?"

Her chin spazzed on me. She rooted in her purse for another tissue. "After the accident they sent her home. Only, she was in no condition … we *had* to keep her here. And one day Mr. Barski came to visit. My father was still alive then. They talked. He offered to pay her expenses, but Daddy chased him out of here. Called him a drunk. That wasn't fair, I thought. He looked like he'd been drinking a long time, and he told us that he'd lost his job at the newspaper because of it. Daddy didn't want to hear it. Gave him back the ring, too."

"Ring?"

"Uh-huh. For a few months he sent money and Daddy sent it back. Finally Mr. Barski called *me* and asked if I could help him set up a fund for her at one of the banks downtown. Ralph and I did it behind Daddy's back. We kept it in our name till Daddy died, then we switched it over."

"And you never *asked* Milo to do it?"

"No, I keep saying we didn't. He *wanted* to. Said he couldn't stop thinking of her and he wanted to help. Did you say you knew him?"

"Yes," I said absently, my mind far away. I watched myself get whacked on the tush for touching a porcelain doll. I watched Barski chase my sisters down the block for winding up a music box. Was that the same man, the same crotchety coot?

Millie touched my arm. "He ever talk about her?"

"Not that I recall," I said. "But what's that prove?"

"I was always curious about their relationship. I got a long letter from Eunice just before the accident, and she told me how he'd finally proposed. She never thought it would happen, because they weren't children anymore. Eunice was always worried she'd end up an old maid. She wanted to travel. Go places. Have fun. That's how she ended up in Hollywood in the first place."

"How long did they see each other?"

"Oh, a little more than a year," Mrs. Eversman told me. "She wrote to tell me that she was so happy. I believed it. That's why me and Ralph did what we did. We didn't think we had the right to slight Mr. Barski like that. That was Daddy's fault."

I was deeply confused now. Munoz had referenced blackmail. But nothing I was hearing sounded like blackmail. His financial support for these people and this woman sounded more like the act of a devoted and grief-stricken lover.

I wondered if I had known the real Milo Barski. I'd known the miser, the sugar bag swiper, the plastic spoon rinser, the white wine guzzler. Would it have been different, I wondered, if this Eunice had been part of his life? Would he have come to New York at all? Would he have ever taken over his family's shop? Hustled and hoarded his dollars? Gotten his skull bashed? It was impossible to know the answers to such questions. I wouldn't, ever. But like someone had once said in an old movie I'd seen: *One person's life touched so many others.*

"How much money are they talking?" Mrs. Eversman asked me. "Do you know what he was worth?"

"They still have to make a valuation to probate the estate," I said. "That's going to take time. With most people that's pretty easy. House, car, money in the bank. But Barski had all those antiques and valuables. Every one of them needs to be appraised. Look," I said. "You said you called Barski. When was this?"

"More than a week ago?" She paused to think, picking at her chin. "Yes, it was a few days before Christmas, the twentieth. I said she was worsening and would he mind ... He knew we didn't like to take handouts like that. It made Ralph so sore. But see, if you run out of money, then the government takes over. We were afraid they'd move her to a cheaper place. A dump, maybe."

Christmas. I saw Barski getting sloshed on New Year's Eve, riding home in a cab with Amos and Bea. Killing bottles of wine alone in his apartment.

"What did Barski say when you asked?"

"'I'll see what I can do,' he said. I believed him."

See what he could do. What could he do? Well, shoot. Barski could have decided to put the screws to someone to raise some cash. Maybe *that's* what Munoz was referring to. But what proof did Munoz have to that effect?

"You think it was fair of me to ask?" Mrs. Eversman said. "Me and Ralph had such an argument about it."

"Fair enough," I said. "Can I see her?"

She took me to a private room and showed me an emaciated body in a bathrobe sitting in a wheelchair, and said it was her sister. I studied the woman's face from several angles, trying to reconcile the person in front of me with the picture of the peacock girl in Barski's bedroom. I suppose it was her. She stared through the window of her room, over the radiator, and watched the flakes of snow flutter down in the yard behind the nursing home. She was fifty-seven years old. She looked eighty.

"Stable condition," I said. Kneeling by the wheelchair, I said, "Miss Mauro?"

"She doesn't speak," her sister said. I'd known that from the moment I saw Eunice, but somehow I couldn't help myself. "Miss Mauro," I said again. I saw the tube under her nose, running to the green tank in the pouch at the side of her chair. Her eyes moved and stared at me and saw nothing.

I took Alison Munro's peacock feather from my coat pocket and laid it on her lap. Her eyes flickered and took it in.

"What is that?" her sister said as I left.

"Only she knows."

FOUR HOURS LATER, IN A CITY FARTHER NORTH, I HAD A nice motel room with two sets of towels and three glasses wrapped in waxed paper. I sat on the bed in my boxers with the TV on low and listened to the hum and *kuh-thunk* of the ice machine down the hall. I dialed the number of Bea's apartment in SoHo. Her first words were, "Where are you?"

"Connecticut," I said.

"You're following my instructions?"

"To the letter," I said.

Somehow she picked up on what I wasn't saying. "Why do you sound so sad?"

I gave it to her in a flash, just for openers. I'd seen Barski's lady friend, I now knew her whole story, and boy, did I really hate places like that.

In the background I heard the strains of some operatic aria. Most likely Puccini. She was a sucker for *Madame Butterfly* or *Turandot*. "Oh, my dear boy," Bea said, her voice barely a whisper. "Are you comfortable? Have you eaten?"

For her the former was impossible without the latter. "I have. Copiously. Abundantly, believe you me."

"So," she said, getting down to business. "Relax and compose yourself, nephew mine. Can you do that?"

"Absolutely."

"Very well," she said. *"Dimmi tutto."*

❧ 22 ❧

THE THINGS WE DO

The school sat at the crest of a flat hill overlooking the Atlantic, its every view blocked by sea gulls and gusting snow. The buildings in the courtyard were red-brick Georgian colonials, except for the dorm and administration building, which were white stone-and-stucco palazzi with terra cotta roofs. Red-brown terra-cotta roof tiles peeked out from under the snow, adding a touch of autumn color to the landscape. Tacked to the right of the administration building was a five-sided wing with stained glass windows (more reddish shades), topped with a cupola. I heard an organ pealing away inside, climbing the scales.

I walked up four freshly shoveled steps, entered the building, and encountered someone who could have been the woman of my dreams. Oval face, reddish cheeks, hair the color of sand. She had a wonderful smile, and offered to help me. It all would have been perfect between us, if she were open to ditching the nun's habit.

I gave her a business card and asked to see the head nun. The card impressed her. She looked me up and down, but her appraisal must have fallen short: I still wore the black suit I'd worn to Barski's funeral, and I'd shaved that morning with a two-week-old Bic razor. So no—today I wouldn't be tempting cute nuns out of their vows of chastity.

"Make yourself at home," she said. "We have coffee and a warm chapel."

"Thank you, but no."

She zipped up the marble stairs with my card in her hand. Her shoes clapped loudly on the stone, echoed under the gilded ceiling and bounced off bare-bottomed stone cherubs.

I sat on an old church pew and fidgeted. This building had clearly been someone's lavish home back in the day. I'd seen those fancy beach houses on Long Island, but this one blew them all away in orders of magnitude. What kind of person builds a mansion with a dorm-sized outbuilding and an attached chapel?

For all its grandeur, the place was unlikely to make an ordinary person feel at home. The space had the same resonant stillness of funeral homes and doctors' offices and empty tombs. On a table near me was a stack of yearbooks. I scanned the dates and carefully selected a particular volume. I found some photos of a spring pageant four years ago. A face leapt off the page. A pretty girl in a white gown, her mouth round in song, the face of a Christmas angel. Voice major Alison Munro entertained parents and guests alike with her selection, "Batti, Batti, O Bel Masetto," an aria from Mozart's *Don Giovanni*.

Mozart?

I put the book back when my unrequited love returned to tell me where I needed to go on the second floor. Up there, the grandeur of the old house had been stripped away, leaving a corridor you would have found anywhere in academia. I passed other offices, heard Xerox machines thumping merrily, and secretaries chatting.

"Mr. Sleet?"

I looked down the runway of carpet. At the end of the hall a woman in a plain brown dress suit stood in a doorway, waving. "I'm Sister Michael Marie."

She was plain and sixtyish. Her thick gray hair framed her lined face like a tossed mop. A simple wooden crucifix hung around her neck. No habit in sight. She was a thoroughly modern nun.

She ushered me into an office that was styled like a living room in a boring retreat house. Commercial carpet. Thickly cushioned indestructible furniture. Tall, fake plants. And a small metal desk. The only signs of the house's former glory were the coffered oak ceilings and a pair of French doors leading to a wrought-iron veranda getting dumped on with snow. The lights were dim, and instantly I felt in need of a midmorning nap.

She waved me into an upholstered monster with legs and wiggled my business card in her hand. "Sleet … is that English? Dutch? Your hair—"

"Forget the hair. I have cousins named Valentine who could pass for St. Patrick's Day poster boys. But my father's side is a mix, and part of it is Irish."

"Where from?"

"Brooklyn."

"I meant where in Ireland. My people came from County Clare."

"Oh, *that* where from. No clue. Not that I care much. As a kid I was told that the surname is Old Norse, and I've been far more fixated ever since on wearing Viking horns than a tam o'shanter."

"Our benefactor, Mr. Kinsella, was a Dublin boy. One of the original Robber Barons. Operated mines in Pennsylvania, and left us this, his summer estate, which became our school."

"That's nice," I said. "But I didn't come for a history lesson. I've come to ask about Alison Munro."

"I see." She cleared her throat. Her legs were crossed primly at the ankle and she rotated my card in her fingers. She tried to smile, but found it difficult. "You must know that I cannot discuss the history of former students."

I was ready for that. I dug in my overcoat for the release Leena had pressured her father to sign. He'd fought us on it, but the John Hancock I demanded was far cheaper than Barski's five grand. Sister Michael Marie held the document at arm's length and read it, squinting. I wondered if her particular order took vows of blindness.

"I see," she said, dropping the letter in her lap. "I didn't realize that they were still inquiring into that business."

"Some parents don't give up."

She scrunched up her face. "But it's *so* painful."

"True. What can you tell me about her?"

"The transcript is the easiest way to understand how she spent her time here."

"I don't care about her transcript. I want to know about *her*. People she knew, her roommate, the kind of person she was. Stuff that wouldn't come in a file."

"Well, as you may know, she didn't stay with us very long. She entered as a liberal arts student, with a minor in voice. She sang beautifully. I didn't know her very well. I don't teach many classes these days. I only knew her from the little problem she had during her first semester."

"Problem?"

"Boys. She had a young man staying in her dorm room. We put a stop to that right away."

"Who was he?"

"Her roommate's brother."

"And who was she?"

"A girl from Providence."

I smiled, gritting my teeth. "Sister, I'm not a dentist."

The side of her mouth dipped and her voice softened. "I can look in the alumni files. I believe her former roommate still has a job in the area."

"Was Alison dating this boy?"

"They were going 'steady,' whatever that means these days. Drugs were also a factor. The boy supplied the girls with marijuana. That's a serious infraction. I notified everyone's parents. Normally a case like that means automatic expulsion. We're an all-girl school, Mr. Sleet, so you really have to go out of your way to fraternize on that level. Families from all over the globe send their daughters here. Families that are not even Catholic. Hindu. Muslim. Our families select us because they *want* that isolation for their daughters. They feel it's entirely appropriate and necessary."

"Is that how she left? Expelled?"

"No. There were some mitigating circumstances. For one, Missy's father can be quite persuasive. So can Mrs. Munro. She came all the way from New York to see me. She said she and her husband were making great sacrifices to send Alison here. She had a heart-to-heart with her daughter, and promised it wouldn't happen again. I believed them, but I split the girls up and put them on probation. We moved them to single rooms on the second floor of that dormitory. The girls call it solitary, but they're actually quite nice. Alison lived next door to Sister Timothy, the dorm monitor."

"Nuns make nice neighbors. So I hear, anyway."

She lifted her eyes heavenward and got no solace there. She plowed on. "It worked. We had no further trouble out of any of them. Alison finished her semester and the year quite productively. Applied herself quite nicely, though she did have to make up some courses that summer."

"Why'd she leave the following year?"

The nun shook her head, probably at the world. "Oh, Mr. Sleet. To understand that you must comprehend the folly of teenagers taken to extraordinary heights. She was going to become ... *a rock star*." She spat the last three words out in a tone of utter derision. "Doesn't everyone?"

She stood and waved Munro's release form. "I'll get those files now. If you don't mind, I'll make a copy of this. Excuse me."

I made a halfhearted stab at politeness and rose with her. She bowed out of the room. The door leading to the thumping Xerox machines clicked and I was alone in the half-darkness. I looked around the room to keep myself from snoozing. On the walls they had the kind of inexpensive paintings you'd find in a religious gift or bookshop. There were also a few old oils in heavy frames, landscapes with billowing factories in the distance, very nine-teenth century.

I opened the French doors. The lace curtains flapped and the wind off the coast slapped me awake. I saw the courtyard and four nuns in gray overcoats sweeping snow off the carmine-colored flagstones. They moved jerkily like pigeons, misty breath hanging before their faces. The youngest nun picked her way over the snow to sweep away the mound of flakes that had collected in outstretched arms of a Virgin Mary statue.

Behind them was the L-shaped dormitory, built in the same Spanish-mission style as the house I was standing in. The back of the dorm faced the Cliffwalk and the sea beyond.

"Sister, oh Sister, *stop!*"

The three shovelers pitched snowballs at the Virgin-duster.

"Sisters! Oh, now stop!"

They didn't. They lobbed them at her and the statue, giggling all the while, pitching them wide and missing her half the time. She adjusted her habit and dipped to Mary's feet to scoop up a killer snowball.

"I'll get you now!"

When Sister Michael Marie returned, I had formulated my question. "Have you ever heard of a man named Milo Barski?"

She stared at the ceiling with growing impatience. "No. Who is he?"

"Was. He was an antiques dealer."

"Ah. No. Most of the antiques in this house were sold more than seventy years ago when we acquired the residence."

"Was Mr. Kinsella fond of books?"

"Yes. They were liquidated in the same estate sale as well. Why do you ask?"

Darn it. It was a promising theory, but headed nowhere.

"Sister, would I be asking if I knew?"

"I wouldn't know, Mr. Sleet. Tiresome questions seem to be your forte."

She rose and jabbed a manila file at me. "I think we have concluded this discussion. Are you still interested in her roommate?"

"The roomie with the persuasive Pop? You bet."

"Well, as you don't have a release form from *her* father, I'm not obliged to share that information with you. But I can say what everyone in the vicinity knows. Her surname is Hettinger. She works in the family business, which I'm sure a detective of your especial talents can easily ferret out." She headed for the door, her face the color of canned beets. "Good day, Mr. Sleet. And, may God forgive me for saying so, good riddance."

I LET THE PHONE RING FIFTEEN TIMES. ANYONE WHO answers a phone on the fifteenth ring will be either very deaf or very angry. He was simply clueless.

"Damn it, man, I'm sleeping."

"Mr. Hettinger? Jeffrey Hettinger?"

"Uh-huh. Who's this?"

"My name is Homer," I said. "Winslow Homer? I'm with Consolidated Mutual of Seattle?"

"Totally not interested—"

"Wait," I said. "This is not a sales call!"

Pause. "It isn't?"

"No. We're the insurance company with those cute little

donkeys in our ads? 'Would you buy insurance from an ass?' You must've seen them, living in California and all."

"Aw, man, you call me at nine in the morning to sell me—"

"No. I'm calling about Alison Munro."

Sheets rustled. The phone rattled and thunked. He picked up again. "What's this about, for real?"

"I'm doing a background check on the family of one Ernest Munro of Brooklyn, New York. He's applied to us for a life insurance policy."

"What's that got to do with me?"

"You dated his daughter, didn't you?"

"Yeah, so? She died, man. It was some weird accident thing. I wasn't involved. That was ages and ages after we broke up."

"Well, Mr. Hettinger, I'm sure you know, being a future medical man and hitting the books so hard at Stanford and all, people don't usually die that young."

"How the hell do you know I'm in med school?"

I knew more than that. I knew, for instance, that he was a balding blond man of the chunky fraternity type. Missy Hettinger had shown me pictures of him at Daddy's highly touted financial services firm in town.

"Geez, I don't believe this! Missy told you to go wake me like this? She know I've been studying for the past week? She know that? No. What jerk gives my phone number to strangers?"

"She didn't give it to me. You're in the book."

I was in top form now. A nerd voice will get you anywhere. A nasal whine will reactivate every human's inbred fear of librarians, teachers, and government officials. "Now," I said. "About Mr. Munro. We're just trying to work up a psychological dossier on the family."

"We only went out for a semester. I broke it off. I had med school to think about."

And Daddy's money to consider, no doubt.

"She date anyone else after you that I could speak to?"

"Who *knows*, man? I didn't go near her after that. She got all weepy. She was a weepy type. Don't get me wrong. I loved her. She was a great gal. But we both had our futures to think about. I had to apply myself. Look—this was *soo* long ago. And we were like kids." He paused. His voice filled with sudden concern. "Uh, is this helping?"

In a fast food joint, I bought myself a large lemonade and a sandwich made of a pinkish, rubbery substance that came as close to resembling roast beef as it could for $2.99. The kid behind the counter tipped his cardboard Stetson at me.

I picked out a table and sat and did some eating. The restaurant was off I-95 out of Providence; the crowd was light but hungry. Near some windows a pretty thirtyish mom shushed her red-headed twins, who had their faces pressed to the glass, watching the snow cover everything in sight. I had a long, lousy ride ahead of me.

Sandwich done, I leaned back in the plastic seat and sipped my lemonade. I wondered how someone so young would deal with being dumped three times, one love after the other. In high school by the lead singer of the Dipsticks. In college, by Jeffrey Hettinger. One night on Long Island, by Tony Crowell. A cavalcade of jerks, and then she was dead.

I knew it wasn't my job to ponder such matters, but I couldn't help myself. I pictured Alison fighting Rosita over Tony, and then later crying alone into her wineglass over him. I thought of Barski moping over his lost Eunice for twenty-five years. It was now clear to me why he'd refused that free oil painting from Walter Kenning, his old employee. The painting had shown a Ford truck, the very vehicle that had annihilated his fiancée's life. That seemed trivial to me, but maybe not to a man in pain.

Ordinary people taking things to dangerous extremes, all because of love.

Outside the restaurant, I pumped quarters into a payphone. I dialed a Manhattan number and listened as a recorded message rattled off times and dates. Funeral parlors were sounding more like movie theaters every day.

I made another call, person-to-person, collect, to the city. I took a chance that the fink would be at home because he usually came into the office late in the day.

"Hellooooo?"

The reporter's voice was as slick as mating eels. I listened to the operator feed him my carefully orchestrated line. "Mrs. Carla Crowell is calling person-to-person for Mr. Bernard Housknecht. Will you pay for the call?"

"Yess! Oh my, *yesss!*" Bedlam rocked his side of the line. I heard plates and cutlery clattering into a sink, then the hasty flip of papers. "Put 'er on! I just have to get my ... hello, is she on?"

"Mr. Housknecht?" I said. Again the nasal bit. "You are the legendary reporter of the *New York Tab?*"

"Yes! Yes, that's me!"

"This is Mrs. Crowell's secretary. You've been trying to reach us, and Mrs. Crowell is ready with a statement."

"Is this an exclusive?" Good ol' Bernie, always driving a hard bargain. I could picture him haggling over Fruit of the Looms tightie-whities in the K-Mart on his day off. "Just put 'er on, put 'er on!"

"Do you mind holding the line?"

"Not at all. Not at all. Waiting's what I do. Heh, heh."

"Good," I said. *"Wait."*

Gently I let the phone receiver dangle in the breeze. Then I walked through the snow to my car, sipping away at my lemonade.

Have a great day, sucker.

🐉 23 🐉

NAILBITER'S JUSTICE

I toggled between FM jazz stations on the long stretch down I-95, and with every bump along the Bruckner Expressway. In those patches when I couldn't raise a note of music, I got to thinking about antiques and the people that owned them. By the time I returned the car to the agency's garage and reached the sedate townhome on the Upper East Side, I had myself a nifty little theory on the subject, one I thought the Crowells would want to hear.

The front door of the townhouse was unlocked, probably the first or second time in its heavily fortified life. A sour-faced dude in a morning jacket must have seen me coming up the steps, because he swung it back before I could even touch the ornate brass knocker with the face of a snarling dragon. The front foyer and the two large parlors on the left and right were filled with upper-crust people milling around with drinks in hand. I scraped a little dab of ketchup off my suit and straightened my tie. No worries. I'd fit right in. We were all dressed alike, in our formal deathwear.

The gent in the monkey suit took my coat and hat, and pointed me in the direction of the bar. A piano tinkled softly somewhere. Guests mingled quietly, chewing and sipping, making somber talk. Servers swirled around them offering little bites. The parlor with the bar had a high fireplace on the western wall; the north wall had tall windows overlooking a snowy rear garden.

Nice place. Rosewood furniture and gold leaf frames, ivory carvings, Oriental rugs on the floors and walls, a folding Japanese screen done up in black lacquerwork and painted with a frolicking gilt dragon. I accepted a glass of white wine and helped myself to a miniature quiche and some speared fruit chunks. I've never been one to pass up watermelon in January. I was nibbling when the wind changed.

I looked up and found Rudy Vranin, the Long Island gunsel, and his master. "Hello, jerk," Rudy said, laying a thick hand on my shoulder.

I patted the top of his paw. "Sit, Rudy, sit. Wow, Nicky, couldn't you have hosed him down before coming? They let him at the service smelling like this?"

"You make your own trouble, you know that?" DiGaetano said.

The Commodore had donned a double-breasted gray suit for Tony Crowell's sendoff. His toupee was slicked back and frozen in place. He stuffed a cheese twist in his mouth. "My eyes refuse to believe what they're seeing. Didn't we ask you nicely to stay away from these fine people?"

"It depends who we is," I said. "When last we chatted, you wanted us off your property, not Mrs. Crowell's. In fact, you made it sound as if you were casually acquainted with the family. I had to knock myself out to find out for myself that you were bankrolling Tony."

"What's a few bucks here and there?" he said, shrugging. "I was like an uncle to that kid. What's the diff? Our business was all in the past. We're here to celebrate a vibrant young man's life. Why bring up issues you know nothing about?"

"Why didn't you save me the aggravation and tell me you knew Barski, too? I haven't got it all figured out. I'm not that smart. But I'm guessing Barski sold you a lot of the nautical knickknacks you've got in that club of yours. And I'm guessing he may have also taken insurance photos for you. Photos for you, photos for the Crowell family."

He waved a finger at me, right under my nose, a smile on his face white and bright enough to keep ships on course. "You're too much. Rudy, is this guy too much or what?"

"I'll get rid of him," the kid said.

DiGaetano held up a hand across Rudy's chest. "What for? He wants to talk, let'm talk." He put a thick arm on my shoulder and gave me an avuncular side-hug. "You're all right, you know that? Smart. It's kind of a shame you're so nosy. Shall we take this somewhere a little quieter? Rudy, get the man's fruit."

"I came to pay my respects to the bereaved mother, who happens to be my employer's client."

"Why not?" he said, with a sweeping gesture. "Right this way. Rudy, maybe Mr. Smartmouth wants another wine?"

On any other day, the parlor would have seemed cozy. It was cluttered with more Oriental rugs and a few pieces of Chinese lacquerware, and a gleaming Coromandel buffet. Porcelain vases. Lots of ceramics of Asian women and pottery men of various sizes.

In short order I was telling the lady of the house, "I doubt Barski sold you any of this. I knew him almost twenty years and never saw Asian pieces in his shop. But he did dabble in nautical items, even used pieces like that as props in his magazine photography. So I'm guessing the connection started with Mr. DiGaetano. He introduced you and your late husband to Barski, and that's how your son came to know him."

"I'm not sure why you find any of that interesting," Carla Crowell said, sipping on a cigarette. "I hired you to find my boy's killer, not trace my social connections."

JOSEPH D'AGNESE

An unusual woman. A chain-smoker, like her son. Gray-blond hair pulled back in a tail behind her head. That style made her look childish, but heaven knew her real age. Me, I'd guess she'd hit sixty a while ago and started using her dollars to turn back the clock. Her pale-olive skin was stretched tight over her high cheekbones and burnished till it shone. She wore a black dress with a high neck. Her legs were crossed at the knee. She sat on a sofa, her shoulder touching her daughter's, all the while puffing away at her Benson & Hedges.

A few feet away, Rudy was slouched over the piano, popping salmon toasts into his craw. DiGaetano hovered in the vicinity, eyes nervously darting from me, to the Crowells, to the carpet.

I felt I didn't have anything to lose, so I just kept unspooling my theories. "Mr. Bray prefers his clients to be clear with him about any associations that may appear … um, *suspicious* to the authorities," I told her. "Mr. DiGaetano bankrolled your son when you wouldn't. So naturally it occurred to me to ask if you and your husband ever had similar financial dealings with Nicky. Like, say, when he was looking to invest in property that had recently become available on the shore?"

I gazed straight into her eyes. If I was hugely off base, I'd know in the next three seconds. "I'm thinking specifically of the tract of land that once belonged to Mrs. Hallquist," I said. "You know—the very land where she was burned out of her home, and on which your house stands today."

She blinked once and her eyes went dead. And that's how I knew.

"Well," she said, casting about for an ashtray. "What should we do about this? How unpleasant, to be upbraided by those for whom you've written nice fat checks. Mr. Sleet, my family has gone through a lot lately. I'd hate for us to have additional trouble. May I suggest that you leave now and tell Mr. Bray to stay in his lane? All I want is my son's murderer apprehended. I want

194

clarity and closure. Peace of mind. What would it take for you to walk out of here and forget this conversation?"

"Mom?" said the young woman beside her. She was my age, and practically invisible all this time. She wore a navy-blue dress with white buttons, probably the most colorful outfit in the entire room, and her eyes and hair reminded me of Tony Crowell's.

"Shush, Deb," her mother said with a swipe of the hand. "Mr. Sleet is trying to think. He's trying to decide how badly he wants to keep his job. I'm sure Mr. Bray would terminate the employment of anyone who jeopardized a major client. Such decisions often require incentives."

She ground out her cigarette in an ashtray proffered by her daughter. "Do you like art, young man? You can have any of these." She waved her hand at the figurines. "Any of them would fetch a fine price."

The girl was shaking her head. "Ma, stop." I believe she meant it, but I could just tell she was unaccustomed to using her spine. Her mother patted her knee like she was still Mama's little girl. "Deb, men like Mr. Sleet rarely have opportunities like this. Let him think."

I finally found my voice. "You want me to let it ride?"

She smiled and waved a hand in the air. "Let it ride! Yes. How about it?"

"Not to be rude, but no way."

I smoothed out my suit and headed for the front door. On my way out, I kept an eye on Rudy over at the piano. I didn't think he'd try something in front of all these people, but I had to consider him as a factor.

Shows you, you never know.

Nick DiGaetano rushed me from the back and threw an arm around my neck. I gave him a quick poke in the gut with my elbow, stepped back to crunch his toes, and tried to swing him over. He was too heavy to bother, so I wheeled around and sent my right fist into his cheek. The whole thing took a second, I think, but for that second I had my back to the room. I heard footsteps behind me, but thought nothing of it. Then I heard Mrs. Crowell say, "Please, Nicolo, let me handle it. Nick, please!"

She was as big a loon as he was. Bigger. She "handled" it with one of those pottery figurines. Smacked me on the back of my head, right on top. I heard the collective gasp of everyone in the room. I sank to my knees and she slammed me again. The statue shattered. Shards and dust flew. I cradled my head in my hands, blood running out of it like a bubbler, and before I conked out, I saw her over me, sticking that damn cigarette back in her lips.

I AWOKE TO A MAN'S FINGERS RUNNING THROUGH MY hair. He pushed the locks aside gently and touched my scalp. The pain started again, like a pendulum set back into motion. I groaned and rolled over. I was on a bed in someone's room. Standing over me was an elderly man with thinning black hair and a face gone slack. He had a good set of jowls flapping under his chin, and a grim mouth. He looked sad, and with good reason. He still made house calls.

He gripped my shoulders and rolled me onto my side. "Easy now," he said, his voice somehow making me think of walnuts rolling around in a lunch bag. I lay on my side in my shirtsleeves, shoes off, and let him go to work on me. At the foot of the bed I saw Deb Crowell, Tony's sister, with a finger in her mouth. I heard the even snipping noise she made with her teeth as she worked her way around a nail.

"And I thought your family made *me* nervous," I said.

She spat out a little white crescent of nail. "Ha ha. He going to make it. Doc?"

The walnuts rattled some more. "Sure, sure. You got a good bump, son. Have to stitch you. It might hurt."

He ran his hand over my skull. "Got quite a few bumps up here. Do you work construction?"

"No."

"Boxer? Football?"

"No," I said again. "I meddle."

"Better be good money in it."

I heard a spraying noise, and then he got busy with his needle and catgut. "Someone should have warned you, son," he said. "Never push Carla. She bites back."

"It's not that bad, Doc," Deb said. She sounded sore, but anyone would sound weird with a few fingers in her mouth.

"Why?" the doctor went on, pushing his luck. "You gonna tell me your mother's an angel, Debbie? Artists are temperamental, so they say. Arnie knew that. Had himself a heart attack to escape this marriage. You ask me, your brother courted disaster. Went and got himself killed. Now they're both at peace."

"You have a strange way of looking at things, Doc," she said. Her hands were on the bedspread now, and she swung her legs like a child.

"Quit that," the doctor said. "Making the whole thing shake."

She stopped.

"As long as you've got an opinion. Doc," I said. "Who killed Tony?"

"Hold still," he said. "Someone who took it upon themselves to correct thirty years of bad behavior."

"Aw, Doc, he was older than that!" Deb said.

"All I'm saying, she pushes the men in her life to be something they're incapable of being, and then she's disgusted when they can't live up to it. First month the condos started going up, I got your father started on anti-anxiety meds. So don't tell me. Hold this."

He yanked something attached to my scalp, and snipped it. Deb stretched across the bed—armpits two inches in front of my face—to hold the wrappings. She smelled like a sachet of lilac petals. I found myself wishing she weren't a Crowell.

They took some time with the bandage. While they were

working, a pencil-neck in a tweed coat walked in and shook freezing rain off on the carpet. He looked familiar, another face from my past. He leaned on a dainty blondwood bureau and waited. They got a little out of hand with the bandage. It covered my head, down to the tops of my ears. I looked like an unraveled runaway from an H.G. Wells convention.

"What you want to do," the doctor said, "is go home and relax. Do something that's not mentally taxing. Watch *Dynasty*."

The pencil-neck cleared his throat loudly.

Deb said, "Hi, Norm. Wet out?" He gave her a stiff kind of bow and said, "Counselor, good to see you." His eyes shifted to me. "Mr. Sleet, Mrs. Crowell has apprised me of the facts in this matter, and I must say, personally, that I find your behavior reprehensible."

"Thank you. I like to go big if I'm going to go at all."

"*... and* legally actionable ..."

"That's what counts now, doesn't it, Norm?" I said.

"I would not make jokes in your position, Mr. Sleet. We're asking Mr. Bray to remove you from this case. Any further attempt to contact, approach, or make communication with any member of this household will result in a civil suit against you yourself personally."

"Me myself personally?"

"This is a time of grief and mourning. We will not tolerate further harassments, Mr. Sleet."

I looked at the doctor. "Can harassment be plural?"

"Norm, can it," Deb said. "He heard you."

The family attorney sneered at her. "For your information, Miss Pro Bono, 'hearing' carries no legal weight. I, for one, am getting tired of running into this particular gentleman. Mr. Emory Bray is a distinguished personage in this city. He can do better than hiring thugs for employees."

That's why the lawyer looked so familiar. I'd seen him at the police department downtown the night Tony bought it. He and two colleagues has sprung into action, late at night, to protect the family's interests.

"I take it you represent Tony and his mother?" I said.

"Precisely."

"*And* Renaissance Estates?"

"Ah, that's none of your business."

I took that as a yes. That's how DiGaetano had known my name and Bea's the day we visited Rockport, Long Island. Despite their obvious differences in style, Nicky and Carla were all curled up in one big bed together, singing that age-old Broadway show tune, "These Are A Few Of My Favorite Scams."

When the lawyer left, the doctor tossed his things in his bag, shook his head and muttered, "Twerp."

They helped me up. Seven stitches, and the hair would grow back. If only I didn't feel like a sick dog. Deb let me use her pink bathroom to splash water on my face and wash away the blood. I found some Bayer aspirin in the cabinet and washed it down.

They walked me down the back stairs to the kitchen, where we found an army of servers loading the last of the *hors d'oeuvres*. The doctor disappeared and returned with my coat and hat. He recommended that I use the back entrance, so as not to inconvenience the lady of the house or her guests.

I slipped out into the garden, swung a right near the ice-encrusted fountain, and slipped down the west alley between their townhouse and the one next door.

Halfway down the alley, I heard a whistle. I turned to find Deb Crowell coming toward me at full tilt, shivering in a flapping, emerald-colored cardigan. She had a brown paper bag clapped to her chest.

"Geez, it is so cold out here! Here. I got it from my room. No, don't open it, just listen. She got rid of the photos before I could get to them, but I saved the rest."

"Say what?"

"I can't talk. You want to talk, call me at the office. Wainwright Terhune & Black. Better yet, leave a message. I'll call you when I can speak freely."

My stomach rolled. "You're a lawyer. Why would you help *me*?"

"There's this thing we have in this country?" she said, up-talking the heck out of her sentence. "It's called justice? We only achieve it when we're at our best?"

People never fail to amaze me. "A good lawyer would stand by her family."

"I know," she laughed, biting her bottom lip. I was starting to find her attractive. "What's that tell you?"

❧ 24 ❧

MUD MAN

In the city, Walt Kenning lived on Lispenard Street in a renovated warehouse with green pebbled windows on the ground floor and columns of yellowed limestone. Outside, the old bricks had been sand-blasted and repointed, leaving them with a dusty look, as if dipped recently in flour. Condos were pricy in TriBeCa, but it was still a neighborhood in transition. Supermarkets were scarce, and you had to walk north several blocks to find the wine and cheese you needed for your weekend hangouts with friends. Walt's place fit the bill: lots of rugs and pillows, a bed, a couple of parson tables, plenty of white light, and big leafy plants in wicker baskets. Maybe he thought they lent the space a tropical air. Memories of the Miami he left behind in his youth.

I placed the brown shopping bag on his coffee table and carefully withdrew the object inside it. On my cab ride downtown, I had been unable to resist tearing off the wrappings.

I carefully spread the tissue paper now, revealing one of Carla Crowell's figurines. It was an ancient Chinese wise man, complete with Fu Manchu beard and moustache. He wore a wide, straw Coolie hat, long flowing robes, and carried a walking staff.

He stood about seven inches high and was coated all over with a thick, milky glaze. His face and hands were less shiny, the color of clay. He stared at me through tiny thin eyes.

"What happened to your face? Why are you wrapped up like that?"

"Head injury," I quipped. "From my days in the war." I pointed at the thing. "What can you tell me about him?"

"Ugly little bastard, isn't he?" Walter said.

"People pay you for appraisals like that?"

It was after dark. I'd caught him coming from the gym, dressed in sweats and smelling of Old Spice. He leaned his back on his bolster and gently examined the bottom of the statue. He shook it gently.

"I tried that," I said. "Empty. What is he?"

"That part's simple. He's a mud man. They used to make them in China from the turn of the century until a little after the second World War. They were made on the cheap, out of clay, but every piece was handmade. What happened was, we imported them, used them as complimentary gifts. Flower shops used them a lot. You'd go buy a plant and find one of these suckers sitting in the dirt. Some people saved them, turned the bigger ones into lamps or whatever, but I'll bet a lot of people broke them and tossed them out with the pot when the plant died."

"Lord, what fools these mortals be."

"You bet. Today the vintage handmade ones are worth a hundred, hundred fifty, more if they're in better condition. This guy's pretty tall. I've seen tons no bigger than an inch or two in height."

I was trying to get comfortable on the floor of his couchless apartment, but even with two pillows it wasn't working. My stitched head throbbed. My legs were stretched out straight in front of me, the bad one stiff as a plank. "This guy worth that much?"

He smiled awkwardly. "It's not vintage."

"A fake?"

"Not exactly. It's a little more interesting than that. This guy would probably fetch you much, much more. Five hundred, easy, more if you went about it correctly. But you'd have to have the certificate of authenticity."

"So the fake is worth more than the real thing? Why's that?"

"You mind telling me where you got it?"

I was not yet willing to tell all. "Finish what you were saying."

He tipped the thing and rubbed a finger under the base of the statue. He cracked a smile. "You see the letters under here?"

He was pointing to something that looked like a pair of letters stamped into the clay, enclosed by a square with rounded edges.

"Yeah. I assumed it was Chinese characters."

He threw back his recently showered head and had a good laugh. "You're hilarious! It's not Chinese—it's the artist's mark. The letters say C.S. That stands for *Carla Schroute*. I know her only by reputation. Schroute's her maiden name."

My mind flashed back to that moment at the funeral after-party when Mrs. Crowell chastised DiGaetano for strong-arming me. Everyone called him Nicky. *She* called him Nicolo. Perfect accent, too. In the words of Nicky himself, they were *paisans*. I didn't know exactly how, but I bet if Rawlsy and I did some digging, we'd find that she and he had crossed paths ages ago. There was some old neighborhood in their past that they had both tried their darnedest to erase.

Walt was still talking. "If you go up to Fifty-Seventh Street, you'll find a gallery up there that carries a ton of her stuff. Huge mail-order business. Ads in women's magazines all over the country. Some idiots would buy *anything* she makes, even this piece of crap."

In my mind I recalled her hands as she smoked her cigarette. The skin of her fingers was rough and grayish, the quick under her nails permanently stained the color of clay.

Walt looked concerned. "Do you ... do you know her?"

I didn't want to explain, so I just shook my head no.

"Well, whatever," Walt said. "Congratulations, pal. You're the proud owner of a Carla original. Not that you should have known this, but the dead giveaway is the face." He rotated the man toward me. He pointed at its cheeks. "You see how goofy and happy he is?"

Yes—he wore an adorable smile. His eyes practically twinkling.

"They all have that same baby face, which you don't find in the original pieces. The vintage ones had a lot more personality. Serious. Whimsical. They almost reflected the personalities of the individual artists who made them. Carla's are just ... oh, I dunno ... commercial and so very obviously Americanized."

As he wrapped up his sentence, I thought I felt a cold blast of arrogance. Either it was his standard art major pose, professional jealousy, or a long-cultivated disdain for anything that wasn't a "true" antique. He set the statue down on his parquet floor and rose, his long limbs folding upward like the legs of an ironing board. "Coffee? Something for the head?"

"Just water," I growled, grabbing the darn thing.

Walt padded off across his Navajo rugs to the kitchenette. I didn't move. I think I could have crushed the mud man in my hands. I pictured Carla sitting there, cool as a gin and tonic, smoking away. "Do you like art, young man? You can have any of these," she had said.

What an unpleasant person.

But what had happened? I said no, wound up with seven stitches, and ended up being a handed one of those pieces by her daughter. Either way, it was the same damn bribe. Deb Crowell had wanted me to believe she was fighting the good fight, but the whole time she was just executing her mother's wishes.

I felt anger rising inside me. My face getting hot. I don't know what came over me. I swatted the figure and sent it sprawling to the floor. When I went to pick it up, I noticed deep gashes on the figure's face. I looked at my fingers. There was a kind of sandy goop under my fingernails. I raised the fingers to my nose and sniffed.

I smelled a faint scent of cinnamon and wax. *Candle* wax.

Kenning returned with coffee and a bottle of Perrier. He saw me rubbing my hands back and forth over the surface of the mud man. He set down my water. His eyes asked the question.

"I don't get it," I said. "His face is wax, his hands are wax, but the rest of him is pottery."

"That's not possible. She works in clay. The whole point is she's trying to appropriate the look of the originals."

"I'm telling you the truth. Look."

He took it from me and poised a single fingernail right over the little man's face. I could tell he was hesitant to damage it. He was, after all, an art lover. His every instinct was to preserve art. But he got over it. Steeled himself and dug his fingernail into the statue's face. A chunk of light brown wax peeled off, exposing hard, fired clay underneath. His eyes narrowed in thought, reminding me of Bea.

"Incredible!" he shouted.

"You see?"

"Here, hold him," he said, thrusting the object in my lap and running back to the kitchen. Drawers slammed. Two minutes later he was back with a candle, a box of matches, and a wad of paper towels. "Maybe I've underestimated her work," he said, dropping to his knees again. "It's possible she's doing something much more profound than I've given her credit for."

He lit the candle and beckoned me to bring the statue closer. "Keep it over the flame," he told me.

I did as he said. Held the mud man's hands in the fire first and watched as the layer of wax dripped away and trickled onto the paper towels. Then I moved the statue down until the man's darling face hovered over the fire. The wax darkened and spat. Hot, gooey brown teardrops spattered onto the paper.

"Keep going," he said.

"His hat's in the way!"

"So? Get under the hat, his hair, everything. Don't burn your-self. Watch the towel. Don't set the place on fire."

I saw the statue's real face now—hard, brown, and unglazed—colored with streaks of scented brown wax. I twirled the statue around, letting the flame reach into the crevice where his head met the Coolie hat. The wax bubbled and hissed and dribbled like mad. We'd struck gold.

"Go ahead," Walt said. "It's probably soft enough now."

"What, his head?"

"The hat, Dante, the *hat*."

"Ouch!"

"Hot?"

"Yeah."

I pulled out my handkerchief, threw it over the head and twisted. Something gave. I put more pressure behind it and the ceramic hat popped off like the lid of a cookie jar. I gave Walt the hat and took the statue. The little man looked like the victim of a bad lobotomy. The top of his head was gone, caked with brown wax. In his head was a hole that ran down the length of his body, as wide and deep as a cigar tube.

Walt was rambling excitedly about how certain Egyptian pieces were relatively similar, except that the secret compartment in the figurine or statue had a door ...

Like I cared.

I poked my finger in and extracted a piece of blue-trimmed cream stationery, tightly rolled. I spread it out on my thigh. A corner of it was brown and charred. Deb said she'd *rescued* it. Her exact words had been, "She got rid of the photos before I could get to them, but I saved the rest."

I handed the now-empty statue back to Walt, who stuck his nose in the hole and fit the statue's hat on and off, just to see how it worked. "Amazing. Never seen anything like it ... I mean *why?* Some pieces have a recess for jewelry, extra cash, but they're big. Why would she need these little holes? Gems, maybe. That's a possibility, or diamonds."

"Walt, shut up." He didn't.

I was holding a piece of stationery and a note written in a man's hand. I rubbed my eyes and read:

A surprise, right? I admit they're a little dark, but you of all people will recognize the virile Crowell features. And you know about the girl. If you don't, Tony has some explaining to do. The deal: Deliver $100K in cash to the above address on Thurs. 1 Jan. at noon. You'll receive everything then. This is a one-time offer. Try nothing. I have taken precautions.

Till then, I Remain Yours.

The note was unsigned, but the name printed at the top of the document was M. Barski Antiques, with the address of his shop on Fourth Avenue.

"What's wrong? Your face looks funny."

I gulped the Perrier in one long chug. I pulled myself up to my feet, and got my stiff leg moving again. Walt looked up at me.

"Tell me again. How long did you know Milo?" I said.

"Long enough, why?"

"And you thought he was a pretty good guy, didn't you?"

His face twitched. "Dante, what's wrong?" His body tensed. "What are you saying?"

"A good guy, you thought. A little quirky, maybe, but basically decent."

"Yeahhhh?" he said, his voice rising cautiously. "He was kind to me. Very bright. A little eccentric, sure. But in all, a nice guy."

I went around the loft, gathering my jacket and hat and coat, then stopped to retrieve the mud man. I stuffed his little hat in my coat pocket.

"That's bull, Walt. Milo was a snake. And none of us saw it."

"What brought this on? What … what did you find?"

I steered my way to the door. "Thanks for the water."

I looked back and saw him sitting barefooted in his specs and his sweats. I knew he had a weird little relationship with the dead man who had sent us all down this path days ago. Milo was educated, sophisticated in ways Walter Kenning's limo-business dad had never been.

Walter looked up to Milo. Looked *up* to the blackmailer and extortionist.

Do I burst his bubble, or don't I?

"Dude, don't leave me hanging like this," he said. "I helped you out and now I don't get to see what it's all about?"

I tucked the statue under my arm and said goodbye. "I'm sorry. Not right now. Soon."

❧ 25 ❧

THEORETICALLY SPEAKING

"Dear boy, wake up."

"Go away. I'm dying."

She shook me again. My head throbbed. My bum leg was numb. I hadn't rested well in two days and now she wanted me up. Face down on her leather couch, I groaned and opened one eye wide enough to read my watch. It said 9:00 p.m.

I wanted to kill her. I'd slept little more than an hour. I pressed myself upright and focused on the apparition in front of me. My Aunt Beatrice loomed over the couch dressed in knee-high black boots, a capacious pair of jodhpurs, a voluminous white blouse, and a brown leather jacket the size of Michigan's Upper Peninsula.

"Look," I said. "If I have to get off this couch to throttle you, I will. Then I'm going back to sleep. They can wake me when they cart your carcass away."

"Go ahead," she said. "Make fun of your aunt."

"I told you everything. *Everything*. I followed your instructions to the letter."

"I know you did. And that's why we are going to Long Island."

I struggled to my elbows. "Can't we go in the morning?"

"No. By then the cretin will definitely be back. Please get up."

"I can't. My head's killing me. I'm exhausted. I'm in no shape to be driving in *that*." I jabbed a thumb at the window and the flurries beyond.

"You needn't trouble yourself. I've taken the liberty of phoning Mr. Rawls. He's brought over one of the agency's vehicles. It's waiting at the curb downstairs."

"I'm not driving," I said.

She threw her arms wide, indicating her sartorial splendor. She pulled on her furry hat with the ear flaps and flung an end of her crimson scarf around her neck. "Isn't it obvious that I'm driving?"

Funny how that made me worry.

"Is that the reason for the get-up? And all this time I thought you were on the trail of the Red Baron."

She plucked one of her heavy walking sticks from the brass canister by the door. Black steel, with the white head of a snarling dog. Or wolf. Or camel. I couldn't tell which.

"Did I mention the car is parked illegally?" she said.

She drove like a monk on crack. Steered the wheel sparingly, braked haltingly. Fiddled constantly with the radio to tune in a classical music station while her right hand roved through a package of anisette sponge cookies on the seat beside her. True, she didn't wrap Emory Bray's brand-new maroon Crown Victoria around a tree, as I'd done with the Mustang that had ended my police career before it got started. But she ignored every other cardinal rule of driving.

"Chief Welty called while you slept. I gather news of Mr. Crowell's death has jarred some people's memories. They found the driver of the car that picked up Alison Munro."

"The little sports car?" I said, almost without thinking. "The MG?"

She chewed her anisette sponge. "Correct. New York license plate *BUCKY*. Bucky is apparently a cosmetic dentist from Staten

Island, you may care to know. He and his family summer in Mastic. Two years ago, he and his wife strolled down the block to attend a Labor Day party, leaving their teenaged son at their rental home. Promptly after their departure, the youth went for a joyride in his sire's vehicle ... Stop shaking your head. It's all quite true. The boy admitted it. He picked up Alison in the inn's parking lot and drove her back to the party and left her there. *Alive*."

"How old is he?"

"Eighteen now. Sixteen when it happened. We needn't speculate on his reasons for keeping silent. Thank goodness we can still rely on the melodramatic idealism of teenagers. His conscience racked, he has signed a statement against the advice of his family lawyer."

"Figures. So why are we rushing there?"

She waved her bitten cookie at me. "Trouble, as I say. Welty has apparently been trying to reach you to review these matters, but you've been unreachable. I told him you'd been on the road. When he asked if you had uncovered some information pertinent to the Munro death, I said that I was not at liberty to disclose that—"

I leaned forward and tugged at my hair. "You are impossible. Can't you just keep your big yap shut? You're *not* a cop, you're *not* an investigator. These guys don't like being upstaged by ... by ..."

"By a woman?"

"... a bookseller," I finished.

"No matter," she glowered. "Well, after that I was subjected to a stream of threats. If we don't settle this disaster tonight, his suspicions will no doubt reach fever pitch and he will quite probably arrest the boy by morning and clap me in irons."

"Won't *that* ruin your day," I said sarcastically. "Hey, how about this? We tell him the truth. Crowell offed the girl. End of story. We give him Barski's letter and call it quits. But that evidence has to be shared with Lieutenant Posluszny as well."

She was already shaking her head. "No. I don't care to release details prematurely. The case—or cases—are far from solved. Can you tell me how Mr. Crowell 'offed' this girl? Can you provide the specifics, hmm?"

"That's Welty's job. It's about time we all got back to basics. I'm only being paid to find a rare book and solve Crowell's murder. Solving Barski's would be nice, but right now I don't care enough about the man to lift a finger in that direction. I hardly care about Tony."

"I cannot do that."

"You mean your damned pride won't let you."

She tapped the brakes gently and we slid slightly on a patch of snow. I swore and shoved my hand out to keep from slamming into the dash. She blasted the horn and barked at the car in front of her. When she composed herself and we were zipping along the expressway nicely, she looked at me, flustered, and said, "You are so clever, dear nephew. Tell me: Why do you suppose Milo was at the house that night?"

"I don't know, was he? Everyone keeps talking about photographs. Milo alludes to them in that letter, but where are they? The cops would have found them if they were in his shop or his apartment. I think the whole thing's a hoax. I'm not even sure you can take photos in the dark that would be good enough to blackmail someone with."

"Wrong," she sang, reaching for a cookie. "Milo was a practiced hand in this sort of thing. We saw evidence of this in his apartment. Newspaper feature pics of adolescents kissing in a darkened movie theater. Hanging out in front of a Los Angeles malt shop at night? How did he manage those, with a flashcube?"

"Put the wipers on. You're killing me."

"Let us continue. What was Milo doing at that party? Is it likely that he was invited?"

"He wasn't. No one's mentioned him being there. He wasn't part of the inner circle. He was just some guy Crowell exploited and stiffed. And if I may be permitted to be unkind, he wasn't cool enough, hip enough, young enough to be in that crowd."

"You're doing quite nicely so far, Dante. Don't give up. Next, if Milo had his camera case with him, he brought it out to Long Island to use it. Did he know there would be a murder? Preposterous. Did they invite him there? As you point out, unlikely. What is the only reason for him to be there?"

I puffed out my cheeks. It came to me on the exhale. "DiGaetano?"

My aunt took the exit and rolled into downtown Rockport. The snowplows were out in force. Their headlights tracked beams of light down the little Main Street. Bea hung a right and headed in the direction of the beach.

"I think it's plausible," she said. "Our social-climbing cretin invites him to photograph some of his pieces and mentions matter-of-factly that his sometimes 'nephew,' the one for whom Milo did freelance work, is having a party up the road. Milo hears this. He is intrigued. Why?"

My conversation with Luzetta, Zephyr's ex-business manager, popped into mind. "Because Tony owed him money and was avoiding his calls."

"Correct. *Money*. The only thing Milo would fight for."

It worked for me. Kinda. Barski wraps with DiGaetano at the club and marina. It's late. He's itching to get back to the city. But he can't resist swinging by the Crowell house. All he wants is a peek. Maybe he stops at one of the trendy fish shacks for a drink and a bite, mulling over his options, stoking his anger. Maybe he gets a few drinks in him and thinks he can take on the world. He drives to the house, intending to barge his way in. To Have Words with Crowell. It's his dumb luck to arrive just as Alison Munro returns.

"Are we thinking he starts snooping?" I said. "Gets out of the car and walks along the beach, using his camera to spy in the windows?"

I squinted into the darkness on the other side of the windshield. The east side of town had not been plowed as recently as Main Street. Our headlights revealed powdery clumps in our path.

"Slow down," I said. "You'll kill us."

"I don't care for your negativity," Bea said and proceeded to drive the car straight into a snowbank.

"The car," she said. "It won't move."

We were right at the entrance of the parking lot where I'd gotten my lovely orange citation. The plows hadn't bothered clearing the lot yet, because who but an insane person would need to park at a beach in the middle of a snowstorm?

She dropped it into second and hit the gas.

"You don't want to do that!"

She gunned it. The wheels spun, going nowhere. She tried edging in, then backing out. Nothing doing. Then she calmed herself by eating a cookie and tried backing up again. If we had a mule in the backseat, the beast would have kicked her out of spite.

After a bit, she announced glumly, "We are stuck."

"Are you sure? Better try again."

"Sarcasm is unhelpful at this juncture. Maybe if you go push?"

"After you dug us in nice and good? No dice. We need a tow."

She ignored me. She shut off the ignition, opened her door, and stepped out into the blustering snow. She opened the back door and took out two huge nine-volt flash lamps. She yanked her crazy furry hat down. "Get out. We'll walk."

❧ 26 ❧

ALIBI SHATTERED

Here's a piece of advice I can offer with utter sincerity. Never go to the beach in January, especially at night. Only an idiot would do such a thing. Only a bigger idiot would follow her. I followed my idiot through the snow to the scene of Crowell's big party two years ago. I felt delirious. My head was hot and pounding, my clothes were three days old and filthy, my fingers were ice. The breath of the sea rose and whipped along the snow, sending grains of sand and snowflakes into my face. My aunt marched along obliviously, planting her walking stick in the ground with every step, and flashing her lamp to illuminate the way.

She stopped when she got up to the boardwalk where Rudy had accosted us last time. She braced herself against the wooden railing and turned to me.

"I know you're in a mood, but do you at least want to know how the girl died?" she said. "If I tell you, can you picture it?"

"Sure."

"Who was calling the shots at the party all night? Who, for example, would have instructed Mr. Nilsson to step away from the front door? To stop waiting for Ms. Munro?"

That was easy. "Crowell."

"They were both at the door, but let us imagine Tony sees the cosmetic dentist's sports car pull up and shuts it before Van can see Ms. Munro step out of it. Earlier that night, she had the effrontery to attack him verbally and physically. You know what does to him … you saw him the day we visited the studio. He struck Miss Starr."

"Right. He's got a short fuse and he decides to settle his argument with Alison in private. So … what happens next?"

She pointed to the side of the house. Raising her lantern as if it could help dispel the darkness. I saw steel railings and the faintest suggestion of a pool and the flicker of our lanterns in the sheet glass windows.

Snow drifted past her face. "The police had already come once to break up the party. They all moved inside. Remember what Chief Welty said? Mr. Crowell instructed his guests to draw the curtains, thinking they'd deaden the sound and keep the police from visiting them again. It didn't work, but now we've got a houseful of people unable to see anything happening outside. I venture to say they could hear nothing either, over the sound of the music. Ms. Munro returns. The two of them have words. She *or he* decides to go upstairs to their bedroom. I propose that they didn't enter the house to do this. Indeed, they didn't have to. The exterior spiral staircase is more than picturesque—it allows one to ascend to the second level terrace without being seen by the occupants of the house." She lifted her lamp in vain. I raised mine as well, but it was of little use. It was hard to see. "This is ridiculous. We should go closer. Dante, I'll need a hand." She turned and marched farther up the boardwalk.

"It's cold, Bea. Wrap it up. Are you saying something happened *here*, on the premises?"

"That's exactly what I'm suggesting. She was struck and fell. Two stories down. Right off that point there—on the south side of the house. There are no doors on that side of the house. And nothing on the ground level but a window into the powder room. We peeked into it the day we were here. So not even the caterers would have heard her fall, not over the music. Ms. Munro was murdered here, Dante. I'm sure of it. She was brutally shoved over by her lover, who had the misfortune of being photographed in the act by Milo Barski, who, I speculate was either standing right where I am"—she indicated the camera angle by aiming her walking stick through the trees at the second-floor terrace—"or just inside the front gate. He snapped his photos, then bolted. And Mr. Crowell returned to the party unaware that his brutal actions had been captured on film."

"But … he had an alibi for the whole night! He never left the party. He spent the whole night with Rosita, if you remember."

She sighed deeply. Sometimes I think she is appalled at the ratiocinative skills of us mere mortals. "Dante, my boy, *never left the party* is quite different than saying he was gone for a *few minutes*. He stepped out for a smoke. Simple as that. And in those few minutes, a young woman's life was snuffed out, and a family devastated."

"But they found her miles from here!"

She waved a hand dismissively. "So? The body was moved. That was obvious from the beginning, wasn't it? The side of her head was marked by moss or mildew. But such things don't grow on a beach. But"—her stick rose again in the darkness, pointing lower—"the south side of the house is afflicted with mildew. We saw it the day Rudy abducted us. The vegetation and humidity would have been thicker on this side two years ago, before the contractors culled some of the trees. Mr. Crowell would have rested easy, knowing it was highly unlikely that anyone would find her until the next phase of his plan could take place."

I beat my shoulders with my hands. "How did she move?" I said. "If it wasn't Tony, who? You think a fleet of horseshoe crabs carried her back?"

She opened her mouth to speak.

But by then she must have felt the muzzle of the gun pressed to her temple.

"Just shut up, lady. Shut up! I could hear you blabbing for miles and miles away."

"Hey there, Rudy," I called to him. "Is that really necessary?"

"Shut up! Get up here," he said. "You go first. Straight up the walkway to the Jeep. Same as last time."

"My dear boy ..." Bea started to say.

He tugged her harder and mashed the gun to her face. "Shut it! Move, Sleet!"

I moved, slipping past them and ahead. The walkway was dark but I could see the headlights of the Jeep up ahead. My heart was racing. I could run, taking the chance that he'd lose me in the darkness. If I raced away in the Jeep, I could summon Welty or his men. But that left Bea in the hands of a dangerous idiot. No, I had no choice. I had to play it his way.

He read my mind the way predators sense your fear. "Nothing funny, Sleet," he said gruffly. "You drive. I'm hanging out in the back with Grandma."

Behind me, I heard the thunk of their footfalls and the clink of her stick on the boardwalk. "I'm his aunt," Bea said, "and I'm hardly of advanced age, young man!"

"Why do you always have to talk, lady?"

"It's what she does," I said, sliding into the driver's seat.

27

ONLY TWO

DiGaetano sipped a dainty demitasse cup of black coffee, only inches from where a bottle of Sambuca Romana stood on his desk. He asked if we wanted any. I declined for both of us. My aunt slid into the larger of the two chairs set up in front of the big man's desk and leaned on her stick. I sat and checked my bandage. It was still tight, but darn wet. I shook my hat, sending chunks of melting snow to the carpet.

DiGaetano sipped his coffee with an extended pinkie. "He clean?"

"I checked him," Rudy said, straightening his tie. Under the camel-colored coat, he wore an Armani suit, double-breasted, a black shirt and tie. Every stitch shone. He went to the bar and poured himself a drink, then plopped into a chair by the French doors that overlooked the terrace and marina. The gun dangled from his hand.

"Careful with the hard stuff," DiGaetano said.

"Go to hell."

DiGaetano finished his coffee and watched us carefully. "Don't feel so good, huh, Sleet? See what happens when you persist with empty endeavors? Got yourself a bunch of stitches in the head. Almost gave me a black eye today. And to top it off, know what I found on my desk when I got back tonight? Wanna guess?"

He waved a folded official-looking document. "Stop work order. They pulled my building permit and shut me down. Pending ... things. That's all your doing. You and the broad."

"Appalling word," Bea said. "With an equally unpleasant etymology. *Broad* once referred to a man's meal ticket. Specifically a pimp's. By its use you are classifying all women as prostitutes, which is ironical since your existence on this shore depended wholly on the Crowell family. They were *your* meal ticket initially, and later, once you got yourself established, you were Tony Crowell's."

Nick held up an index finger. "Shut it, lady. I'm trying to be nice. But you know what? I'm *sick* of being nice, extending courtesies that are not returned."

"I surmise that two years ago Mr. Crowell made a late-night phone call from his home," Bea said. "The police didn't find a record of it, so it had to be a local call. I believe his call rang *that* phone on your desk. Tony may have been frightened. Frantic. Desperately trying to put on a brave face. He had only hours before the sun came up and revealed his crime. In such a position, who might he call? His unsympathetic mother? His jaded sister? Attorneys? Unlikely. He knew only one man who would not balk at getting rid of a young woman's body. As you are hardly a fine physical specimen of a man—"

"Hey, watch it!"

"... you sent Rudy to take care of the mess. You didn't have to trouble yourself with her vehicle. She'd already left it behind, further deepening the mystery of her last hours. Come morning, I can imagine that Rudy was pressed into service again. All he would have needed to do was power-wash that side of the house. You'd have the necessary equipment here at the marina and club.

Moss and mildew are a nuisance on marina walkways. By the time the police arrived asking questions, the crime scene was spotless and dry. The rest is merely icing. Milo Barski saw the whole thing and had photographs. He needed money badly and for all we know he may have blackmailed Tony for two years before approaching Mrs. Crowell for the final score."

"Bull!" DiGaetano said. "Tony would have come to me. He wouldn't have played a patsy to some blackmailer."

My aunt's lips pursed. She gave a slight shake of the head. Like she wasn't buying it. "He was used to shelling out what is known as *payola*, so it's possible he did pay. And he was probably a little afraid to bring you back into it. This may be hard to hear, Mr. DiGaetano, but weak individuals are apt to perceive you as a terrifying figure."

"I don't scare you, lady?"

"I said weak individuals. I myself am not. I find you repulsive and predictable. You do not even have the saving grace of eccentricity to redeem you. I pity the police and district attorney who will have to suffer you through your trial and long imprisonment. Now, are we quite finished?"

DiGaetano shot a look at me. "What did she just say? What was all that?"

I wasn't in the mood to help him. If he had a dictionary on those shelves of his, I would have tossed it on his desk so he could look up some of the words Bea had just used. But we had bigger problems to deal with. We were alone with two psychopaths in the middle of the night.

DiGaetano's mustache wiggled on his lip. Serious thought going on here. He blotted his lips with a cloth napkin, then drummed his manicured nails on the desk. They were pink and shiny, as square as a row of garden spades. He looked over his shoulder at Rudy. "We're going to need the boat," he said. "It's got to be done properly this time."

The kid nodded, his mouth wide open.

"Swell, Rudy," I said. "And when you get back from your disturbing night-time errand, Nick here will have the cops waiting to collect you. 'Oh, Officers, I don't know what got into him. He shot up all these people. He's been acting a little strange lately. Always did like playing with dangerous weapons.'"

"What're you talking about?" Nick said. "You stupid?"

"It's the truth, isn't it?" I continued. "Tony's dead. Barski's dead. After us, the only ones who know what happened that night are you and Rudy. You can pin it on Rudy or he pins it on you, and right now he's the only one I see with a gun around here."

"That's bull. The kid knows he's got a good thing going here. Huh, Rudy?"

Rudy was quiet. His eyes went from me to Nick to Aunt Bea. He might have been thinking, but a feat that insignificant probably wouldn't register on his face. Nick came around the desk to his seat and opened the top right drawer.

"Tell you what, Rudy. Go get the boat. I'll finish up with them." He peered into the drawer. His face went white. "Hey," he said. "Where is it?"

"Right here."

We looked. Rudy was holding a tiny blue .32-caliber revolver. He aimed it at DiGaetano and squeezed it off three times, hitting him in the chest and neck. The Commodore slumped back in his chair and slid, his toupee crawling down his forehead.

The door behind us popped open almost immediately. It was two cleaning ladies, their faces curious at first but instantly horrified. Rudy threw the H&R revolver on the desk and swung his automatic at them.

I jumped two feet and grabbed him by the wrist, slammed my right fist once into his cheek, then his neck. He got off one shot to the ceiling, then whirled me around, using his gun hand as a pivot. I grabbed his blazer and took him with me. Together we smashed through the French doors, four hundred fifty pounds of protoplasm shattering them into splinters of wood and glass.

We landed on the slate patio, and there I thought I had him, but he stopped himself from falling and yanked hard to free his wrist. I held on. I battered him with my right, and felt my shoulder warming up just as I threw another punch. I heard a crunch and his nose melted away, showering us with blood. He shrieked and froze for a second, and that's when I shook his wrist and sent the gun sailing over the gray railing. It skittered and spun across frozen snow and sand.

Rage filled him. He wrenched his right arm free and went for my neck. He shook me hard and sent a blood-soaked fist in my stomach, and shoved me against the railing. I hit the steel hard, felt my scalp stitches rip. He kicked me once in the ribs and left me there.

I wrenched the bandages off my head. He was on the other side of the railing, pawing through the snow.

A voice came out of the shadows. "Stop it! Stop it this instant. Don't move."

We both squinted into the night. The motion lights affixed to the exterior fascia of DiGaetano's office had flipped on, but the beams only went a few feet. Somewhere out there was the water and the marina, and heaven knows what else.

"Bea?" I said.

No answer.

Rudy's hand went for the gun. The air whistled. Then came a vicious crunch. Rudy yelped and coiled his arm to his chest. Something long, thin, and black whipped across his jaw and sent him sprawling into the snow.

I climbed over the railing and ran to where he rocked in pain.

My aunt stepped out of the shadows and kicked the gun away. By the time I reached her, she had the tip of her walking stick pressed to his throat. Not that he was giving her any trouble, mind you. He was weeping like a baby, cradling his gun hand with his other.

"You broke my wrist, lady!"

"Of course I did, you ignoramus. You moved."

❧ 28 ❧

HARSH TRUTHS

F riday I woke to find a dark-haired angel hovering near my bed. Leena Munro wore a rabbit-fur jacket like the one her sister had owned, tight white stretch pants, legwarmers, and a green-and-white striped sweater. Hanging from her left ear was the Eiffel Tower in white plastic.

The one window in my bedroom hovel revealed a gray morning with flurries cascading gently past the brick wall next door.

"You *have* to stop doing this," I said. "I could have killed you out of fear alone."

"Not the way you were sleeping," she said.

"You laugh. But my karate chop is a lethal weapon. The slightest scare, and it springs into action out of sheer instinct. Did Trey let you in again?"

She jingled a set of keys. They were attached to a heavy pewter charm in the shape of Michelangelo's *David* that I knew all too well. "Your aunt said you might be sleeping in."

"I like how she gives my spare keys to strangers."

She gazed at me with mock horror. "I'm a stranger now?"

"You know what I mean. This is Manhattan, lady, not

Mayberry. Besides, I could have been *very* indisposed. People don't appreciate the fact that I have a *very* active love life."

Her eyebrows arched in disbelief. "My words exactly, Casanova," she said with a chuckle. "But Aunt Bea said that was *highly* unlikely. I'm supposed to tell you she needs you. Your face looks like crap, by the way. Are you okay?"

We'd had a miserable night and a long throbbing ride home only hours before dawn. I had hoped my head and face would be better by morning, but I was so swollen that I felt as if I'd grown a second head instead.

"It sounds like there's real official business to discuss," she went on. "Some dude named Mr. *Rawls* was stopping by the shop?"

"If it's Rawlsy, it *is* official," I said. "Unless it's close to happy hour."

"I was kind of hoping we could speak privately first. Is it true what they're saying? They might know how my sister died? The news on the radio and in the papers is real weird."

"We can talk," I assured her. "In fact, we should."

"There's a lot of innuendo, but no specifics."

"It can get like that," I said. "Might be that way for a while."

She leaned forward, her eyes moist. She had the kind of warm, joyful eyes that should never be asked to cry. "So much stuff is happening. My parents are not real good at grokking the details. Dante, I need to understand it before they freak."

I felt for her, I really did. Our late-night adventures on Long Island had been exhausting yet disturbingly fruitful. Through sheer stupidity and a little brain power on Bea's part, we had forced a break in the case. It was tempting to think that we were mere inches from solving the Barski-Crowell murders, but midnight hope often died in the light of day. I needed to think. That meant coffee. Probably eggs. Ham, or possibly bacon. And before that, a scalding shower and a careful inspection of the wounds I'd suffered at the hands of a gun-toting man-child.

"What time is it?" I said, almost afraid to look at my alarm clock.

She told me. I yelped and ran for the shower, my ribs smarting.

Thirty-six minutes later we were tucked into a booth at the soup and burger joint across from Astor Place. The gum-snapping waitress in the pink leather pants set down my second coffee, my first breakfast, and Leena's banana shake. My mouth disappeared into my Greek omelet and the accompanying mound of steaming home-fried potatoes. Leena fiddled with the volume on the mini-jukebox that was high-piping the Bangles.

"By the way," I said. "I feel I should point out that your hair is green."

She ran her hand through it, the Eiffel Tower shaking as she tilted her head to the side. "Sure. It matches the outfit. Aunt Bea said it was outrè."

"She would."

The story she told me was the kind cops heard a million times. Her parents had always suspected foul play in her sister's death. The prospect of closure was tantalizing, but the resurgence of media coverage tore open old wounds and exposed fresh ones. For two years they had lived without details. Now details were close; they were terrified to hear them, but they craved them nonetheless. Unfortunately, at the moment it felt as if the press knew only half the story.

Indeed, the news was sparse. Rudy Vranin had been arrested for DiGaetano's murder. The press reported that the young man was cooperating with police, and had already confessed to being a party to the death, by arson, of one Mrs. Gertrude Hallquist—the very blaze that had allowed DiGaetano to acquire property on the shore in the first place. Chief Welty and the district attorney believed that their suspect was also implicated in the death of Alison Munro two years earlier.

But none of the reporters knew what I did. They didn't know

that since Christmas Milo Barski had become frantic about raising cash for his fiancée's care. They didn't know that the poor fool blackmailed Mrs. Crowell for a hundred grand to keep silent about the truth of her son's involvement in Alison's death. Barski had carefully prepared two book safes to hold the cash he expected to realize from the Zephyr affair—*The Winds of War* and *Gone with the Wind*.

But those books had remained empty for another reason the reporters did not know. Mrs. C. had asked her dear friend Nicolo to look into the matter. Last Thursday DiGaetano and Rudy had paid Barski a visit in his shop and had worked him over, breaking his nose. The reporters didn't know that these two knuckleheads had forced Barski at gunpoint to hand over negatives, plus any other records he may have had of the DiGaetano-Crowell antique collections, thus eradicating any link between himself and those two families. Barski's copy of *Gone with the Wind* had probably held the negatives, and been nearly destroyed in the process. The press didn't know that after that visit, Barski had become desperate to skip town.

So yeah—you can't always trust what you read in the papers. At least, not right away. The reporters didn't know any of the stuff I told Leena as she bravely fought back tears over her milkshake.

And to that long list, I should note that the reporters also didn't know that attorneys for Mrs. Crowell had paid Rudy Vranin a visit in the hospital late last night. They'd stayed with him an hour, leaving only when he started shouting for the district attorney and wisely demanding his own counsel.

"So it's all going to come out," I said as Leena blew her nose into a paper napkin. "It just won't happen right away. You have to prepare yourself for that. Right now all they have is a young punk who's pointing a finger at a lot of rich people. The Crowell attorneys are going to make it look like he's doing it to save his own skin. Rudy admits he moved your sister's body, but denies having anything to do with Tony's or Milo's death. I believe him, but he's still going to look like a finger-pointer until Welty and his team get the proof they need to satisfy the DA."

"But the proof is gone," she said. "You said so yourself. If Barski gave them the negatives, we'll never know."

"Bea has a theory on that. Photographers can shoot an awful lot of film in a few minutes. Most likely he had more than one camera loaded with film and ready to go."

"You think he set aside some photos that he didn't give to these thugs?"

"It would have taken superhuman willpower and craftiness, but Barski was just that way. He may have reserved some for his own protection, should Mrs. Crowell and her friends ever come back to haunt him. But then he got the idea to sell the extras to your father before he skipped town. By then, he must have hated the Crowells so badly that he wanted them to burn. He just didn't want to be the one to hand the photos over to the authorities."

"Is my father in big trouble?"

I shook my head. "No one knows he was ever approached," I said. "And they never will."

"But it's true, then?" Her eyes started again. She reached for the napkin holder. "Tony killed her? That's for real?"

"Yes," I said. "That's what Rudy said, and what Nick appeared to confirm before he died. The cops will go back to everyone who was at that party and try to jog their memories. Someone is bound to remember that Tony stepped out, and that he later made a phone call from inside the house. There's also a possibility they can compel Tony's sister Debbie to tell what she knows. There's no love lost between her and mom. But that's all in the future. To answer your question, I have no qualms saying yes, it's true. Tony Crowell killed your sister."

It didn't seem right to eat while she sobbed, so I sacrificed the remains of my meal and waited. After a bit, I reached across the table and held her hand. She shook it awkwardly, but with gratitude. As she dried her eyes, she told me that she was going to move to her own place in the spring. After much badgering, her mother had agreed to act as a cosigner on a rental lease for an apartment she was thinking of getting with a few other girls in the East Village.

"I can't stay in that house any more," she said. "It's not that I don't love them. I *do*. That's the problem. I can't keep being both daughters to them. I have to be me." She paused. "Do you think they'll find that proof? We can all really use the closure."

"It's a maybe," I said.

"If you or the cops can't come through, I guess I can pin my hopes on Aunt Bea. That is, if she's really as good as you say she is."

"She's good, and she may still have some ideas up her sleeve. Which reminds me ..."

When we entered the bookshop, Rawlsy was standing under the lights of the demo kitchen, rolling meatballs. He was dressed like my aunt—in a frilly pink apron. "That's it," she was saying, hovering over him, arms akimbo. "Roll them gently but swiftly. Stop when the seams disappear. You mustn't overwork the meat."

Amos Horne was nowhere in sight. The theater major, Russell, was reading a paperback of *The Glass Menagerie* behind the cash register.

"They smell delicious," Rawlsy said. "I could eat them raw."

Steam rose from a bubbling pot of sauce on the fire.

"Well, of course!" my aunt said. "They're fifty percent ricotta cheese and parmesan." She looked up when the bell rang. "Dante! Finally, you have roused yourself. Mr. Rawls, let us conclude the lesson. Into the oven we go! We have more pressing matters to attend to."

When they joined us under Verdi's bust moments later, Rawlsy had a thick manila envelope under his armpit. It stayed there while he meticulously dried his hands of any remnants of ground meat, spices and ricotta cheese.

"Love the apron," I said. "Goes with your eyes."

"Stick it," he said.

My aunt slumped into her armchair, still apron-clad and clutching a wooden spoon. I made the introductions. The slicked-back operative nodded at Leena and said, "Hiya," but his hands were already busy spreading a series of black-and-white photos on the coffee table.

They showed a well-dressed young man leaving his apartment in the morning. Descending in the maw of the subway. Walking slushy city streets. Arriving for work at the Grouser Club. Clearing off tables. A shot of him lighting a patron's cigarette. And then the same man going home. Buying stuff in a Korean-owned grocery. Taking clothes to the cleaners. Picking up the evening paper. Out for a stroll. Meeting some friends for drinks at a bar. Heading home. And the next day, doing it all again.

"That would be our boy, Samuel," I said. "Chief flunkie at the Grouser Club."

"Exactly," Rawlsy said. "Last name, Wells. Age twenty-six. Unmarried. Studio apartment on West Eighty-First Street. A boring life—"

"But not without guile," my aunt said.

"When you asked for the tail," Rawlsy said, "I balked 'cause I didn't think it was justified. Four men for two days equals mucho moola. And I thought I was vindicated when I didn't see him going into any rare bookstores to palm off Haverstrom's book."

"Understood," my aunt said. "But then you completely over-look the true purpose of having him surveilled."

Rawlsy looked up, abashed. "I did? You thought he offed Barski and took the rare book."

"I never thought that, Simon," said Aunt Bea. "I merely knew he was lying about something."

"Yeah," Rawlsy conceded, "but we can't tail everyone in the

world who looks suspicious. One, there's not enough green to pay for it all. And two, you'd have operatives tailing themselves."

"Samuel clearly knows more than he was letting on," Bea said. Her eyes shifted to me. "Dante, you saw his face!"

"Who *are* these people?" Leena said. "What does this have to do—"

My aunt tapped her knee with the wooden spoon. "Forgive us, dear. Matters are often best gleaned from context. Gentlemen, I tell you: Samuel *knew* something."

"What did he know?" I said.

With some effort, she shifted her butt forward in the chair and started rearranging the photos. When she was done, she had removed all but four photographs from the table. Shots of Samuel paying for his groceries, and one of him picking up clothes at the dry cleaners.

"The man has to eat, doesn't he?" Rawlsy said.

"Yeah," I nodded. "And working where he does, he probably blows through tons of dry-cleaning bills. So what?"

She held up a photo in front of my face. "You say he eats. Fine. But look at his purchases. Does a single young man with a job outside the home need half-and-half for his coffee twice in one week? Does a twenty-six-year-old man need denture adhesive and Geritol?"

Next she raised a photo of Samuel walking out of a dry cleaner carrying a tweed suit jacket in a plastic bag. "Does a strapping fellow like him look like he wears a jacket that small?"

Disgusted but triumphant, she flung down the photos and glared at us. "I'll remind you that only one person was capable of overhearing Mr. Haverstrom's plans at the Grouser Club. That was Adrian Balsam, a man who has apparently vanished into thin air, and whom you have not been able to locate in a week. We are left with the same question that we faced on Day 1. Where, I ask you, is the elusive Adrian Balsam?"

♔ 29 ♕

MOUSE MEETS SNAKE

"Package for Mr. Wells," I said.

The buzzer sounded. We were in.

The apartment house was old and massive. Cast iron windows, Renaissance-style red brick, varnished wood doorway, and a polished brass speaker set into the doorframe. Not the sort of place you'd try the oldest trick in the book and expect to pull it off.

We found the apartment four flights up. Bea and Rawlsy stood out of sight of the peephole. I knocked twice and heard locks being thrown back. The door finally swung open, but only as far as the security chain would permit. A gray-headed, spectacled face peeked around the door, then shrank back.

"Stick it through," the face said. It was the voice of an elderly man.

"Won't fit," I said. "See?"

I held up a completely empty box that we'd gotten at a liquor store and wrapped in brown paper to look enticing.

"Oh, all right," the voice said in an exasperated tone. The man grunted and excused himself while the door closed again. I heard the clink of the chain being pushed back. When the door opened again, I dropped the box in the hall, stuffed my foot in the door, and pushed it open with my right hand. The resistance on the other side of the door lasted a millisecond before collapsing.

I heard footfalls as he tottered backward.

When the door finally swung ajar, we spied a little man in shirtsleeves and brown tweed suit pants breathing heavily on the other side of it.

"Hey! Hey, what is this? I'll call the police!" His eyes boggled behind rimless specs, staring at the three of us in the doorway. "Who are you people?"

Bea closed the door gently and proceeded to remove her leather gloves. The way she did it—a half-mad look in her eyes— took forever. She might have scared the bejesus out of me if I didn't realize she was trying to hide the fact that she too was out of breath.

But our little host didn't know that. He trembled in his tweeds. He was skinny and pale, looking one size smaller than his dress shirt. Face as bony as an angelfish, and roundish glasses perched on his twitching nose. His balding head was encircled with wispy white hair in need of a cut. Great, I thought, we're roughing up Grandpa.

"Now look here," he started, and stopped, waiting to stoke his courage. He cleared his throat, then started up again. "I don't know where any of the valuables are. It's not my place! So ... I couldn't tell you where he keeps his money. I ... I have some cash ..."

"You have wasted a good deal of my time, sir," Bea said, unbuttoning her trench coat, removing her fedora, and shaking it out on the carpet. She pointed at a worn chair with sagging upholstery. "Sit."

"You have no right to barge in here—"

"I said sit!"

The gray mouse sat, plucking at his knees nervously. Across the small studio apartment, the TV blared. A woman was tearfully explaining to Phil Donahue why she'd beaten her vegetarian husband. Phil was patting her shoulder and nodding sympathetically.

Bea's show was better. She took a slow walk around the living room. A neat but shabby place, a few well-watered plants, some copies of *Vanity Fair*, and a small shelf of paperbacks and hardcovers. Finally, with some disdain, she lowered herself slowly into a worn, brown corduroy-covered couch that looked like it might have been rescued from a street corner trash pile. I could tell the stained fabric disgusted her, but then again she was well swaddled in acres of water-resistant fabric. She leaned back and carefully draped one of her leather gloves over the armrest, no doubt to keep her flesh from coming in contact with any germs. When all threats to her person had been minimized, she began drumming her glove with the fingers of her right hand. "Mr. Adrian Balsam, I presume?"

Mousy gulped. "Y-Y-Yes? How do you know me?"

"You have been absent all week from your customary habitat at the Grouser Club. And you have been equally absent from your residence on the West Side of Manhattan. Were the club actually a locus of camaraderie, which it is not, you would have several chums concerned about your mysterious disappearance. Unfortunately, as you are friendless, interest in your whereabouts and well-being has fallen to me, a position I find appalling and enervating."

A quick smile flashed across his face. "I don't understand … the club doesn't admit women."

"Mr. Balsam, I do not have time for stonewalling or flummery," Bea said impatiently. "What role have you played in the matter of Mr. Haverstrom's missing book?"

At the mention of that name, Mousy's shoulders snapped as if he were waking from a nap. His lips puckered. "I should have known he was behind this. He's been trying to upstage me for years in that place, all these little games. He wants to embarrass me? Let him try, see where he ends up." He ended his speech with a dramatic nod of his chin that he probably thought was a brave show of decisiveness.

He and Bea were both silent for a moment. On TV, the poor woman was saying, "I remember him yelling, 'You didn't steam the broccoli right.' I just snapped."

Rawlsy chuckled at the screen, shaking his head.

Bea ignored his outburst. "I applaud your pathetic but brave stance against the forces of injustice, Mr. Balsam," she said. "I detest Mr. Haverstrom myself. I am far more interested in Milo Barski."

Balsam shot to his feet. "I didn't do it! I swear! I swear! Oh boy, I'm telling you, I had nothing to do with that awful, awful mess! Look, I don't know who you are but you're not the police, are you?"

"Sit!" she commanded. "Keep talking."

He dropped into the seat, nose snuffling. I offered him a handkerchief and then went to lower the volume on the TV. Just a bit. I would have switched it off completely but Rawlsy was engrossed by the drama.

"I never did anything like that in my life. You would know that if you knew me, really you would. I'm a respected man. I used to do Fiorello LaGuardia's taxes. Men of influence relied on me. I was a highly capable individual. I don't *kill* people. That's not who I am."

"But you were there," Bea pressed.

"Sure, I admit it. I got to, right? But how you knew that, I'll never figure."

"You just told me."

His hand shot up to his mouth, surprised by his own admission. "Now look—I just *found* him there. I didn't do anything *to* him."

Remarkably, Rawlsy had been following our conversation all

along. He suddenly piped up, "Oh golly gee, Inspector, he was dead when I got there!"

"He was!" Balsam insisted. "Just like that. Dead. *Dead!* Deader than anyone I ever saw in my whole life!"

"When was this?" Bea demanded.

"Sunday. Twelve forty-six. I was supposed to be there at one in the afternoon, but I always like to get where I'm going at least fifteen minutes before, and wait around."

"You had an appointment, then?"

"Sure, it was all on the up-and-up, very aboveboard. If I tell you, maybe you'll understand, see what I had to put up with. The club, we're historically collectors of serious volumes. History, biography, and, well, the gentlemen like me who are Am-Litters. It's been that way for years. Now a few of the new crowd are dabbling with genre crap. Mysteries, science future, romances. In other words, potboiler trash."

"You don't bother with that junk," I said. "You're a Faulkner man."

His eyes lit up in an expression of happiness we hadn't seen since we'd entered. "Why, yes, I am. How did you know?"

"Stick to the facts, Mr. Balsam," Aunt Bea said.

The veil of joy disappeared. "It's all so simple. I don't know how it could have gotten into such a mess. Haverstrom's been in high spirits for days and I couldn't think why. Then Samuel, who works for us, happened to confide that the old curmudgeon had located his very last want. Mr. Barski apparently had a volume that would tip Haverstrom over the edge and complete his annual pursuit." His eyes darkened. "Me, I'm still waiting for my *Intruder* signed first edition. I can't begin to tell you when it might come through. The market is fickle, and swift. I can't imagine you understand—"

"Don't presume," Bea said.

"You just don't know when a bookseller will come through for you. With my luck, it's always when I can least afford to plunk down the cash. I've got my wants scattered all over the city. In bookstores down south, even, but nothing's turning up. So you can see why I acted the way I did. I was not going to be forced to write a check to that man's charity."

"How did it happen?" I said. "Tell us right now."

"Last week, at dinner, Samuel told Haverstrom that Mr. Barski was on the phone. They'd met on Friday and Samuel heard the whole conversation. Mr. Barski was holding out for cash. They moved the transaction up to Sunday. I knew he wanted a thousand, so I thought it couldn't hurt to offer him more money and get hold of the book. That would delay Haverstrom's win and I could also liquidate the book later. So, Saturday night I called Mr. Barski on the phone, and offered him *two* thousand. He says, 'Will that be in cash?' When I said yes, he insisted I come down the very next day at one in the afternoon. It was a Sunday, but he was meeting someone there anyway."

Bea exhaled. She leaned forward on the couch. "Think carefully. This is important. Did he mention the name of the person he was meeting?"

"No, not at all. Why would he? It was none of my concern."

She made a face. "I told you to think carefully. Consider his choice of language. Did he, in other words, hint at the person's gender by the way he spoke of them? Don't just blurt. *Think.*"

The poor fellow tried, but came up empty. "I'm telling you. There was no such reference, either to the person or the content of their meeting. But I can tell you that his other appointment was on my mind. When I got to the store, I briefly considered walking around the block to kill time, since I'd come so early. But the weather's been so miserable I thought I'd catch my death of cold. I looked in the windows and saw him on the floor. I touched the door and it was unlocked—"

At the same time, Rawlsy, Bea and I all said the same thing: "*Unlocked?*"

"Yes! I went in, thinking he had dropped something and was

searching for it. A watch crystal or something. Then I thought he had one of those ... I don't know what they call them—embolisms? But there was all that blood. And then I jumped when I heard the sound out back. Scared me half to death!"

Bea was resting serenely on the couch, eyes nearly closed. "You heard the back door slam shut."

"Yes!" Balsam said, his voice quavering. "All I could think was that whoever did this was coming back. I should have run. But I wasn't thinking straight. My first instinct was to hide. I ducked under the folding table. Wasn't easy at my age, but you do incredible things when you're scared. I crouched and waited. But no one came."

Bea's lips moved wordlessly. Something like anger flashed in her eyes. Then she spoke. "And as you waited, Mr. Balsam, your fear transformed itself to opportunism."

"Well, it wasn't like that—"

"Nonsense. You saw that he was dead. You were inches from his body. You were alone among his possessions, one of which you desired greatly."

"Look, lady, I've been very patient with you!" he said, waving a finger. "I don't even know why you're asking these questions. You haven't shown me any identification."

"You stole Haverstrom's book, didn't you?"

His jowls dropped to the carpet. Then he had his own personal flash of anger. "That book wasn't doing him any good up on those shelves, was it? He wasn't breathing. Not moving an inch. Why *not* take it? I mean, don't get me wrong, I was sick to my stomach, trying to push that table away from the breakfront. I picked up this brass bird. It was covered in blood, but I didn't know what else to use. It was so heavy I had to use two hands to smash the glass."

"Why smash it?" I said.

"How am I going to get the book if I don't?" He looked at my aunt and shook his head. "Smart, these kids."

"The point begs to be clarified, Mr. Balsam," Bea said slowly. "Are you saying that when you found Milo the breakfront cabinet in which he stored his books was locked? No glass broken?"

"That's correct. Why—"

"Milo's keys, his wallet ... were they anywhere in sight?

"Not in sight, but he might have had them in his pockets. But I wasn't going to touch him."

"But you *did* touch the books."

Balsam nodded vehemently. "I had my gloves on the whole time. They were covered in blood from the statue. I was afraid to get blood all over the books, so I peeled them off before I touched the volumes. But when I broke the glass, I saw that there was already some blood on the shelves inside."

My aunt shot me a glance. I wasn't sure what I supposed to make of it. "And then?"

"I didn't want to make a mess, but I had no choice. The books were in no kind of order I could understand. Not alphabetical by author. I tried reading their spines, but it was taking too long. After a while I just started pulling them off. It was a god-awful mess. Things got out of hand. Haverstrom's book was on the bottom shelf. When I finally had it, I saw I was covered with blood. Blood on the gloves in my pocket. Blood on my shoes. I didn't know what to do. I had to get out of there! I wiped my feet on the rug going out. I switched off the lights. I used my coat sleeve to push that little button on the back of the doorknob. You know, to lock it? I pulled the door shut and wiped the knob the way they always show you on TV. I pulled the grating down over the shop so no one would see inside. And then I left."

"How did you decide to lay low?" Bea said.

"Well," he said. "I walked up a few blocks in kind of a stupor, I don't mind telling you. I took the subway uptown to the club. They were still having Sunday brunch, and I went and found Samuel in the pantry and told him what I'd done. He's a good fellow, Sam. My daughter, she married a guy that reminds me of Samuel. A chiropractor, but that's another story. 'Mr. Balsam,' Samuel says. 'You have to get out of those clothes. They might find fibers or something.' I almost died. That's all I had to worry about, these fibers! He took me into the staff locker room and had me wash and change. Gave me some waiter's pants to put on. 'We need to get these cleaned,' he says. He showed me the blood on my trouser cuffs and knees and shoes where I must have touched something. He gave me his rain boots to wear. They were big, but I had no choice. He gave me his raincoat and hat, and the keys to his apartment. 'Go there and wait it out,' he says. 'Anyone here asks about you, you're sick.' And that's what I did. I've been here ever since." He paused in his tale, exhausted. Balsam moved his foot in circles on the carpet. Keep rubbing, I thought. Dig yourself a hole to China and run. "I've still got the book, if you want it back."

"We do," Bea said.

He started to rise, but my aunt waved a finger at him. "Mr. Balsam, tell me this: Do you remember the lock on the breakfront cabinet?"

"Sure … of course. Heck, if that wasn't there, I would have been able to open it, wouldn't I?"

"Indeed," my aunt said. "You left the lock as it was? You didn't touch it, move it?"

"It was locked, lady. How could I move it?"

"And the feathers in the cabinet? You knocked them to the floor, did you?"

"Those two pretty peacock feathers? Yeah, I knocked them out of the bowl. Why?"

"Two?" said Bea. "Where was the third?"

"Third? Oh! When I was dragging the table away, I saw it in that big bowl."

"Chamber pot," I said.

Bea's eyes burned. "Are you certain of that?"

"Yes, I'm telling you. I remember thinking it was a funny place to put it, actually."

Bea sighed gratefully. She sank back into the depths of the couch with her hands in her lap. She was quiet. Her eyes stared over Balsam's head to the small kitchenette. I don't think she saw a thing. She waved her finger at me, murmuring, "Get the book."

Balsam led Rawlsy and me behind a partition, which hid a full-sized bed, a dresser, and a wardrobe. There was a framed poster on Samuel's wall depicting a hot air balloon festival in Hunterdon County, New Jersey. That was the extent of the artwork. On the bed was a stack that consisted of a spare blanket, top sheet and pillow, all neatly folded.

"He lets me take his bed," Balsam said, "on account of my back. He's a good kid that way. He takes the couch."

We watched him pull out a dresser drawer, peel back some underwear, and produce something square wrapped in brown paper. He put the underwear back slowly, neatly, looking once at us, perhaps to see if we were impressed with this highly original way to hide things. He handed over the parcel. I gently unwrapped the paper. In the end, it was just a funny-smelling, brown-edged book in old buckram.

The Curious Mr. Tarrant, by C. Daly King. Copyright, 1935. The first story in the book was called "The Episode of the Codex' Curse."

That was all fine and dandy, but nothing I saw about that book made it look like it was worth a thousand, two, or even more. It was just a book. But then, I've been saying that about my aunt's profession all my life. If by now I didn't understand the allure of boards and cloth and paper and ink and glue and stitches, I never would.

True to form, Rawlsy asked if maybe we could have something to drink. Balsam perked up and led us into the kitchen, assembled a big green bottle of Schweppe's ginger ale and some glasses and ice, and went to town being hospitable. The kitchen window, framed by faded yellow curtains, had a nice view of someone else's apartment across an air shaft.

"Boy, I sure need this," Balsam said, taking a good gulp. I sipped mine. The ice cubes smelled like stale breadcrumbs. Rawlsy eyed his glass as if hammerhead sharks were lurking in the bubbles. Balsam drained his and washed out the glass in the sink.

I wanted to ask him about his daughter and her husband the chiropractor and whether he had any other family, any grandchildren, anyone he could have gone off and hid with instead of a glorified bachelor busboy who lived alone and drank ginger ale. But I passed on that.

He wiped his hands with a towel and gave us an uneasy smile as he replaced the ginger ale. When Rawlsy drained his glass, we all went back to the living room. On the TV a woman was discussing detergents with a little green man in her dishwasher.

Bea's gaze was still far-off and distant. She twirled her finger like a cowboy signaling a round-up to the other pokes. "Have him get his things," she said. "He goes with us."

"Why?" I said. "We've got the book and his story. He's old and scared. Why hassle him?"

"He's an adult," she said. "And adults answer for their choices. Besides, Posluszny won't believe us without him."

She launched herself off the couch and went to wait by the door. Rawlsy and I helped the mousy guy pack. Behind the partition, he asked what was going to happen to him. I promised him very little would, but I could tell he wasn't buying it. He was still spooked. His hands shook so badly that we finally packed his few belongings for him, bundling them all neatly in a brown supermarket bag.

On the way out, I snapped off the TV. Phil Donahue was waving his mic in the faces of the audience members, asking, "How do the rest of you feel about that? Yes—how about you?"

❦ 30 ❦

CENTER OF THE WEB

A few years back I made peace with the fact that despite what it said on my business card, I was a professional waiter. Not the kind who works for tips. The kind that sits and waits, and waits. The truth of my job description was driven home once again that afternoon as I sat waiting downtown with Adrian Balsam, accountant and book nut, while Lieutenant Posluszny cleared her docket and finally whisked us into a drab concrete room to listen to the little man's story. Four minutes into her spiel, feeling the walls closing in, Balsam wisely announced that he probably ought to have a lawyer present.

This necessitated more waiting, while the litigator daughter of one of the Grouser Club members was pressed into service and summoned from her midtown offices. Abby used the time to issue me a receipt for the precious book. As the hours wore on, I realized how fortunate (or un-) I was to have grown up in Aunt Bea's world. For better or worse, I had absorbed an inexhaustible fount of facts about the rare book world that needed to be painstakingly explained to neophytes like Abby and the poor counselor, whose eyes glazed over at the mention of *first editions*, *want lists, dust jackets,* and the obscure literary obsessions of rich old men.

When we wrapped later that afternoon, Balsam fled in the company of his new friend, who was treating him to a very expensive cab ride back to his uptown digs. That's when Abby gripped my upper arm and motioned me into a chair in her office. "That's two witnesses and two major revelations in less than twenty-four hours," she said. "Does Bea have more up her sleeve, or am I going to be the last to know?"

My turn to feel the walls closing in. "If she had something, I think I'd know."

I started to rise, but she held up her hand. "Maybe I wasn't clear, Sleet. The killer or killers are still unknown. I better *not* be the last one to know. I don't want another Coltharp. Emory Bray does not get to walk out of this looking like a genius."

"Correct," I said. "There's room for only one of those in town."

Our conversation was still ringing in my ears when I returned to Fourth Avenue. I expected to sink into one of the comfortable armchairs at the Book Lady & Friends, preferably with a hot, cheesy chicken parm sandwich in my mitts, but the bell over the transom had hardly stopping jangling when I heard my Aunt Beatrice baying *"Ruuusssseeellllllll!* Where is that boy?"

"Down here, ma'am," I heard the college student call from the depths of the Nature section.

"Did you find anything?"

"No, ma'am."

She had changed into one of her free-flowing garments—a one-piece dress decorated with orchid blossoms—and was dangerously perched at the top of the rolling library ladder. Bifocals perched on her nose. Book clutched in her fists. And her eyes flashing with exasperation. "How many times have I told you to *enunciate?* For heaven's sake, you're an *actor.* Has no instructor taught you to project your voice? Must I inculcate you in the niceties of *elocution*?"

"*NO, MA'AM. I'M STILL LOOKING, MA'AM!*"

She looked around aimlessly. "Amos, what about *you?*"

The little man spoke from the realm of Gardening, but I could not rule out Textbooks. "You have some Time-Life books—"

"I need something a little more authoritative than the hacks at Time-Life, thank you very much."

My hand was on the door handle, hoping to sneak out unnoticed, when she spotted me. "You!" she said. "It's about time! I was beginning to think you'd taken the day off."

"You're busy. I'll go."

"*ON YOUR LIFE, DO NOT LEAVE!*"

She propelled the ladder along its squeaky bar by pulling herself toward the next set of shelves. Her garments fluttered in the breeze. "You're just in time, thank heavens. I'm looking for a book on sea creatures, marine life, anything of that nature."

"Lady wants fishes," Russell said, streaking by with an armload of books.

"Not fish," she snapped. "Well, no, that's not correct. Fish would be helpful, crustaceans ideal."

She stomped down the ladder and set foot on dry land. In a second she sailed across the room and was pinching my biceps in exactly the same spot Abby had gripped me earlier.

"Balsam made his statement—"

"Never mind that," she said, lowering her voice. "I'm ashamed to say I have overlooked something very important. A fact so simple an almanac might have it—*RUSSELL! AMOS! FIND THE ALMANACS!*"

"If you're busy with a work thing," I said. "We can speak by phone—"

"It's *not* a work thing. It's a murder thing. A most infuriating, niggling detail. You need to go back to Brooklyn. To do what you should have done in the first place."

"Which is what?"

"Read someone's mail."

MOTHER AND DAUGHTER TORE INTO EACH OTHER downstairs. Doors slammed, a dish shattered on a countertop, and the six o'clock news squawked away.

"You're late, I call the shop and what do they tell me? 'She didn't come in today. She's sick.' Why didn't you tell me?"

"I wasn't sick!" Leena said.

"Then why didn't you go to work?"

"I had stuff to do!"

"Is this the way you talk now? What 'stuff'?"

"Important stuff."

"Why is he back? Why is he making that racket? If he touches anything in her room—"

"He's in *my* room, Mom!"

It's true. I was in *her* room making a racket. You couldn't *not* make a racket. Leena had two closets; one for storage, one for everyday clothes. I was doing my Fred Allen routine on the storage one. Tennis racquets. Water shoes. A silly blue snorkel-and-flipper set, complete with beach pail and shovel. Tons of old paperback bodice-rippers. Their enticing covers distracted me, and I missed the box, flinging it down on the bed with the books and not noticing it until I heard the swoosh of letters flipping out and scattering across her flowered bedspread.

I said it before, I'll say it again. The reason my Aunt Beatrice and I work well together is that she always remembers the things I forget. In this case it was one little throwaway line uttered by Leena Munro days ago, speaking about the time her sister quit college to become a rock star.

"*Mail came from school ... Dad trashed it all ... Yelled at me when I tried picking it out.*"

And tonight, as we'd ridden the subway back to her parents'

house, she unpacked that little factoid even further. "The week she died was the worst week of my life," she said. "I don't think the police asked me for them—"

They wouldn't. Because when a person dies, the focus of the investigation is on the very recent past. You don't really start digging into the long past until you're up against a wall with no leads. Even if the cops had searched her bedroom, it would have never occurred to them to search her sister's.

Here was the thing we'd overlooked. Alison's mail. Ten or twelve letters, more than I'd expected. A few magazines, too, the ones she'd had rerouted before heading home to pursue her musical career. I sat on the bed and picked through them, one by one. I was working blind here. I didn't exactly know what I was looking for, or why Aunt Bea was so worked up. All she'd told me was that if I found what she was looking for, I'd know when I saw it.

I picked through the letters, growing increasingly annoyed that my aunt was pulling another one of her stunts—keeping me out of the loop. As I read, I felt my heart working its way up to my throat. Come on, I thought. Give me something. Don't let me go back to Fourth Avenue empty-handed.

But there were slim pickings indeed. A flyer from some misguided office at Magnificat College, offering Alison a great deal: "You'll want to cherish forever your fond years at Magnificat. Why wait till senior year?" Why indeed. Leave school and order your yearbook later.

None of the envelopes were from her roommate, Missy Hettinger, or Missy's brother. I found one from Sister Michael Marie and got a funny feeling as I opened that stiff white envelope, and scanned the nun's words scribbled in the Palmer Method. "I'm sorry you have chosen to leave us. I wish you well in all your endeavors. As I have not had you in any of my classes, I am perhaps unsuited to offer you help in the future. But know this: Should you ever need advice on any matter, do not hesitate to call me. You are our daughter forever."

The nun's words surprised me. You don't know the girl, but you still care. Why? What makes you care?

I flipped to the next letter and froze. It was a small brown, thank-you-note-sized envelope. The return address was somewhere in Portsmouth, Rhode Island. No name.

I had it open in a second, and the plain white card flipped into my lap.

Allie —

You might have waited. That's about all I can say. You were the one who said we were crowding each other, not me. I step back, let us have some space, and now you don't care? This guy Tony cares? Be real. I didn't know you were really leaving until I went to the Bastille on Sunday and saw Sister Tim cleaning the place out. She yells at me for being there. I tell her I'm looking for you, that some of the girls said you'd gone, and she shows me your empty room. I felt like crap, Allie. Had to learn the whole thing from Tiny Tim! You could have told me. No one knows where you are. Everyone's talking. I know you're with him, and I know you think you love him. All I can say is, call me. Maybe we can think this thing through. I know I've been a jerk, but believe me, I love you. I'll leave the dump and come see you. How about it? Call me!

Love you,
Me.

No name, just a handwritten note. I struggled to place the handwriting. I had the faintest glimmer, but I couldn't be sure. I sat digesting the letter over and over, seeing if its content would come out differently on a second, third, fourth read. It didn't. My stomach churned itself into knots. After a string of breakups in which she is the dumpee, a pretty girl dumps someone for the first time in her young life. What happens then? How did this letter change things?

I slid the note in my pocket and rumbled down the stairs. Mom and daughter were still arguing. Mrs. Munro was shouting into the telephone, probably at her husband. The kitchen and foyer were filled with the smell of butter and frozen spinach burning on the stove. I let myself out and hopscotched around the treacherous patches of ice in my mad dash to the subway.

TIMES SQUARE. CROSSROADS OF A BILLION COLORED lights. A tall, powerfully built black man with gray hair sat behind the security desk in the lobby of the Bray Agency's building. He tapped his hands in time to the music from radio station WBLS. Reginald Boame. Detective, First Grade. He was dressed as a rent-a-cop.

"What's this?" I said when I came through the revolving doors.

His beautiful brown eyes rolled slowly in their sockets and stared at the electronic LED clock on the wall over the TV monitors: 8:28 p.m.

"They're expecting you."

I peeked at the sign-in book on the desk. The only visitor to the Emory Bray Agency this evening was Beatrice Valentine.

Upstairs, the glass doors to our suite were open, the lights out. All the office doors were locked, except Bray's. I knocked and entered. Only half the room was lit. In the partial darkness I saw my aunt sitting at Bray's desk. She flicked on the green desk lamp. She wore the same dress she'd worn hours ago at the shop, only now there was a thick, fuzzy, purple shawl thrown around her shoulders.

I walked over and flung down the letter. Venetian blinds sliced Times Square into planes of neon reds and blues. Her fingers went for the letter.

"You were right," I said.

Her face was calm, but the pits under her eyes danced with tics. She finished reading and said, "Where?"

I told her about Leena's closet. "Go inside," she said, gesturing with her head.

"What does it mean?"

"I'll explain later."

"Are you sure about this?"

She pointed toward the bathroom that connected Bray's office with my father's. I went through the passage, closed the pocket doors after me, and emerged in the darkness of the other office. My eyes adjusted. Abby Posluszny paced the floor like a caged animal. Rawlsy peered at the closed-circuit monitor on my father's etagere. On the TV screen I could see Aunt Bea sitting at Bray's desk.

I peeled off my coat and jacket, and dug some aspirin out of my father's desk. On the blotter was a note, dated the day of my hasty departure from our offices:

DANTE—
YOU ARE AN IDIOT AND YOU ARE FIRED!
BRAY

What a lovely welcome home. The light on the phone blinked and Abby hit the speaker button.

"Lieutenant …?"

Boame's voice.

"Go on."

"Coming right up. Signed the book with an alias. You want me up there?"

"Give me ten minutes."

Beside the desk, Rawlsy extracted his Smith & Wesson .38 revolver from his shoulder rig and placed it on the etagere shelf in front of him.

I swallowed my aspirin dry and stared at the monitor. The three of us heard a knock at the door.

Bea called out in a sing-song voice: "*Yeeee-eeeesssss?* Well, hello! I didn't expect you so soon. Come in. Come in."

Said the spider to the fly.

31

ELUCIDATION

"When's your nephew getting here?"

"Oh, he'll be along," Bea said, settling herself behind Bray's desk. Of all the chairs in the city, Bray's is possibly the only one comfortably suited to my aunt's girth. But she detests task chairs on wheels. Thinks they're too fiddly. "He had a few errands to run, so he sent me ahead. Good nephew I have, always willing to humor me."

Her guest looked a bit uneasy. "You said you needed my help."

"We do. Just last night the police made an arrest."

"Oh? I didn't hear."

"Yes. Foolish boy from Long Island. He hasn't fully confessed, so the police want Dante and me to give a statement explaining our involvement before they put the screws to him. We'd be happy if you could help refresh our memories."

"Sure. Why not?"

"Excellent. Now ... the crux of the problem, I think, lies in the appearance of Milo's shop on the morning he was discovered dead. Books everywhere, broken glass, the peacock feathers ..."

"Blood."

"Oh yes, that too. Milo lay under the debris, making it obvious that the robbery was committed *after* he was struck down. This appearance of a scene led us and the police to assume that one person was responsible for *both* Milo's death *and* the robbery. Mistake No. 1. This very afternoon I learned that Milo's murderer didn't break into the cabinet, or move the drop leaf table, or even ransack the books."

"He didn't?"

With complete candor, my aunt sketched out how Balsam came to swipe the *Tarrant*. Then: "So in order to arrive at our solution, we must subtract the panic-stricken chaos inflicted by Mr. Balsam. That alone will give us an accurate picture of the room as the killer wanted us to see it."

"You think the robber left a setup?"

"Not robber—*killer*. And yes, it was most certainly a setup. I'll get to that later. First, the use of that absurd, top-heavy peacock suggests the crime was not premeditated. I say *suggest* because the killer could have come armed with another weapon, but then used the peacock instead. Second, let us consider also that Milo had been attacked in his shop earlier that week."

"He was?"

"Yes. By a young Neanderthal named Rudy Vranin and his employer, the late Nick DiGaetano. Now, if a stranger had walked in one day and had broken your nose, wouldn't you be a little leery if the same men appeared again? Wouldn't you seize a weapon to protect yourself the second they entered? But we found no sign of a struggle. No indication that Milo tried to arm himself. Why?"

"He didn't suspect danger."

"Right again. You know, you are as good as Dante at humoring me. If Milo didn't fear his assailant, I can only conclude that he either knew his visitor or perceived him as a harmless customer. And if I subtract Balsam's intrusion, I am left with what? An unbroken, locked breakfront cabinet, a peacock feather in a chamber pot, and tellingly, some spots of blood inside the cabinet. These things told me everything, I'm pleased to say. Without them, I was lost."

"I don't see how."

"No? It's simple. Milo *treasured* those feathers. They reminded him of a woman he once loved, *still* loved. He once gave one of those feathers to a lonely young girl. Perhaps he saw something in her that reminded him of his past love. A certain innocence. But that's another story. My point? If Milo had opened the cabinet, he would never have allowed one of those feathers to flutter down into the chamber pot. He simply wouldn't have. They were too important to him. The blood observed by Mr. Balsam inside the cabinet makes it abundantly clear: After killing Milo, the murderer used Milo's keys to open the desk drawer, retrieve the padlock key and unlock the breakfront, dripping some blood on the shelves in the process." She paused. "Now. Which drawer did he keep the key in?"

The words came out punchy and staccato: "Top right."

"Precisely what the killer needed to know," Bea said.

"So? Any customer of his could have answered that question. You know, I don't think I like your tone in all this."

Aunt Bea drummed her fingertips on the desk. "Forgive me, I meant nothing by it. Yes, everyone knew where Milo kept his keys. He made such an elaborate show of it, didn't he? I've come to believe that the killer was after a book containing some photos Milo had taken. To access that book, the killer had to extract the pertinent volume from the bookshelf. He would have needed to move the drop leaf table to swing open the breakfront doors. When he was done, the killer replaced the table and locked up, leaving the padlock to the left of the doors, as was Milo's habit. In all this, the killer duplicated Milo's habits precisely."

"Which proves what?"

"Familiarity. He's just killed Milo and robbed the store. In any moment, anyone could walk in off the street. Mr. Balsam was probably only minutes away. And yet, despite that pressure, our murderer was able to pluck the book he wanted from those shelves. Minutes later, Mr. Balsam would attempt the very same feat, and unwittingly create chaos! So the killer knew where to locate a book on those encoded shelves."

"You're saying the person was calm, cool and collected. Big shock. Crooks are like that."

My aunt's head wagged, seeming to say, *Well, I have to disagree ...*

"But the killer was still enraged. Milo said something in the course of their talk that drove our killer to this act of passion. He dropped a feather and didn't notice it. That tells me he was distracted. The slick theft from the cabinet was governed by instinct, not thought. The killer didn't have to think because he knew exactly what to do."

"And that's how you got your man? This Long Island boy?"

My aunt snorted. "Hardly. There was still the theft to consider. The police found an intact copy of Volume 1 of Dreiser's *An American Tragedy* in the dumpster. We assumed Milo discarded it because it had a forged signature. We fell for the killer's trap. I am convinced that the last thing the killer wanted us to know was that he'd stolen a book. He needed to draw attention away from the shelves and fasten it onto something else, like Milo's stolen watch and cash. That's why he left the cabinet as Milo would, and took the padlock key. If all went well, the breakfront would attract no attention from the police. Indeed, with the key missing, the breakfront could not be opened. The missing Dreiser wouldn't be noticed until Milo's executor inventoried the estate. The killer might have hoped he'd be invited to help do that; or even better, he thought he'd been named executor, in which case the secret of the stolen book was safe in his hands. It was a fine plan, but it depended on the neatness of the shop to misdirect the police. But Mr. Balsam destroyed all semblance of neatness. The police saw the shelves had been ransacked and demanded to know what was on those shelves. Conveniently, only hours later, Dreiser's *Tragedy* materialized in the trash, with a perfectly intriguing note intended to make us say, 'Don't worry about this one. Milo threw it away!' And we fell for it. But think about it: Milo would never have discarded a book, no matter how defiled. And if he *had* discovered a book he thought had been signed by Dreiser, he would have noted it in his ledger. He didn't, so the book had been tampered with and planted."

"Maybe the killer brought a substitute."

Bea shook her head slowly. "He couldn't bring a book because he didn't know he'd need it. He didn't know he'd be committing murder. And if you're suggesting that he returned to the shop after Balsam, ran out and found a replacement book somewhere in Manhattan on a Sunday, and returned again to plant it, you can forget it. Who'd risk being seen near that shop three times in one day? No, I'm sure he spent Sunday doing what any self-respecting killer would do — getting himself an alibi."

"So when did he plant the book?"

"The book we found late Monday morning was planted late Monday morning. It was probably dropped by the same teenager Detective Munoz saw running from the dumpster. The child was cajoled with money or pizza to plant the book. Who cajoled him? To answer that, I had only to ask myself this: Who knew the police were investigating Milo's books? News of his death wasn't broadcast until evening. So how did the killer know? Only one way. He was in the shop that morning! Who could that be? Not the police, the coroner, or the assistant DA—they were neither friends nor customers of Milo. Four people. Only four knew Milo's habits with some degree of intimacy. All four were in his shop Monday. All four saw the books and heard the police focusing their investigation on the content of those shelves. Dante and I were together constantly from the moment we left the shop until our return nearly two hours later, when we heard of the Dreiser's discovery. Milo's landlady will testify that we were in Brooklyn for most of that time."

In my father's office, Abby Posluszny shot me a nasty look.

Bea continued, "During that period, Amos Horne—Suspect No. 3—was being questioned most vociferously by Detective Munoz. He never left my bookshop. I had my doubts about Amos anyway; his arthritis makes him incapable of clubbing a man to death or lifting the table clear of bloodstains. Mr. Balsam is about the same age, and ended up *dragging* the legs across the rug, leaving streaks. That leaves you, I'm afraid. Monday the police questioned and released you, allowing you to roam the city for nearly two hours in search of a substitute book. More than any of us, you knew how Milo's mind worked. You spent days alone in that shop, and you're certainly bright enough to have figured out how Milo shelved books."

"It looks bad, doesn't it?" Walter Kenning said.

"It doesn't look good."

Silence. My aunt rose to get something out of Bray's refrigerated sideboard. I think she did it so that we would have an unobstructed view of Kenning's face. He sat there the whole time wearing a lopsided grin. I couldn't tell what he was feeling. That's the odd thing about killers. The good ones hide it very well. The best ones get away with it. Walter Kenning was good, but only good.

When Aunt Bea returned with a cup of orange juice, Walt said finally, "Does Dante know?"

My chest tightened. I felt crushed. From the moment I'd begun working in the family business, I'd surrounded myself with longtime friends. This was like losing one of those.

My aunt shook her head no. Bluffing.

"You were always the strangest woman, Bea," Walt said, the edge finally creeping into his voice. "Always thinking. Always noticing. Always *snooping*. You know about the other, then?"

"Tony Crowell? Yes, that was simpler, actually. That same night I felt the killer must have entered the building early and hid somewhere, waiting for his chance to strike. But why do that? Why make an appointment with Mr. Crowell? There was an excellent reason, which I'll share in a moment.

"And then there were the cigarettes. Mr. Crowell was a chain smoker, like his mother before him. He had a wasteful habit of leaving his current cigarette at Zephyr's front desk when he came out to meet someone. The night you killed him, he left one cigarette in the ashtray out front, and lit another in his office just before you killed him. The one in the ashtray out front told me that he'd come out to meet someone, escorted the person back his office, and was killed.

"That suggested that the killer was someone who had never visited Zephyr Records. Anyone familiar with the place would have crept into his office and killed him by surprise. But you couldn't exploit the element of surprise. You didn't know where his office was, and you couldn't waste time wandering about the suite, looking. That would have been too dangerous. So you rang the bell and let him come to you. So on the very night of Tony's death, I knew we could eliminate as his killer anyone connected with Zephyr Records or anyone who had ever visited Zephyr Records. That was a vast group of people—everyone from current to former employees to his own family members. I could also eliminate the most suspicious of characters—his surrogate 'uncle' Nick DiGaetano and Nick's bodyguard, Rudy Vranin. All had been up to the studio at on one time or another."

"You ran out of people, so you picked me?"

"Hardly. I was left with a city full of suspects. It was *possible* that both murders were committed by the same person, but far from certain. I had to tentatively proceed as if the two murders were linked and see if that avenue of thought led me anywhere productive. Unfortunately, that left me a circle of suspects that included the members and staff of an organization called the

Grouser Club, the Munro family, anyone investigating both cases, or Milo's own close circle of friends. That's the point I'd reached in my analysis when I spoke with Mr. Balsam this afternoon. Once I heard his story, the rest was painfully clear."

"Everything but motive," Walt said.

"Mr. Balsam stole the *Tarrant*, which means *you* stole Milo's copy of Dreiser's *An American Tragedy*, in which, I suspect, Milo had tucked away highly sensitive photographic negatives. Milo had used that very word—tragedy—when talking about the death of a young woman named Alison Munro. Now why should *you* turn against your beloved mentor for the sake of a poor girl? Why would you be interested in those negatives? I had no idea, unless of course, the girl meant more to you than Milo … When did you know her?"

Walt shifted his weight, but his hands remained on the arms of his chair. A good sign. "After my father died," he said. "I bummed around. Lived in the Newport, Rhode Island, area, for a change of pace. I met her at one of those winter festivals. An arts and crafts show where I was trying to sell my work."

"You were lovers?"

"I hate when people use that word. It's so … whatever. Yeah, Bea, yes, we were, okay? I shared a house with a bunch of artist types … I saw her a whole year. All summer, then fall. It was really … *nice* …" His voice faltered. "Then Tony and the others showed up … and I lost her. I tried telling her they were losers but she cut me off. Dumped me and left town."

"But later," Bea said, "she helped you. She met Milo at a photo shoot and lobbied for a job on your behalf. She made the introduction to Milo when you came to New York. I can't imagine why, but I suspect she felt some modicum of guilt for the way she left you."

"I don't know how you figured that out, but yes. By then it was solidly over between us, but I suppose I was being mopey, calling her and telling her that I'd moved to the city for her and was broke. She hooked me up with Milo because she was a decent person, and because she probably just wanted to get me off her back. I was always interested in fine art and the decorative arts, so the job was a lifesaver, *and* interesting. I worked, I went to school, and stayed the hell away from her. I was sore about our breakup for a long time after, and never spoke about it with anyone. Milo thought we were just old friends. I guess that's what she told him." He peered up at the ceiling, his face twisted in pain. "I wonder if that's what she felt? I mean, *really* felt?"

He'd gone to pieces when she died. In Milo's shop they had observed her passing quietly, privately, Milo mum. Two years passed, Walt moved on, and suddenly his former employer was asking favors: Could he recommend a good estate liquidator? He was retiring, leaving town in a hurry. Would Walt mind coming down Sunday?

"I got there around twelve, and I saw immediately that someone had worked him over. He tells me, 'Can you come open the shop Monday and show the appraiser around?' He announces that he has business with Ernie Munro. It was all matter-of-fact. Like he remembered that I knew the family but couldn't recall exactly how? I pressed him on it, and he was so scared, he was dying to confide in someone." His shoulders dropped, then heaved. "He told me all of it, the fink! Told me someone had to know the truth of what happened to Alison. Someone had to put these monsters behind bars. But it wasn't going to be him. Oh no! He was blowing town, and selling the negatives to Alison's father. What a bum! Can you believe it? He wanted my help!"

"You could have refused," Bea said softly. "You could have called the police."

Walt's mouth was a grim, straight line. "Oh really? Is that what you would have done, you pompous windbag?"

The insults rolled off my aunt's face. "I would not have killed him, Walter. I *could not* have killed him."

"Figures you'd get pious on me. You don't know what it was

like. He watched a girl die! And he was subjecting her parents to horrible torment all over again. How could I help a man like that?" He twisted the hair above his ears and wiped the sweat from his forehead on his coat sleeve. "I didn't think about it. I just acted. Grabbed the first thing I could and did it. He'd referenced the book, so I knew which one to look for. When it was over, I was appalled at myself, but I've since come to see that he deserved it. *Absolutely* deserved it. You're right about the rest. That's the thing with you, isn't it? You're always right. When the cops let me go, I left your shop and went down a block to The Strand and asked if they had a Dreiser. They didn't have any first editions, so I just made the rounds of the shops I know in town.

"The book I took was a fourth printing, but I could only find a *sixth* printing of the first edition. It saved me a bundle, but it wasn't quite the same thing. I didn't think Milo would have noted the printing in his logbook, but then again I didn't really have a choice, did I? I had to cross my fingers and hope the cops—or you or Amos —wouldn't flag it as different from the one in the ledger. I went to the office, typed the note, and packed it up in a used envelope. I went back and slipped a kid a few bucks to drop it off. It felt like the only way to get the cops' minds off that book. Oh gosh, this *sucks* ... And of course when I studied the photos, I knew I *had* to get Tony. That loser met me only once, and didn't even remember. I reminded him when I got him. The rest, I just lied. To the cops, to your nephew, to everyone asking. I told them only half the story. Lies on top of lies. But it was never easy. You must believe that. Both of them got what was coming to them. Any reasonable person who knows the story will understand. I won't serve time for this. I won't."

"Little late for that," my aunt said. "The further you get from the scene of Milo's death, the less your actions look like a crime of passion. The police will match the typewriter in your office to the note and mailing label that you so coolly typed. They'll canvas every used bookstore in the city if they must, but eventually they'll find clerks who remember the attractive man in glasses who quite sanely purchased a first edition Dreiser on Monday. And there is always your trash."

"My what?"

"An hour ago, you left your apartment with a plastic bag. You walked six blocks and threw it in a trash can on the sidewalk. Shall I tell you what the police found in it?"

"Police?"

Bea reached for a sheet of paper on Bray's blotter. "Yes, you were followed. Ah … let's see … 35mm photographic negatives, close to thirty-six exposures, a butcher block kitchen knife holder, six holes, four knives … You left one knife in Mr. Crowell, so that leaves one knife unaccounted for."

Walt rustled in his overcoat. "I have that that right here."

In my darkened office Abby yelped. *"Get in there!"*

I was first through the bathroom passage. Detective Boame and Rawlsy burst through Bray's office door. Walter loomed over the desk, the knife high over my aunt's face. I snatched his wrist and wrenched him back. He flew back into the chair, toppled out of it, and onto the floor. I held his wrist and stomped my foot in his left armpit. Boame, still dressed in his rent-a-cop duds, yelled at me, "Better hold that hand tight!" He planted a knee in Walt's chest and snapped the first cuff on his left wrist. Rawlsy loomed between us, calmly pressing the cold steel of his nickel-plated Chief's Special to Walt's forehead.

"It's okay," Rawlsy kept saying. "We've got him. We've got him!"

But I found it hard to stop. I kept screaming at him till I was hoarse, and didn't relax until I'd pried the blade out of his hand and let it drop to the carpet.

Abby had an arm around Bea's shoulders. Still seated at the desk, my aunt sipped her orange juice and gathered the shawl tighter around her. She was playing it cool, but I could see that

JOSEPH D'AGNESE

her cheeks were bright red from nerves. "You should be ashamed, Walter!" she scolded him.

"Damn you, lady," he snarled. "I really cared for her!"

Bea croaked, "Isn't that how it starts? Love is the ruin of many men."

32

SUBPHYLUM: CRUSTACEA

If you were to carefully analyze the newspaper coverage announcing the arrest and resolution in the Barski-Crowell murders, several troubling facts would emerge.

One is that while Lieutenant Abigail Posluszny credited her own team of Homicide Task Force detectives—and two devilishly handsome operatives of the esteemed Emory Bray agency *by name* —for assistance leading to the successful apprehension of the killer, for some reason fifty percent of the city's newspapers still ran a headshot of the great Emory Bray.

The *New York Tab*, and Bernie Housknecht in particular, had outdone themselves. The front page of the Sunday paper featured an outrageous image of Rosita Starr in a one-piece bathing suit and a grainy candid of Emory Bray sucking down a large soft pretzel (with brown mustard), under a headline which read,

ACE PI CRACKS DOUBLE HIT!

The center spread featured photos of Andy Kay in a punked-out 'do, a few of Tony Crowell and Alison and the others, and one of Barski's shop. The Bray Agency's illustrious founder was quoted as saying, "No one was as shocked by this outcome as I, but justice must prevail."

A sidebar by the paper's music editor, Lupole, traced the pop/rock/heavy metal career of underrated performer Andy Kay, and announced that Kay—now released from his Zephyr contract by the tragic death of his producer—planned to front a new heavy metal, Christian rock group called HungerPang. According to Andy's new manager, Van Nilsson, the musical genius could not wait to record his new album.

A Los Angeles rock critic announced a series of articles on that misunderstood and troubled visionary, Tony Crowell. Days later the same critic signed a deal to pen a true crime book on the case described as "a cross between *Rebecca*, *In Cold Blood*, and *No One Here Gets Out Alive*."

An attorney for Rosita Starr issued a statement saying that the much-maligned songstress was suing *the Tab* for invasion of privacy, and the Crowell family for sexual harassment at the hands of their departed scion. No comment from the Crowells.

On Long Island, a consortium of Japanese investors had bid an unspecified amount, "rumored to be in the tens of millions," for the yacht club and uncompleted real estate developments, pending settlement of the DiGaetano estate.

Someone had even tracked down Ernie Munro, who said, "Get out of my face." They'd printed that, too.

Nowhere in any of the coverage, which lingered in the media over the course of a week, was there mention of the rotund bookseller who may have had something to do with the disposition of the case. Not a peep, not a jot, not an iota. Which was the way Beatrice Elodia Valentine liked it.

When I finally got over to the Grouser Club, I had the pleasure of watching Haverstrom fling down our bill and receipts and glare at me. His face was a grizzled red plum.

"This is extortion!" he rumbled. "I won't pay it!"

"Fine," I said. "I don't care one way or another. But if you choose not to, we'll recommend that the estate not sell you the book at the previously agreed-upon price. They'd be happy to have you walk away, since we all know Milo Barski knew little about books, and the *Tarrant* will fetch boatloads more at auction, if it comes to that. Frankly, I think two thousand and change is fair for the time we put into the case. Mr. Bray happens to possess one of the finest minds in this city, and that doesn't come cheap. Come on, Judge. I happen to know you paid four times this amount for a first edition by Artie Doyle three months ago."

He slapped the arms of his chair. "Where did you hear that?"

"Doesn't matter."

"Enough!" He withdrew his checkbook and began his tight-fisted scrawl. Ten minutes later, he capped his Mont Blanc and tore out two green-tinted checks. The rips crawled up my spine. He held the finished documents up for my inspection.

Pay to the order of the Emory Bray Agency. The second was made out to *The Estate of Milo Barski*, but was ultimately destined for the Eunice K. Mauro Trust Fund.

"My book," he said.

"Your book," I said, placing the brown-wrapped package on the desk in front of him.

He proffered the checks, but held onto them when I reached for them. "Do I have your word that no one from the club was involved in the theft of my property?"

"Technically, it wasn't your property yet. But yes, you have my word." I felt comfortable saying this, because Adrian Balsam's strange contribution to the case was months from being disclosed at the trial, if at all.

And later that night, the man everyone thought possessed one of the greatest minds in the city poked at the white sauce that drenched his linguine, and said, "I think they cheated me. How many clams did you get?"

Bray, Aunt Bea and I were at the Fontamara Restaurant on Mulberry Street. Good, cheap food. Venetian watercolors on the walls, a few dried starfish hanging from fishing nets. Go for the food, not the decor.

"You want to count clams or you want to listen?" I said. "Sooner or later, some reporter is going to ask, and you need to know how it went down."

He blotted his lips and three chins and leaned forward intently. "I'm listening, I'm listening. Go ahead, Valentine."

My Aunt Beatrice was dressed for a night on the town in a gold lamé turban and equally subdued yellow caftan. Later tonight, once we ditched the big man, we were headed west to the Caffe Reggio, where we were expecting to join Leena Munro and her current beau, Russell, the theater major who worked at Aunt Bea's shop. The two lovely young people had apparently bonded the day we'd left them in charge of the shop, not to mention Bea and Rawlsy's plump, ricotta-infused meatballs.

The case had been troubling and traumatic, and we could think of no better way to put it behind us all than to drown our sorrows in foamy cappuccini and creamy tiramisu, possibly with a side of profiteroles drenched in chocolate sauce.

For now, though, Aunt Bea kept a vigilant eye on the possibility of flying sauce as Bray twirled linguine and hoovered it up like an industrial vacuum.

"I was merely being cautious," Bea said. "Balsam's confession told me everything I needed, but I still felt uneasy about accusing a family friend of murder."

"Ex-friend," I murmured.

"I needed evidence to link him to the girl. I felt certain their paths must have crossed, but everything we knew about him placed him in Indiana or Miami—nowhere Ms. Munro had ever been. Background checks run by the police and Mr. Rawls told the same story. Then I remembered Walter's art. A man's art must tell of its creator's peregrinations. We know Monet was in Giverny because his water lilies practically scream of place. Gauguin's canvases plant him indelibly in French Polynesia.

Dante, you recall the painting Walter gave Milo? The one we found in Milo's apartment? Fishing boats on the sea, with fishermen hauling in their lobster pots? I saw the painting twice days ago, but the inconsistency didn't hit me until I was forced to look for it."

"Inconsistency?" Bray said.

"Lobsters," Bea said.

"Lobsters?" Bray said.

"Lobsters. There are none in Miami. None in Florida, either, for that matter. In the continental United States they inhabit the waters from Maine to North Carolina. The scene as presented on that canvas was quintessentially New England in tone. Therefore Walter must have been in the region for some period of time, during which he must have met Ms. Munro."

"Hah!" Bray said, thumping his fist on the table and nearly spewing us with bits of linguine. "*That's* what you had to look up in your precious fish book? Where *lobsters* come from? What a joke! Forgive me, Valentine, but I think I would have figured that one out." He slapped the table again, this time with his open palm. Glassware clinked. "Hah. Who would have thought? Lobsters!"

"You think you would have done better, then?" Bea said, steepling her fingers.

"Uh, I think so!" He guffawed merrily. His already pink face was turning dangerously red.

"I find that hard to believe. You are, after all, a man who doesn't know his elbow from his butter dish."

Bray stopped chewing pasta. "My butter dish?"

"Yes. Your elbow is in it. More wine, Dante?"

END

PLEASE LEAVE A REVIEW

If you liked this book, I'd be extremely grateful if you'd leave a brief review at your retailer's site. Reviews are one of the best ways a reader can help an author. Reviews increase visibility and help other readers find out about the book.

JOIN THE VIP CLUB

Let's make this a regular thing. Building a relationship with my readers is the best thing about being an author. The Daggyland VIP Club is the best way to stay in touch. You'll alway be among the first to learn about upcoming books and deals.

As a welcome gift, you're entitled to download any or *all* of the range of ebooks in my Starter Library, completely free of charge.

One of the books—*The Mesmerist: Aftermath*—is a short, explosive, never-before-seen chapter that was cut from the original manuscript of the novel, *The Mesmerist*. It's not sold in any store online. It's exclusively for members of the VIP Club.

Your contact info will never be sold or shared with anyone. You can easily opt-out at any time. Did I mention it's free?

VISIT JOSEPHDAGNESE.COM TO SIGN UP

ALSO BY JOSEPH D'AGNESE

IN THE MESMERIST SERIES

The Mesmerist

The first in a spellbinding series of thrillers about an underground culture of gifted individuals who can kill with a glance or heal with a touch. If you like noir stories and occult detectives, this is for you.

Ear of God

(COMING SOON!)

When a kidnapping attempt goes tragically wrong, occult detective Ishmael Soul fights for his life—and the life of a young psychic child. Second in the acclaimed thriller series.

King of Thinks

(COMING SOON!)

A long-rumored mastermind is killing the city's most powerful psychics, forcing them to off themselves in a battle of the minds. Can Soul stop the diabolical "king" from gaining control of the White House?

OTHER FICTION

Sorceress Kringle

(COMING SOON!)

Everything you know about Santa Claus is a lie—and that's just the way *she* likes it. A stunning fantasy epic about the story behind the world's most beloved bringer of gifts.

Murder on Book Row

Beatrice Valentine is a larger-than-life bookshop owner with a penchant for three things in abundance—delicious Italian food, *vino*, and murder. The first in a series of delightful whodunnits set in a world of rare books and copious snacks.

Jersey Heat

A gorgeous scientist. A duffle bag of cash. A tough guy's only chance to do the right thing. An action-packed, full-length thriller with all the twists, turns, savage wit, eccentric characters, and black humor found in the work of Elmore Leonard or Carl Hiaasen.

The Marshal of the Borgo

Part whodunnit, part ghost story. A troubled cop and a teenaged witch rain down vengeance in a small village in Italy. If you enjoy the work of Magdalen Nabb, Andrea Camilleri, Michael Dibdin, or Donna Leon, you will absolutely love this evocative, sun-drenched story in the career of Captain Scarpone.

Arm of Darkness

A demonic prankster visits earth to punish do-gooders and evildoers alike with equal fury. Six horrifying tales of horror in one slim volume.

Daggyland #1 & #2

The easiest and most complete way to read the author's award-winning short stories. Most of these tales first appeared the world's best mystery magazines. Some appear in print for the very first time.

NONFICTION

Signing Their Lives Away

The true story behind the 56 men who signed the Declaration of Independence. Entertaining, essential, inspiring.

Signing Their Rights Away

The true story behind the 39 men who signed the U.S. Constitution. Praised highly by the *Wall Street Journal*.

Stuff Every American Should Know

What's the difference between the Declaration and Constitution? Who invented blue jeans? What's the story behind patriotic American songs? A pocket-sized hardcover perfect for stocking stuffers or gift-giving.

The Money Book for Freelancers

A critical guide to wealth-building and debt eradication for self-employed people. The *only* personal finance system for people with not-so-regular jobs.

The Scientist & the Sociopath

Incredible true-life stories collected from the author's in-depth reporting for the world's top science magazines.

Blind Spot

A ground-breaking "Big Think" book about why we fail to perceive solutions to intractable problems—even when they're staring us right in the face.

Big Weed

A Colorado millionaire's rollicking story of life in the cutting-edge world of legal marijuana entrepreneurship.

The Underground Culinary Tour

An eye-opening account of how the restaurant industry is being quietly transformed by Big Data.

The Indiana Jones Handbook

A beautifully designed hardcover volume that delights armchair archaeologists of all ages. (Warning: Out of print and hard to find!)

FOR CHILDREN

Blockhead: The Life of Fibonacci

The award-winning children's picture book about the medieval mathematician famous for the number pattern that bears his name. The book the *New York Times* called "charming and accessible."

American History Comic Books

Contains 12 educational comic books for classroom use. Designed to be easily photocopied by teachers for students in grades 4 to 6. Published by Scholastic, the biggest name in classroom learning.

ABOUT THE AUTHOR

Joseph D'Agnese is a journalist and author who has written for children and adults alike. He's been published in the *New York Times*, the *Wall Street Journal*, *Wired*, *Discover*, and other national publications.

In a career spanning more than twenty years, his work has been honored with awards in three vastly different areas—science journalism, children's literature, and mystery fiction.

His science articles have twice appeared in the anthology *Best American Science Writing*.

His children's book, *Blockhead: The Life of Fibonacci*, was an honoree for the Mathical Book Prize—the first-ever prize for math-themed children's books.

One of his crime stories won the 2015 Derringer Award for short mystery fiction. Another of his short stories was selected by mega-bestselling author James Patterson for inclusion in the prestigious annual anthology, *Best American Mystery Stories*.

D'Agnese's crime fiction has appeared in *Shotgun Honey*, *Plots with Guns*, *Beat to a Pulp*, *Ellery Queen's Mystery Magazine*, *Mystery Weekly Magazine*, and *Alfred Hitchcock's Mystery Magazine*.

D'Agnese lives in North Carolina with his wife, the *New York Times* bestselling author Denise Kiernan (*The Girls of Atomic City*).

To claim your free Starter Library, sign up for Joe's newsletter at his website: josephdagnese.com

twitter.com/JosephDAgnese

instagram.com/JosephDAgnese

amazon.com/author/josephdagnese

bookbub.com/authors/joseph-d-agnese

goodreads.com/JosephDAgnese